Her name was Lily . . .

and she was the most beautiful thing he'd
ever seen. In all his fifteen years, Trace had
never seen anyone or anything like her. She
stepped out of the worn truck into the dusty
yard, and the flat Oklahoma prairie faded
away.

From a distance her bones seemed too delicate
to support her. Her skin was pale, like the
white china teacup that was his mother's
prize possession. And her hair was like the
wings of some tropical butterfly he'd seen in a
picture book.

Then Lily stepped onto the porch and fixed
her gaze on him. Up close he saw her face—
too beautiful for childhood, her eyes large and
thickly lashed, the most brilliant shade of
green he'd ever seen. She held out her hand
and he took it. And Trace suddenly knew he
would be forever lost in her gaze.

Dear Reader,

Dallas Schulze has written a truly special—and very different—book for you. Because of its unusual format, I'd like to highlight a couple of features you'll be encountering as you read *Together Always*.

Dallas tells the story in two parts, and both are contained here. Book One features Trace and Lily as fifteen- and eight-year-olds, respectively, as they meet for the first time and form their magical lifelong bond. Book Two picks up on their lives in the present day, when they have reached adulthood and are grappling with the emotional risks that such a bond entails.

You'll notice, too, that the story is told entirely from Trace's point of view, giving us his thoughts and feelings about life, love and, of course, Lily.

Dallas and I are sure you'll be moved by Trace and Lily's story and that your lives will be touched by theirs.

Please let us know how you feel about this tender, poignant love story told in a manner not usually used in romance fiction. Write to us at the address below.

Debra Matteucci
Senior Editor and Editorial Coordinator

Harlequin Books
300 East 42nd Street
New York, N.Y. 10017

Together Always
Dallas Schulze

Harlequin Books

TORONTO • NEW YORK • LONDON
AMSTERDAM • PARIS • SYDNEY • HAMBURG
STOCKHOLM • ATHENS • TOKYO • MILAN

Published April 1989

First printing February 1989

ISBN 0-373-16291-X

Book One

Chapter One

Her name was Lily and she was the most beautiful thing he'd ever seen. In all his fifteen years, Trace had never seen anyone or anything like her. She stepped out of the worn truck into the dusty yard and the flat Oklahoma prairie faded away.

His mother had said that this new member of the family was eight, but Trace wondered if that was right. She was tiny—smaller even than Ned Higgindorf, who lived at the farm down the road, and Ned was only six. From a distance her bones seemed too delicate to support her, her limbs too fragile to be real. Her skin was pale, like the white china teacup that was his mother's prize possession, and her hair— How could he describe her hair? It was black but not just black. Where the sun caught it there were blue highlights, like the wings of some tropical butterfly in a picture book. It fell in a rich black cloud past her shoulders.

Trace stood on the porch, caught between the need to get closer to such beauty—to see if it was real—and the urge to back into the shadows of the tumbledown house.

His stepfather slammed the driver's door of the truck and came around the front, his boot heels scrunching on the thin layer of gravel that served as a driveway. He carried a cheap vinyl suitcase in one hand and a sack in the other. Trace barely glanced at him. The suitcase would be the girl's things; the sack would be from Joe's liquor store.

"Come on, Lily. Come meet your new family."

The words floated over the yards between them, the voice slurred, indicating that whatever the bag contained, the old man had already more than sampled it.

Lily. Trace rolled the name over in his mind. Lily. There were some lilies growing in old Mrs. Grady's flower bed near the school. He remembered seeing them and thinking they looked too delicate to survive the cold winters that blew down out of the north. Lily. The name suited the child who was picking her way across the rutted yard.

"Don't just stand there, boy. Come and meet your new sister." The old man stopped at the foot of the stairs and set down the suitcase, stripping the paper bag off the bottle and twisting the cap off the whiskey. The bag skittered across the yard, pushed by a late summer breeze. It caught in the branches of an overgrown rosebush, the thorns holding it tight. The rosebush was all that was left of the rose garden his mother had planted. The rest of the bushes had succumbed to bitter cold winter winds, searing hot summer sun and neglect. The bag dangled from a cane, its rustling reminding Trace of a cricket trapped in a shoe box, scrambling to escape.

"Well, boy, ain't ya gonna come meet Lily?"

Before Trace could answer, the screen door squealed a protest and his mother stepped onto the porch, squinting against the sun.

Addie Roberts had been a pretty woman once, but time and life had worn the prettiness out of her, leaving her dried up and old before her time. Her hair, once the same dark blond as her son's, was streaked with gray and her face bore lines of worry. It was only when Trace closed his eyes and thought real hard that he could remember the pretty smiling woman she'd been when he was little.

Her brow furrowed now, her eyes anxious. "I'm sorry I wasn't here to greet you, Jed, but the sink clogged up again and I was trying to fix it."

Jed Roberts grunted and lifted the bottle to his lips, taking a long pull of the amber liquid before answering his wife. "I can't leave the house even to go pick up my only brother's little girl without something going wrong around here. It's a wonder how you manage when I go to work."

Trace's upper lip quivered in contempt. They did just fine when the old man went to work, but that wasn't very often.

"I know, Jed, and I'm real sorry about the sink."

"Never mind about the sink." Jed waved the bottle, the liquid sloshing in it. "You haven't said hello to Lily. Trace wouldn't even come off the porch to make her welcome. What's a matter, boy? You afraid of a girl child?"

Addie cast a worried glance at her son but Trace only shrugged. After thirteen years he'd learned that most of his stepfather's comments weren't worth bothering about. The old man was just trying to get a rise out of him and it was more satisfying to frustrate him by ignoring the remark. Seeing that there wasn't going to be trouble, Addie turned her attention to the little girl, who'd watched the exchange without expression, her wide eyes taking it all in but revealing nothing.

"Hello, Lily. I'm Addie. I hope you'll be happy with us." She held out her hand and the child took it in one of her own; her other hand clutched a stuffed dog. Lily climbed the three steps onto the porch, stopping just out of the sunlight.

"Hello."

"I'm very sorry about your mommy and daddy but your uncle Jed and I will take very good care of you."

"Thank you." The self-possessed little voice left little room for sympathy, and Addie stared at the child for a moment, at a loss for words. Lily looked around the porch and then fixed her gaze on Trace, who still hung back in a corner. Those eyes drew him forward and he took a step, then knelt down in front of her to meet her face-to-face.

"Hello. I'm Lily."

"Hi. I'm Trace." Up close her face was all delicate angles and lines, too beautiful for a child. Her eyes were large and thickly lashed and the most brilliant shade of green he'd ever seen. Her beauty was enough to catch at your breath. She held out her hand and he took it, feeling the fragility of her bones contrasting with the strength of his callused palm.

"Trace?" She wrinkled her nose, her face crinkling in a purely childish expression. "That's a funny name."

"I think Lily is a beautiful name."

"Thank you. This is Isaiah. He's my best friend." She held up the stuffed dog and Trace nodded solemnly, taking the dog's paw in his hand and shaking it.

"I hope you'll let me be a friend, too."

Lily stared at him, those fathomless eyes thoughtful, and then she nodded. "I think so."

"Let's get Lily settled in her room." Addie's voice broke into the strange rapport between her son and the little girl. Trace stood up, feeling an odd glow when Lily slipped her hand into his, her tiny fingers curling trustingly around his, as if she had no doubt that he'd be staying with her. He'd planned to walk the five miles into town and look for a job he could take on at nights when school started in a couple of weeks, but that didn't seem so important now.

Addie led the way into the house and Trace and Lily followed her with Jed bringing up the rear. Trace had helped clear out the old sewing room only that morning. The sewing machine still sat in one corner but a narrow bed and a dresser transformed the space into a bedroom. Addie hurried into the room, smoothing the worn blue coverlet with anxious hands.

"It's not much. Probably not near as nice as what you're used to, but we can fix it up. Some paint maybe, and new curtains." She dusted at the scarred window frame as if the neglect of years could be repaired with a flick of her apron. She turned to smile at Lily, her expression apologetic. "You probably had a real nice room at your folks' home."

"You're very kind to let me stay here." She was obviously parroting something she'd been told to say. Trace wondered who'd coached her. Maybe the neighbors she'd stayed with after the small plane crash that had killed her parents.

"You're my brother's only child. Of course you're goin' to stay here." Jed pushed into the room and Trace wondered if it was only his own distaste for the old man that made him think Lily shrank a little closer.

Jed dropped the suitcase on the floor and took another pull at the bottle. He caught his wife's eyes as he lowered it and his mouth set in a sneer. "Don't say a word, Addie. I'm tired of your whining every time I take a drink. It's gettin' to the point where you'd think I was drunk all the time or somethin'. Is that what you think?"

"Of course not, Jed. I just worry about you." Addie's eyes skittered away from him, settling on nothing in particular.

"Well, stop worrying. Never could stand to have a woman fussin' over me." He turned and looked at Lily. "When you're growed, don't you go fussin' at a man, you hear?"

This time Trace knew it wasn't his imagination. The child edged back slightly so that she was partially behind his leg, her wide eyes fixed on her uncle. She didn't say anything. Jed looked as if he might like to press for an answer and then changed his mind. He left the room, his walk still reasonably steady. But that wouldn't last long. Pretty soon he'd have finished the bottle and then maybe he'd start in on another.

Addie watched her husband leave and then met her son's eyes for a moment before looking quickly away. She'd long since given up trying to answer the questions she knew he'd never ask.

"Well, Lily," she said. "I hope you'll be happy here." She looked around, seeing the worn paint and scuffed floors, the tattered curtains that hung at windows that had been painted shut years ago. Her smile flickered quickly. "I'd better go water the vegetable garden. The sun gets real hot this time of year. Trace will stay with you and show you around the place. There's all kinds of things to see."

Trace watched her leave and then looked down at Lily. She was staring around the room, her expression unreadable. He wondered what she was thinking. He wondered if he'd ever know.

LILY SETTLED into the household as if she'd always been there. Trace couldn't remember what life had been like without her. She tagged along after him whenever he wasn't at school or work. He might have found her a nuisance, but somehow she fit so neatly into whatever he was doing that he didn't mind having her along.

He taught her how to look for eggs, discovering all the places the hens liked to hide their nests. She followed him when he went fishing, sitting quietly on the creek bank, watching his pole with more interest than Trace had himself until she'd fall asleep, her head pillowed on the stuffed dog that was her constant companion.

She rarely talked about her family. When he asked, she said that her parents had been gone a lot, leaving her with various sitters, all of them nice. She didn't seem to miss them much, though sometimes he thought he saw a deep sadness in her eyes.

She made friends with Addie and helped to weed the garden and snap beans for canning. She was slow and awkward with the tasks but Addie didn't hurry her. A few minutes either way didn't matter.

It was only with Jed that Lily failed to display the friendliness that seemed to be so natural with her. She watched her uncle with wary eyes, speaking to him only if he asked her a direct question.

Summer edged into September and Trace started school. In years past he'd looked on school as an opportunity to be away from home all day, away from the tension and hopelessness. Now he found himself looking forward to getting home. He took a job at the grocer's in town, and Lily learned what time to expect him. She'd wait by the road, Isaiah in one hand and a fistful of papers in the other, eager to show him what she'd learned in school. And Trace wanted to know.

If he'd tried to analyze his reaction, he would have said that Lily was an orphan, alone in the world, and that was why it was easy to be kind to her. But the truth was, Lily brought something into his life, something he couldn't define, couldn't explain. He wanted to protect her, keep her from the harsh realities of the world as he knew it.

She'd been with them almost two months when Jed came home one night roaring drunk. Jed's drinking always got worse as winter approached. It was a pattern Trace had learned to live with. He simply stayed out of the old man's way as much as possible.

Dinner was tense that night. Jed drank steadily. Addie watched him, her eyes nervous. Lily picked at her food, her big eyes darting to her uncle's flushed face and then away. Trace watched his mother, hating the fear he saw in her eyes.

As soon as the meal was over, Addie sent Lily off to get ready for bed. Trace retreated to his cramped room and shut the door. It didn't help. He could almost smell the anger and fear and resentment. He had homework but he didn't pick up a book.

He leaned against the window and stared out into the darkness. There was no moon that night, but he didn't need light to know what lay beyond the window. Flat prairie stretched in all directions—featureless, monotonous, never changing.

Jed's voice rose in anger and Trace closed his eyes. He couldn't hear what his stepfather was saying but he could guess at the general theme. If Jed hadn't married Addie and taken on her and her son, he could have made something of himself. He would have been a big star by now, working out of Nashville. Everyone around here knew he could have been a star.

And Addie would apologize and tell him she was sorry she'd held him back, sorry she'd had so many miscarriages and had never given Jed a son of his own.

Trace's hands clenched into fists. He opened his eyes. Somewhere out there beyond the flat prairie there had to be something more. Something better.

He turned away from the window. Jed's voice still rose and fell in the living room, the whining note coming through even when he was shouting. Trace knelt next to the bed and reached under the mattress, drawing out an old cigar box. He set it on the rumpled blanket and lifted the lid. Worn bills stared back at him, a few fives and tens, a couple of twenties, but mostly ones. He didn't pick up the money to count it. He knew how much was there. Three hundred fifty-three dollars.

It had taken him almost four years to save that much. Most of the money that he made at odd jobs he gave to Addie to help stretch the meager sums Jed grudgingly allowed her. But he always saved some. He'd never said it out loud but he knew what the money was for. Escape. When he had enough, he was going to walk away from this place and never look back. He'd go somewhere and get himself a job, and as soon as he had earned some money he'd send for his mother, and neither of them would ever have to see Jed Roberts again.

Staring at the money, he could almost picture the life he'd have. A new car and a house and maybe a maid for his mother so Addie would never have to wash another dish. He'd wear nice clothes—no more patches on the elbows or knees. And he'd buy Addie a Sunday dress for every day of the week.

"Trace?" He jumped, slamming the cigar box shut before turning to look at the door. Lily stood just inside, Isaiah clutched in one hand, the other holding the edge of the door. With the door open, Jed's voice could be heard more clearly, droning the familiar theme of how much he'd given up. Trace stood, crossed the room to draw Lily inside and shut the door behind her.

"What's wrong? Did you have a nightmare?"

"No." She watched him, eyes enormous in her pale face. "He sounds awful mad."

Trace lifted the mattress and shoved the cigar box back into hiding before glancing over his shoulder at her.

"He's just hollering because he's too lazy to do anything else."

Lily looked at the closed door and then looked back at Trace. "Could I stay here with you?"

"Sure."

She ran across the room and dived onto the bed, curling up on her side, her arms wrapped tightly around Isaiah.

Trace sat on the edge of the bed, listening to the rise and fall of Jed's voice, hearing occasional whispered apologies from his mother.

"Why is he yelling like that? Is he going to hurt her?"

"Nah. He just yells a lot. Nothing to worry about. You go to sleep now and tomorrow I'll take you for a picnic."

"It'll be too cold." The protest came out on a yawn and he could see that her eyes were heavy with sleep. Trace reached to pull the covers up around her shoulders, his expression tender.

"We'll bundle up. My mom used to take me on picnics in the snow."

"Really?"

"Really. Now go to sleep."

"Okay. You won't go away, will you, Trace?"

"I won't go away." That seemed enough to satisfy her. Within minutes her breathing was light and even. Trace watched her sleep, reaching out to brush a lock of inky hair off her forehead.

She looked so young, hardly more than a baby. Anger stirred in him as he remembered her fright. She shouldn't have to be afraid. Not of anything. She should be happy and carefree. Every child had a right to that.

He leaned his head back against the wall. Jed's voice droned on, though quieter now. Pretty soon he'd pass out and then the house would be quiet except for the sound of Addie's weeping. Trace stared up at the cracked ceiling, trying to remember what it was like to be carefree. His memory didn't go back that far. Maybe if his father had lived, things would have been different. But he hadn't and things were the way they were.

Sometimes Trace thought they'd never change, that he'd grow old and die without ever seeing anything beyond the prairie. The flat endless landscape would border his birth and his death, like a picture frame. He'd die here, hemmed in by the sheer nothingness of the land.

He pushed the thought away. That wasn't the way it was going to be. He was going to escape this place. He was going to make something of himself. Somewhere there had to be something better than just surviving.

Lily stirred and whimpered in her sleep. Trace rolled his head to look at her. She didn't belong here. She was like the flower she was named for, exquisite and delicate. She'd wilt here. Sooner or later she'd break, all her beauty drained away, leaving her as worn as his mother. Fierce denial came on the heels of the thought. He wasn't going to let it happen. He wasn't going to see her destroyed the way Addie had been.

The house was quieter now. Jed had stopped talking; he'd probably passed out on the sofa. The ever-present wind caught in the cracks of the old house, a muffled background to the soft sobs coming from the living room. Trace shut his eyes, his fingers clenching against his thigh. There had to be something more to the world than this. And he was going to find it.

AS THE WEATHER got colder, Jed's drinking grew worse. It was the usual pattern, but it seemed to Trace as if his stepfather were even worse this year than most. Construction work tapered off and then disappeared as the prairie settled in for winter. No one wanted to be in the midst of building a house when winter hit.

Trace began to dread leaving for school, afraid of what he might find when he got home. He remembered the nightmare of coming home to find his mother's face bruised and

swollen, her eyes blotched from tears. She'd always told him
that she'd fallen, but he'd been younger than Lily when he
realized what was really happening. He'd been helpless to
stop it until he grew big enough to confront his stepfather
and threaten to dish out a little of the same treatment. Jed
hadn't hit Addie since then but there was an ugliness to his
mood lately that frightened Trace.

If this was what it was like even before the first snowfall,
he couldn't imagine what would happen when the weather
grew colder, trapping them inside the little house. And then
everything shifted and he realized that there was more to
worry about than Jed's rapidly worsening moods.

"I saw Lisa Mae Watkins at the market today. Her
grandfather says the signs are it's going to be a real cold
winter."

Jed grunted sullenly in answer to his wife's comment,
poking his fork into the plate of beans and hocks. "Don't
know why you sound so cheerful. Just means we'll be
snowed in more'n usual. Nothin' to crow about."

"I wasn't crowin', Jed. I was just making conversation."
He said nothing and Addie looked at him anxiously before
turning her attention to her son. "How was school today,
Trace?"

"Fine." He shrugged, forcing himself to swallow despite
the tension in his throat. "Everyone's real excited about
having the long weekend off for Thanksgiving next week."

"That'll be nice. Do you like Thanksgiving, Lily?"

"I like Christmas better. I'm going to be an angel in the
play this year."

Addie smiled but it was Jed who spoke. "I bet you'll
make a pretty angel. All that beautiful hair and all. They'll
hardly have to give you a costume."

He reached across the table to lift a lock of her hair, letting it sift through his fingers. Trace had the urge to knock

his hand away. His throat closed up tight and he could hardly breathe. He looked at his stepfather's face and felt a sick uneasiness he couldn't define. There was something there he didn't like. Something ugly.

Lily shifted slightly and Jed's hand fell away. He continued to look at her and Trace felt his uneasiness growing. It wasn't just tonight. It was something that had been swelling inside him for weeks now. He'd seen Jed watching Lily, looking at her, making comments about how pretty she was. He couldn't put his finger on what it was that bothered him but there was something there that made him uneasy. He glanced at his mother but she was staring at her plate.

The meal over, Trace and Lily cleared the table while Addie started on the dishes. Jed continued to sit at the table, a bottle and a shot glass in front of him. He didn't say anything. Most of the time he stared at the wall, but several times Trace caught him watching Lily. Trace wanted to snatch her away, put her out of sight, as if that would keep her safe. But safe from what?

He still didn't have an answer when it was time for Lily to go to bed. He didn't have an answer but the uneasiness was as strong as ever. The TV was on but no one was watching it. Addie was bent over some mending, squinting in the light of a too-dim bulb. Jed was slumped in a chair, the bottle beside him, his eyes on the screen, his thoughts elsewhere. Trace sat in the corner of the sofa, a history book open in his lap, his mind on other things. Lily came into the room after her bath. As always, her delicate beauty was out of place among the worn furnishings and scuffed floor.

"Good night, Aunt Addie. Good night, Uncle Jed. Good night, Trace."

"Aren't you going to give your old uncle a good-night kiss?"

Lily hesitated, her eyes flickering uncertainly. This, too, was a new habit of Jed's. In the past couple of weeks he'd started insisting on her kissing him good-night. Trace glanced at his mother. She kept her head down as if the mending were absorbing all of her attention. But her hands were still.

"Come on and give me a kiss."

Lily's eyes flickered to Trace as he stood up, stretching elaborately. "I'm beat. I think I'm going to hit the sack, too. Come on, Lily. I'll tuck you in. Good night, Mom. 'Night, Jed."

He took Lily's hand, pulling her from the room before anyone said anything.

"Are you going to bed, too, Trace?"

"Sure am." He stopped in front of her bedroom door and stared at it. It looked so thin. No protection at all. Now why was he thinking in terms of protection? "I'll tell you what. How'd you like to sleep in my room tonight?"

"How come?"

How come? He didn't know how come. He just knew he didn't want to leave her alone in that room tonight. He shrugged.

"Just for fun. What do you think?"

"Isaiah, too?"

"Sure."

"Okay." She hurried into the room to get her faithful companion. Trace looked over his shoulder, not knowing what he was looking for. When Lily came back out, he took her hand again, shutting her bedroom door before leading her down the hall to his bedroom.

She was asleep within minutes of his tucking her in. Trace settled into a chair, a book in his lap. The room was cold. The old heater didn't reach into this back corner. It would have been warmer under the covers but he was too restless to go to sleep. He sat there, flipping a page occasionally, barely noticing what he was reading. After a while he heard his mother and Jed go to bed, their bedroom door clicking quietly shut. Still Trace sat there, waiting, though he couldn't have said what for.

His head was nodding over the book when it came. A sound beyond the restless whisper of the wind. His head jerked up. Muffled footsteps came down the hall, as if someone were tiptoeing. He reached out to shut off the small lamp, blinded for a moment until his eyes adjusted to the darkness. Trace stared at the wall as if he could see through the dirty paint to the dark hallway beyond. The footsteps stopped and his fingers knotted over the spine of the book. He hardly dared to breathe.

"Lily? It's me, honey. Uncle Jed. I thought you might be scared alone in the dark."

Trace heard Lily's door open and close and then silence. After a few minutes it opened again and Jed's footsteps came down the hall. They stopped outside his room, and as he stared at the door Trace could almost hear his stepfather's breathing. The tension grew inside him until he thought he might burst. After a long moment the footsteps moved away, but Trace didn't relax until he heard the sound of a door closing and knew Jed had gone back to his own bed.

He stared into the darkness. His hands were shaking so badly that he almost missed the table when he tried to put the book down. He swallowed hard against the acid taste of bile that rose in his throat. Getting up, he leaned his forehead against the window. It felt no colder than he did inside.

Lily stirred, turning over and muttering in her sleep. Trace squeezed his eyes tight, feeling the sting of tears behind his eyelids. She was so little. She had no one but him to take care of her. He had to protect her. But how? He had to get her away from here, away from Jed.

He rubbed his forehead over the chill glass. There had to be a way. All he had to do was find it. Come what may, he wouldn't let her stay here. He couldn't.

Chapter Two

In the morning Trace wondered if he'd imagined the events of the night before. Maybe his imagination had been working overtime. But sitting across from Jed at the breakfast table, he knew that wasn't the case.

Though it was barely seven in the morning, Jed had already been at the bottle. The smell of bourbon wafted across the table, a strident addition to the scent of bacon and eggs. Addie set a plate of charred bacon and hard-cooked eggs down in front of her son. Trace stared at the unappetizing food and he didn't say anything. He'd seen the way her hands shook.

"These eggs'd break a window if you flung 'em at one. You'd think after all these years you'd've learned to cook a decent egg." Jed's tone was more whining than angry.

Out of the corner of his eye, Trace saw his mother's worn hands twist in the faded gingham apron and he didn't have to look at her face to see the uncertainty and hovering fear. She knew as well as he did that Jed's mood could swing from whining to rage in a matter of a drink or two.

"I'm sorry, Jed. I'll cook you some new ones."

"Never mind. If Trace can eat his, I reckon I can manage mine. How'd you sleep, boy? Anythin' disturb you?"

Trace swallowed hard, forcing down a mouthful of rubbery egg white. He looked up, meeting Jed's eyes. What he saw there almost brought his meager breakfast back up.

Jed knew. He knew it was no coincidence that Lily hadn't been in her room the night before. He knew that Trace had kept her with him deliberately. He should have been angry or ashamed or defiant, but that wasn't the emotion Trace saw. There was a kind of sly amusement in his bloodshot eyes, a challenge. Trace swallowed hard, dropping his eyes to his plate. He didn't care that Jed would see his action as fear. If he looked at his stepfather for another instant, he was going to go for his throat. Rage like he'd never known before threatened to take control of him. He wanted to feel Jed's flesh beneath his hands, wanted to feel the life draining out of him. He wanted it so badly he could taste the desire to kill.

He jerked, startled, as a small hand touched the fist that lay clenched against his thigh. Hidden beneath the table, Lily's tiny fingers closed over his hesitantly. Trace looked up, meeting her gaze. Her emerald eyes were wide, holding a tinge of fear. She sensed his anger but was uncertain of its origin or target. Staring into her eyes, Trace felt his rage shift from a white-hot need for violence to cold determination. This was one battle Jed wasn't going to win.

He turned his hand, squeezing Lily's fingers in reassurance, giving her a half smile. The uncertainty faded and she turned her attention back to her breakfast, her world safe again. Trace lifted his head and stared across the table at his stepfather.

Jed looked into the boy's eyes and his satisfied smirk faded, replaced by a hesitancy that even the bourbon couldn't drown. Trace's eyes were a cold, cold blue, too old, too controlled. He glanced away, reaching for the bottle that was never far from his side. He splashed another shot of bourbon into his glass, his lower jaw setting sullenly.

The boy had always been too old for his own good. From the time he was a toddler, he'd look at you with those cold blue eyes that seemed to see deep inside a body. He always seemed to see things that shouldn't be seen, know things you wished he didn't know. Too damned uppity. He'd told Addie time and again that the boy needed a good whipping to take some of the spirit out of him. In thirteen years of marriage it was the only time she'd ever shown any signs of a backbone. He'd never quite forgotten the look in her eyes when she'd told him never to lift a hand to her child.

He took a swallow of liquor, feeling it burn its way down his throat and settle in a warm pool in his stomach. Looking at Trace again through a haze of alcohol, Jed wondered if he'd imagined the cold threat in the boy's eyes. The liquor made it easy to believe he had.

TRACE FOUND IT IMPOSSIBLE to concentrate in school that day. His mind kept racing round and round, looking for some way out. There had to be a way to protect Lily. He had to find it.

The light snowfall two days before had melted, leaving the ground muddy. It sucked at your feet when you walked, threatening to strip off your shoes. The warm breeze that had melted the snow had shifted to a cold northerly wind. When he stopped into the gas station to get a candy bar for Lily, old man Hanover commented that it sure did look like they were going to get a real snowfall before long. Shaking his head, he edged closer to the electric heater. "Goin' to be a real cold winter, I reckon."

Trace walked the rest of the way home, thinking about what winter might bring. With cold winds howling outside, there'd be few opportunities to escape Jed's surly drunken moods. He hunched his shoulders inside his thin coat, knowing that the wind that chilled him now was nothing compared to what January would bring.

He kept Lily in his room again that night. She accepted his suggestion with a trust that Trace found both a blessing and a curse. It was a blessing that he didn't have to try to explain the unexplainable. And it was a curse in that it increased his feeling of responsibility.

He wedged a straight-backed chair under his door and crawled under the covers, only to lie awake staring at the door, waiting. He didn't know quite what he was waiting for. He couldn't believe that Jed would actually come into the bedroom while he was there. Still, sleep, when it came, was fitful and unsatisfying, leaving him more tired than rested the next morning.

Walking home from school that afternoon, he faced the fact that this was something he couldn't handle alone. He had to have help. The decision made, it seemed like providence when he found his mother alone in the kitchen. Jed wasn't home. He was either out on a job or out drinking—neither would do much for his mood. Lily was watching cartoons in the living room. It had been a long time since he'd gone to his mother for help, but she was his only hope.

"Mom? Could I talk to you about something?"

Addie started nervously, her eyes lifting from her mending for a moment to look at her son's face. She glanced away, her fingers plucking at a crooked stitch.

"What about, Trace?"

"It's about Lily. I'm worried about her."

"I don't know why. She seems to be settling in real well. Follows you around like a puppy, too. She's a pretty little thing, isn't she?"

"Yes, but that's not what I wanted to talk about." He hesitated, watching her thin hands weaving the needle in and out of one of his shirts, mending a ripped seam. He was torn between his love for Addie and his need to protect Lily. What he had to say was going to hurt his mother and surely she'd known enough hurt in her life. Yet he couldn't stand by and let his stepfather destroy Lily.

"It's about Jed, really."

Addie jerked, jabbing herself with the needle. A bright spot of blood welled on her finger, dripping onto the faded blue flannel of the shirt and disappearing into the fabric. She didn't move for a moment and Trace might have wondered if she'd heard him if it hadn't been for that single bright drop of blood.

"Mom, he's—"

She broke into his words, her voice holding an edge of panic. "I know you and Jed have never gotten along all that well, Trace, but he don't mean no harm. Jed has a lot of things on his mind—things we don't even know about. You got to be patient with him."

"Mom—"

"You know, I really think we're going to have to buy you some new shirts this winter. This old thing is about to give up the ghost. Maybe we'll go into town after the first of the year and see if we can pick up something on sale."

"Jed—"

"Don't you worry about Jed. I'll talk him into the money. He's not as bad as you think he is, Trace. Really he's not." Addie looked up, her eyes pleading with him, her fingers knotted in the old shirt.

Trace stared at her, feeling the last fragile illusions of youth break into a million fragments. There was a dull pain in his chest, and for a moment it was hard to breathe.

She wasn't going to help him. She couldn't.

The realization washed over him, bringing pain and a certain sharp relief. A part of him had known all along that this was how it was going to be. It was out in the open now. No more pretending. No more hoping. It was up to him.

In that moment he left the last traces of childhood behind. Looking at Addie, he saw her clearly and he couldn't hate her. She had no strength left, nothing to give. Not to him, not even to herself. She couldn't help him protect Lily. He'd been foolish to think she might. She hadn't been able to protect herself.

He saw his mother now through adult eyes. At thirty-five she looked like fifty. Her shoulders were hunched, her face was drawn. Her eyes, which had been such a bright blue when he was a child, seemed to have faded to a dusty gray, like an old woman's. He looked at her and felt a great pity.

Addie seemed to sense something of his feelings. Faint color came up in her thin cheeks and she glanced down, her eyes on her fingers twisting aimlessly in the worn shirt.

"It's okay, Mom. Don't worry about new shirts. I guess what I've got will see me through winter." He wasn't talking about shirts.

Addie's flush deepened, her mouth pulled tight with shame, but she only nodded stiffly, still not looking at him.

They sat there without speaking. Trace accepted her inability to help him but there was a part of him that couldn't walk away. He'd sat down in this chair still half a boy. When he got up, he'd have to shoulder a man's responsibility. He'd leave childhood behind forever. His thoughts didn't run so clear as that. He just knew he didn't want to leave his mother yet.

From the living room came the faint chaotic sounds of cartoon mayhem. On the stove a pot of watery beef stew bubbled. Where the steam from the pot met the chilled windows, a mist formed, shutting out the cold prairie. Addie made a few clumsy stitches in the shirt, her head bent over the work. Trace watched her, wishing things were different.

"You know, things would have been real different if your father hadn't died." Addie's hands stilled but she didn't lift her head. "I wish you could remember him, Trace. He liked to laugh. Nothing he enjoyed more than a good laugh."

Trace didn't say anything. It was so seldom she spoke of his father. He'd been barely a year old when Robert Dushane was killed in a car wreck. There was a faded picture in the cigar box where he kept his treasures and he'd worn the paper thin studying the image of a smiling man whose eyes seemed to laugh into the camera.

"You know, you have an uncle." Addie smoothed the flannel across her knee, her eyes on the aimless movement, at odds with the intensity in her voice. "He lives in Los Angeles, worked at Lockheed last I heard. Probably still there. Philip. I only met him once. He came to our wedding. Seemed like a good man." Her fingers smoothed imaginary wrinkles. "Los Angeles has a real nice climate. Your dad used to say we'd move there someday."

Trace sat very still. Now he understood why she'd brought up his father. It wasn't his father she wanted to tell him about. It was his uncle. An uncle in Los Angeles.

Lily couldn't stay in this place. He couldn't protect her forever. He'd known that, even while he hadn't wanted to consider the results of that knowledge. His mother, in her own soft way, was telling him how it was going to have to be. She couldn't deal with the problem head-on, but she knew something had to be done. And Trace would have to be the one to do it.

LILY SLEPT IN HIS ROOM again that night. If she thought the situation was strange, she didn't say so. She curled up on his lumpy mattress, Isaiah cuddled against her, and fell asleep instantly, content that as long as Trace was there, all was right with her world. Trace only wished life could be so simple.

Jed had been drinking heavily at dinner, and just the memory of the way he'd watched Lily was enough to make Trace feel sick. How could Jed look at her like that? She was hardly more than a baby.

He stirred restlessly in the hard chair. There'd been something particularly ugly about Jed tonight. Twice he'd caught Trace watching him but he hadn't looked away. Instead, there'd been a sly challenge in his eyes, as if he knew he'd win sooner or later.

It was that look that had Trace sitting up in the old chair as midnight approached. The room was dark except for the moonlight that shone in through the open curtains. Outside, the prairie lay still and empty, at peace before winter howled down out of the north. But Trace wasn't interested in the moon-kissed scenery.

He was watching the door, his ears strained to hear any sound in the quiet house. His hands lay in his lap, loosely curled around the grip of an old Colt .38. It had belonged to his father, and on Trace's fifteenth birthday, his mother had given it to him. She'd given him the package after Jed left for work one morning and he hadn't needed to ask if Jed knew about the gift.

Trace's head bobbed, exhaustion winning out over tension. It was so late. Maybe he'd imagined the look in Jed's eyes. Maybe there was nothing to worry about. A floorboard creaked in the hallway, the sound loud in the quiet house. Trace's head jerked up, his eyes sharpening on the door. Another floorboard popped and he could suddenly feel the pulse in his temples.

It could just be the old house settling. But then the floor shifted outside his bedroom door and he knew. Jed was standing out there, staring at the door, just as Trace was staring at it on this side.

He tightened his hold on the gun, easing the safety off, aware of his sweaty palms against the wooden grip. He lifted the gun slightly, wondering why it suddenly felt so heavy. Was Jed going to try the door?

His mouth was dry, his tongue thick with the coppery taste of fear. There was no sound from the hall but he knew Jed was there, waiting, watching. Trace's head began to pound, the ache centering in his temples. For one insane moment he almost hoped Jed would force the door. In one moment of crystal-clear thought he knew he could kill his stepfather without regret.

And still there was no sound from the other side of the door.

Trace had no idea how much time passed while the bizarre standoff continued. It might have been hours but he suspected it could only have been a few minutes when the floorboard groaned again. He sensed Jed leaving more than he actually heard him.

Still Trace didn't move until he heard the click of a door latch and knew that Jed had gone back to the bedroom he shared with Addie. His breath exploded out of him on a sob, making him aware that he'd been holding it so long he felt light-headed. He slumped in the chair, easing the safety back on the .38 and setting it on the table before wiping his sweaty palms on the legs of his jeans.

"Trace? What's wrong?" Lily's sleepy voice came out of the darkness, startling him. He turned, making out the vague lump of her under the covers.

"Nothing's wrong. I was just studying late. Go back to sleep."

"Okay." She snuggled deeper into the thin pillow and was asleep instantly, only half-awake to start with.

Trace listened to her light breathing, his thoughts painfully sharp. He no longer had a choice. And he no longer had any time. Tonight Jed had walked away, but if he'd had a little more to drink, maybe he wouldn't have.

No, he had no choice. No choice at all.

"LILY, WAKE UP." He kept his voice low, clenching his teeth against the nervous shivers that threatened to set them chattering. "Lily, come on. We've got to go now."

"Trace?"

He'd turned on the table lamp, throwing a towel over it to mute the light. In the dim glow he saw Lily's eyelids flutter and then lift. Her sleepy gaze settled on him as her arms tightened around Isaiah's scruffy form.

"Is it morning?"

"No. It won't be morning for a long time but we've got to get going now."

She sat up, rubbing her fists into her eyes. "Where're we going?"

"Away from here. We're going to California to visit my uncle." He tried to keep his voice calm, hoping she wouldn't notice that his hands were shaking as he helped her tug a heavy sweater over her head, leaving her pajamas on under it.

"California?" He pulled her hair out from under the sweater and handed her a pair of jeans.

"That's right. It'll be real nice there."

She stood up, obediently poking her foot into the boot he held, balancing herself with a hand on his shoulder. He bundled her into a heavy coat and tugged a wool cap down over her ears.

"We have to be real quiet, Lily. Don't make a sound, okay?" Her eyes were wide green pools of questions but she nodded.

"I'll be quiet as a mouse."

"Good girl." He switched off the lamp, plunging the room into darkness. Trace waited until his eyes had adjusted to the lack of light and then he picked up a battered satchel with one hand and took Lily's hand with the other. The house was dark and still around them as they crept down the hallway and into the kitchen. Trace held his breath at every creaky floorboard. Once the satchel banged against a corner of the wall and he froze, but nothing happened and he tugged Lily forward.

He hesitated in the kitchen, staring at the back door. The enormity of the step he was taking struck him. For just a moment he wanted to turn around and go back to his bed. But then Lily's fingers tightened around his and he knew he couldn't do that. There could be no going back.

His hand was on the latch when he heard a quiet click. He spun around, pushing Lily behind him, wishing he'd thought to tuck the old gun into his belt instead of putting it in the satchel. But it wasn't Jed's drunk and angry figure who stood in the doorway. It was Addie, an ancient flannel robe wrapped around her thin body, her hair lying about her shoulders.

Her hand dropped from the switch of the small lamp and their eyes met across the room. Light spilled out over the counter and onto the floor, illuminating without revealing. In this light Addie looked almost young again, the gray in her hair smoothed by the shadows. Trace stared at his mother, wondering what he should say, what he should do. In the end, he said nothing.

Addie came forward and the illusion of youth was lost in the stiffness of her movements, the slump of her shoulders. She opened the pantry door and pulled out a heavy paper bag, the top folded down to seal in the contents. She held it out toward Trace and he took it automatically, his eyes never leaving her face. There was a small part of him that still hoped she would tell him not to go. She'd help him protect Lily.

"You won't have to worry about food, at least not for a couple of days."

The hope died without taking full wing. Trace's hand tightened over the sack and he straightened his shoulders. Addie's eyes softened.

"You're goin' to be as tall as your father was."

Her eyes flickered to where Lily stood so quietly, half-hidden behind Trace. Addie looked away and the room was quiet for a moment. Trace said nothing, fighting the urge to break down and bawl like a baby. His mother reached into the pocket of her robe and brought out a wad of faded green bills.

"I want you to have this." Trace set down the satchel and reached out automatically, only realizing what he was holding as his fingers closed over the money.

"That's your egg money," he protested. "You can't give me that."

"It's my money and I can do what I choose with it and I choose to give it to you now."

"But, Mom, you've been saving this for a long time."

"That's so, but I want you to have it. I think you're going to have more use for it than I ever would. It's not much but it ought to help the two of you." Her voice quivered and she stopped. "I want you to have it, Trace."

And he understood. It was all she could offer him. It shamed her that she didn't have the strength to do what needed to be done, and this was the best she could do to make up for her failure. He nodded jerkily and stuffed the money in his pocket.

"Thanks."

Addie looked at him, her eyes bright with tears. She reached up, touching his cheek with trembling fingers. "You write when you can."

Trace nodded, swallowing hard on the urge to cry. He was too old for tears. Besides, they wouldn't change the way things had to be. Addie looked so frail, so old. He bent to kiss her cheek, feeling the trembling she was fighting so hard to conceal. For an instant he couldn't bear to leave her. With him gone, who would protect her from Jed? Who would take care of her?

Behind him Lily stirred, her hand tugging on his coat. "Trace? I'm sleepy. Can we go back to bed now?" The plaintive question ended on a yawn.

Trace closed his eyes, feeling torn between the need to protect his mother and the need to keep Lily safe. There was really no choice. Addie had made her choices a long time ago. Lily was only a child. Her whole life was ahead of her and she had to have a chance of her own. He couldn't do anything for his mother, but maybe if he kept Lily safe, it would somehow make up for some of the choices she'd made.

Addie saw the decision in his eyes and she nodded jerkily. He was doing the right thing, the only thing he could do. "You take care now. Both of you."

"We will." Without another word he turned and opened the back door. Cold air swept into the room and Addie shivered, wrapping the old robe closer around her thin frame. "Come on, Lily. We've got a long ways to go." She yawned but followed him without protest.

The moon cast a pale glow over the ground, more shadows than light but enough to see by. Trace hesitated once, looking back over his shoulder. Addie was standing in the open door, her fingers knotted on the worn flannel robe, her shoulders hunched like a woman twice her age. He had only that one glimpse of her before he set his sights firmly on the road ahead of them. He didn't look back again.

Chapter Three

Frost scrunched under their feet. Trace hunched his shoulders inside his coat, hardly noticing the cold. He had too many other things to think about to pay much attention to the physical discomfort. The money his mother had given him felt like a lead weight in his pocket. Conscience money. He couldn't remember where he'd heard the term and he wasn't sure exactly what it meant, but it popped into his head now and wouldn't go away.

Trace knew Addie was doing the best she could, and on one level he couldn't be angry with her. But there was another part of him that felt a deep resentment. He was fifteen. It wasn't fair that he should have to shoulder all this responsibility by himself. She was his mother and she'd failed him just when he needed her most.

He sucked in a deep breath of cold air. If there was one thing he'd learned in his life, it was that life couldn't be counted on to be fair. Fair was something only children expected from the world. And he wasn't a child anymore. No matter how much it hurt, he had to accept that his mother had done the best she knew how. If that wasn't good enough, he'd just have to make up the difference himself.

"Trace, I'm tired. Where're we going?"

"You keep hold of my coat, Lily. We're not going far to-night. Just to Hoffman's. We'll spend the night there and go on in the morning."

"To California?"

"To California."

"How come we're going to stay at Hoffman's barn?"

"Just for fun, Lily. Don't you think it'll be fun?"

"I suppose." She sounded doubtful and he could hardly blame her. It was the best reason he could come up with on the spur of the moment.

By the time they got to the neighbor's property, Lily was beginning to stumble sleepily. Trace held the satchel and the bag of food in one hand and put his other arm over her shoulders, letting her lean against him.

The barn door was open, only a crack, but wide enough for them to slip inside without shifting it. Inside it was cold but not as cold as outside. Trace dug in his pocket to find the small flashlight he'd purloined from the kitchen and shone it around the cavernous building until he found what he wanted.

"Come on, Lily. We're going to climb up that ladder and sleep in the hay."

"I'm too tired, Trace." She hung back, rubbing her eyes.

"It's only a little ways and then you can sleep in the nice soft hay. Come on, Lily. It'll be fun." For a moment he thought she was going to argue further, but perhaps the promise of a bed at the top of the ladder won out. He un-zipped her jacket enough to tuck Isaiah into the front of it, freeing both her hands for the steep climb. It seemed to take forever for her to get to the top of the ladder and Trace kept glancing over his shoulder, half expecting old man Hoff-man to come running through the door with his shotgun.

They reached the top without incident and Lily was asleep within minutes, covered with an old blanket Trace had found in one corner. Rumor had it that Jimmy Hoffman had always brought his girlfriends up here before he left for college. From the supply of blankets, Trace could believe it was true. He could only be grateful. He curled up next to Lily, shivering more with reaction than cold.

His life would never be the same after tonight. He'd taken the first steps down a road whose ending he could only guess at. It was not a reassuring thought, but tiredness won out over worry and he fell asleep at last, not waking until the roar of a truck engine outside woke him to morning light.

They picnicked in the hayloft, eating the thick sandwiches Addie had packed for them. Lily was in good spirits, giggling at the hay that clung to Trace's hair. He looked just like the scarecrow in *The Wizard of Oz*, she informed him. Trace amused her by doing his best to imitate a rubber-legged walk. He wasn't very successful but his attempts drew peals of laughter from Lily. Despite his worries, he felt his spirits rise. Whatever happened, he'd been right to take her away from that house. He was old enough to know just how frightening a step he'd taken and young enough to feel some optimism about its outcome.

That optimism faded as they crept out of the barn and started walking along the road again. It was cold. The sun was up but its light seemed weak and filtered, giving little warmth.

"Trace, why are we going to California?"

"My uncle lives there."

"Are we going to walk all the way?"

"Nope. We're going to catch a bus just as soon as we get to town."

Lily came to a halt in the middle of the road. Trace stopped and turned to look at her, trying to rein in his impatience. "What's wrong?"

"Trace, we're going the wrong way to get to town."

"We're going to another town, Lily."

"How come?"

He hesitated a moment and then decided that it would be easier to tell her the truth than to try to think up a reasonable lie. "Because I don't want anyone we know to see us."

She considered that, digging the toe of her boot into the hard ground.

"How come we snuck out last night? How come your mom or Uncle Jed didn't drive us to catch a bus like Mr. and Mrs. Lauder did when I came here?"

"Jed doesn't know we're leaving."

"Are we running away?"

"Yeah, I guess we are."

"How come?"

"I . . . just thought it would be a good idea." How could he possibly explain the reasons? "Do you mind?"

"Nope." She shook her head, sending her hair flying under the knit cap. "Long as you're here, it's okay."

"You're going to like California, Lily. We both are."

"Okay." She hitched Isaiah higher under her arm and tucked her hand in Trace's. Her confidence in him terrified Trace. She believed in his ability to take care of her far more strongly than he did.

They continued walking. Trace kept his eye on the horizon. Heavy storm clouds were banking to the north and he watched them uneasily. He knew what they could mean. To be caught in a snowstorm in the open could be fatal. It was just past noon and they were still several miles from town when the first fat snowflakes began to fall.

They were deceptively soft, harmless seeming. They floated to earth gently, only a few at first and then a few more until the ground was covered with a thin layer of white. Trace scanned the area for some shelter but there was nothing to be seen. Nothing but prairie and more prairie.

They had to keep walking. He set his teeth and pulled Lily closer to him, sheltering her as much as possible.

The snow thickened with frightening rapidity. A wind kicked up, driving the increasingly heavy snowfall in diagonal curtains across the roadway. It took all Trace's concentration to make sure they were staying on the road. Lily stumbled along beside him, clinging to his coat, her face muffled in a scarf, only her eyes exposed. If she was frightened, she chose not to say anything. Trace was just as glad. He was too scared himself to be able to offer her much reassurance.

He was just beginning to wonder if they should stop and try to build a shelter of some sort when he heard a low rumble coming from behind them. It took him a moment to realize what it was. A truck. If they didn't get off the road, they could be run down, yet they couldn't risk falling into one of the drainage ditches on either side of the road. He wasn't sure he had the strength to pull them out if they fell in.

He hugged Lily closer, backing as far as he dared. The truck loomed up behind them. The driver had the headlights on, trying to penetrate the thick curtain of snow. Trace crowded back another few inches, convinced that they were going to be run down. Instead of sweeping by them, the huge vehicle slowed. Trace could hear the change in engine speed as the driver geared down. He stopped when the cab was just level with them. There was a moment's pause when it seemed as if even the snow was waiting to see what would happen, and then the passenger side door was thrust open from the inside and a deep slow voice rasped out at them.

"What the hell are two kids doing out on the road in the middle of a blizzard? You need a ride?"

Trace hesitated only an instant. He couldn't see anything beyond an outline of the man who was leaning toward them. But it was a sure bet they couldn't stay where they were.

"Trace, I'm cold." Lily's plaintive whisper made the choice for him, not that there'd been much of a choice to start with. The stranger seemed to agree.

"Boost her up, kid. I'll lift her in. Then climb up yourself before we all freeze to death."

The interior of the truck was warm. Trace hadn't realized just how cold he was until he felt the tingling in his face and hands as the warmth started to penetrate his icy skin.

"You two okay?"

"We're fine. Thanks, mister."

"Name's John."

"I'm Trace and this is Lily."

John nodded, putting the truck into gear and easing forward.

"Pleased to meet you. This isn't really strolling weather. Where are you two headed?"

Trace looked up from helping Lily out of her coat, his eyes wary. "We're going to L.A. to stay with my uncle."

"The weather is a hell of a lot better there. Does this road go straight through to the highway? I took a wrong turn a few miles back and I've been expecting to find myself at a dead end in some farmer's yard ever since."

"It meets the main road in a couple of miles." Trace allowed himself to relax a bit. It didn't look as if he were going to have to answer any impossible questions.

"Good. I wasn't really anxious to back this thing for ten miles."

Trace stared out at the swirling snow as he shrugged out of his own coat, letting the warmth of the cab ease into his chilled body. If the truck hadn't come along, they would still be out there. They could have died.

"You two seem a little young to be heading for L.A. by yourselves." The words weren't quite a question but the tone hinted at wanting an explanation. Trace hesitated a long moment. Pride forbade him telling a stranger any details of their personal troubles. But he couldn't risk having John decide that it would be in their best interests to return them home.

"We've got good reason." It was all the explanation he felt able to offer.

Their eyes met for a long moment before John returned his attention to the road outside. Trace waited without speaking, knowing that his words were being weighed somewhere behind that still expression. Studying John's face, Trace realized that he wasn't as old as he'd thought at first. Not much more than twenty-five. But his eyes were older and held depths of memory that didn't suit his young face.

"All right. I'll accept that." John glanced at him again, weighing and measuring. "Your uncle expecting you?"

"Yes." Trace didn't hesitate over the lie. John's eyes narrowed for a moment, as if he could see the truth, but he didn't question further. He nodded, making up his mind about something.

"I'm heading as far as Denver. You could catch a bus from there. You're welcome to ride along with me."

Trace didn't say anything for a moment. They would have changed buses in Denver anyway. The money they'd save would be welcome. He didn't want to arrive on his uncle's doorstep without a penny to his name. On the other hand, he didn't know anything about John except that he'd shown up just when they'd needed help. Not much to go on. He'd heard enough stories of what could happen to hitchhikers to be a little cautious. And yet . . .

He looked from John to Lily. She'd fallen asleep, Isaiah clutched tight against her chest, her head pillowed on his shoulder. He shifted her, easing her into a more comfortable position.

"Thank you. We'd be obliged if you'd let us ride with you."

"No problem. I could use the company. A man gets a little antisocial driving one of these things." He reached for a pack of cigarettes and lit one with one hand, keeping his eyes on the road. "Not that I'm a real sociable kind of a guy anyway, but even I get tired of my own company."

"We're grateful that you came along." Trace looked out at the snow that was falling steadily outside the huge cab. His shoulders twitched in an involuntary shiver. John followed his gaze.

"You'd have been frozen colder than a well digger's butt by now." He took a long draw on the cigarette. "You know, if I believed in fate, I might think it had something to do with this. I've been driving this route for four months and this is the first time I've taken a wrong turn." He shrugged and his mouth twisted in a wry smile. "But I don't believe in fate."

Trace didn't say anything. At the moment he couldn't have said whether he had any belief in fate or not. He'd never been much for religion but he had to admit that he'd sent up a garbled prayer or two when they were stumbling along in the snow. His mother would undoubtedly say that John was the answer to those prayers. He wasn't sure whether he believed that or not, but just in case he sent a quick glance upward and a mental thank-you. It didn't hurt to be careful. He wouldn't want anyone thinking he was ungrateful.

Lily woke up after a nap of less than an hour. She blinked sleepily at John for a moment, as if trying to place him, and then gave him a sweet smile.

"You're the man in the big truck who picked us up."

"That's right. Did you have a nice nap?" Trace noticed the way John's face softened when he looked at Lily. He understood the feeling. There was just something about her.

"Yes, thank you. This is a very big truck."

"It's pretty good sized."

"I'm hungry, Trace."

"There's a truck stop about five miles up ahead," John answered for him. "If you can hang on until then, I'll treat the two of you to a couple of hamburgers."

Trace's hand closed over Lily's arm, stilling her acceptance. She looked up at him, puzzled, but didn't say anything.

"Thanks, but we've got some food with us." His voice was stiff with pride and John slanted him a look from under dark brows.

"Stale sandwiches?"

Trace flushed but he didn't back down. "We don't need any charity. I've got plenty of money."

"Let me give you a little advice. There's no such thing as plenty of money. It always goes twice as fast as you'd thought it would and only half as far. And don't let your pride get in the way of accepting a little help. Pride is a good thing but you can't let it run your life. I can tell you that from experience. And the last piece of advice is never turn down a free meal."

He turned off the road, parking the huge truck in a lot full of similar vehicles and shutting off the engine. He turned to look at Trace, resting one arm on the wheel. "I'm going to eat some lunch. I'd appreciate your company."

Trace hesitated, pride warring with common sense. Lily had no such hesitation. "I'd like a hamburger, please. But no onions. I don't like onions."

John's expression cracked into a grin. "Put on your coat and we'll see what we can do about that order, little one."

In the end, Trace went with them. He'd have felt absurd sitting in the truck by himself. Besides, he had to admit that a hot meal held more appeal than the cold stale sandwiches his mother had sent with them.

They didn't linger at the truck stop. They ate and John refueled and then they were on their way again. The snow continued to fall, sometimes heavily, sometimes barely drifting down. Lily dozed, lulled to sleep by the smooth rhythm of the wheels. John and Trace talked sometimes and sometimes were silent. Only once did John come close to asking why the two of them were on their own.

"Great little kid." He nodded to where Lily slept, her head pillowed in Trace's lap. "Your sister?"

"No." Trace answered without thinking and then wished he'd lied. "She's a . . . cousin."

John slanted him a look that told Trace the lie had been too little, too late. "You two are a bit young to be traveling on your own like this."

"I told you, I've got an uncle in L.A. We're going to stay with him."

"Well, I don't know about an uncle but I do know someone who's running when I see him. I did it myself once. You got a good reason, kid?"

"We've got good reason." Trace didn't add anything more to the flat statement. Just the thought of Jed was enough to make his stomach tighten. John glanced at him, the look measuring. Trace met his eyes without hesitation, man to man, not man to boy. After a long moment John nodded.

"I reckon you do." He didn't ask any more.

The drive to Denver was long and tedious, with little to see outside the cab of the truck. They eventually drove out of the snowstorm but the land remained gray and cold, as if to make sure they didn't forget that winter had arrived. John drove at a steady pace, his hands competent on the huge wheel. Trace found himself relaxing, letting some of the burden of Lily's care slip from his shoulders. At least for a few hours there was someone else to help care for her.

But it was only for a short time. All too soon John was pulling the big truck to a halt near the bus station in Denver.

"This is as far as I can take you."

Trace looked at the busy station and squared his shoulders in an unconscious gesture, as if shouldering a burden.

"We really appreciate this."

"No problem. It was nice to have company for a while." John lit a cigarette, his eyes narrowing through the smoke. "You got enough money?"

"We're fine." Despite himself, Trace's tone was stiff, bristling with pride.

John's mouth twisted in a smile but his eyes showed his understanding. "You've got a lot of pride, Trace. But remember what I told you before—it can get you in trouble. Sometimes you need to be able to ask for help."

Trace swallowed the urge to tell him that they didn't need any help from anyone. "Thank you for the ride."

John nodded as if he knew just what was going through the boy's mind. "Like I said, I enjoyed the company." He looked from Trace to Lily, who was staring out at the bus station with wide eyes, Isaiah clutched to her chest.

"L.A. is a big place. It's easy to get swallowed up in it." His tone carried the implication that if they were running from something, they'd chosen a good place to go.

"Have you been to Los Angeles, John?" Lily turned wide eyes on him as if she were asking if he'd been to the moon.

"Born and raised there, Lily. Only I ran away from it, while you two are running away to it. Guess the world's a strange place, huh?" He grinned at her but Trace thought he could hear pain underlying the light words. He hesitated a moment, as if debating with himself. "Look, I'm going to give you an address. If something goes wrong with meeting your uncle, you can go here and get some help." He scribbled on the back of an old envelope and then hesitated before handing it to Trace. He stared at the envelope as if seeing far more than a simple address. "The man at this address isn't always the easiest guy in the world to get along with but he'll help you."

Trace took the envelope from him and slipped it inside the satchel. "Thanks, but we're going to be staying with my uncle."

"It never hurts to have a backup."

Trace lowered Lily out of the cab and then climbed down himself. They hurried across the street, stopping on the other side to look back at the big truck that had been a welcome shelter for a few short hours. John lifted a hand in farewell and Trace waved, aware of Lily doing the same. Neither of them moved until the truck turned the corner and disappeared.

"Well, let's go in and see when the next bus to L.A. leaves."

"John is very nice, isn't he, Trace?"

"Yeah, he's a pretty nice guy."

"He seems awful lonely, though." Lily looked up at him, her big green eyes shadowed. "We won't be lonely like that, will we, Trace?"

"Not as long as we're together."

"Are we going to be together always, Trace?" She slipped her hand inside his and leaned against him confidingly. Trace felt a funny bump in his chest and his hand tightened over hers.

"Always, Lily. Always."

THE BUS RIDE from Denver to L.A. was tedious beyond belief. Lily tolerated it better than Trace did, entertaining herself with puzzles out of the book he bought her before they left Denver. During all the long hours of the journey, Trace thought about his uncle, wondering what he was like, wondering if he'd want to be saddled with two kids.

In the end it didn't matter what his uncle would have thought, because Trace couldn't find him. He didn't work at Lockheed anymore, his phone wasn't listed in any of the towns that surrounded the plant. Just looking at the phone book made Trace's head spin. There were more cities listed in one phone book than he'd been to in his entire life. And he called every one of them. Not one of them had a Philip Dushane listed.

After two hours of fruitless calling, Trace hung up the phone and leaned against the wall. For the first time since he was a boy, his eyes filled with frightened tears. If he turned his head he could see Lily sitting on a hard plastic chair, her face puckered in concentration over the words in a picture book. She believed in him. She believed in his ability to take care of her.

Trace squeezed his eyes shut, taking deep breaths and trying to think of a next step. It hadn't occurred to him that he wouldn't be able to find his uncle. All his hoping and planning hinged around them having a place to go, somewhere to stay. With a few phone calls, all those hopes and plans were gone and he had to start over again.

"Is something wrong, Trace?"

Trace opened his eyes, blinking away the shameful tears. Lily was standing next to him, her eyes questioning. "Nothing's wrong. I . . . can't find my uncle right now so we're going to be on our own for a little while."

"Is your uncle lost?"

"Yeah, I guess he is. We'll keep looking for him but we'd better find someplace to stay until we find him."

"Okay." She slipped her hand into his. "Isaiah and me are hungry."

"You are, huh? I guess we'd better find you something to eat." He gave one last look at the phone. But he was out of places to call. Maybe some food in his stomach would spark some new ideas.

But a meal didn't make a difference. They were still alone in the middle of a very big city with nowhere to go and no one to go to. Trace pushed his fears away and tried to think of the next step. They needed someplace to stay. A motel seemed the obvious answer. But it wasn't as simple as it seemed.

He hadn't thought about the picture he and Lily made. Both of them a little scruffy from travel, a worn satchel their only luggage. No one wanted to rent a room to a couple of kids. They tried five motels before he finally convinced a clerk that they were waiting for their parents, who would be arriving the next day. That solved their problem for that night, but it didn't take care of the following night or the night after that.

The money, which had seemed like more than enough in Oklahoma, disappeared with frightening speed. No matter how carefully he spent, the worn bills kept dwindling. Thanksgiving came only a few days after they arrived in California, and Los Angeles celebrated the holiday with clear blue skies and sunshine. Trace and Lily celebrated with turkey sandwiches and coleslaw eaten in a park.

Christmas came more quickly than seemed possible. There was something unnatural about seeing the garlands and Christmas lights when there was no snow on the ground. But Trace had more to worry about than the weather. The money wasn't going to last much longer. They had to move from motel to motel, never staying longer than a few days in one place. The story that they were waiting for their parents wore thin quickly. The clerks would begin to look suspicious and then they'd start asking questions, and Trace had no doubt that the next step would be to call the police. The police meant the Welfare Department, and that meant he and Lily would be separated. So he always took Lily and moved on before that could happen.

They spent Christmas at an old motel in Santa Monica. There was no tree but he bought a cheap doll, wrapping it clumsily and leaving it beside Lily's bed for her to find on Christmas morning. He almost wept at the look of excitement on her face when she saw the present, because he knew it couldn't possibly be anything she wanted. And yet the excitement didn't fade when she saw the simple baby doll with the impossibly bright blue painted eyes.

"Oh, Trace, she's beautiful." She cradled the doll in her arms, looking up at him with a happy smile. "I'll call her Esmeralda and she'll be friends with Isaiah."

Trace looked at her and he wanted to tear the doll away from her and throw it in the trash. She shouldn't be spending Christmas in a run-down hotel, receiving a doll from Woolworth's as her only gift. She should be living with a loving family, people who'd give her the things she deserved. She should have been the angel in the Christmas play.

Sometimes he thought maybe Lily would be better off if the Welfare Department did find them. Maybe they'd find her a good home, a real home. Or maybe they'd send her back to Oklahoma. One way or another, he'd lose her forever. She might have been better off without him but he couldn't bring himself to let her go.

"I have a present for you. I made it myself." She reached under her bed and pulled out a coloring book, opening it to the back and tugging out a raggedly torn piece of paper that had obviously once been attached in the book.

"It got a little wrinkled." Lily smoothed the sheet of paper on the bed, her face intent.

"That's okay. A few wrinkles never hurt nothin'."

"I was going to wrap it only I couldn't figure out how." Trace took the scruffy piece of paper from her and solemnly studied the crayon drawing. It wasn't difficult to recognize the sticklike figures. Bold strokes of black crayon flowed around the head of the smaller one and tucked beneath one arm was a pink dog. The other figure was much taller. Yellow crayon had been streaked through with brown in an attempt to get the right dark blond shade. Two bright blue spots in the middle of the face were clearly eyes. His arm was around the smaller figure.

"It's the two of us, Trace." Lily leaned on the bed next to him, her eager face bent over the drawing. "It's a portrait just like they hang in museums. I was going to do one of just you but you looked lonely so I put me and Isaiah in it and then it looked better. Do you like it?"

Trace kept his eyes on the drawing, ashamed of the tears he knew must be visible in his eyes. Out of the mouth of babes. So he'd looked lonely when she drew him by himself. That was exactly what he'd been before her. Alone and lonely.

"Trace, do you like it?" Lily's question was a little more anxious this time and he cleared his throat.

"I think it's the most wonderful present anyone has ever given me." Her face lit up in a bright smile.

"Really?"

"Really."

She threw her arms around him, pressing her face against his shoulder. Trace hugged her awkwardly, still enough of the boy left for him to feel uncomfortable with open affection.

"I love you, Trace."

"I . . . love you, too, Lily." The words were rusty. He couldn't remember the last time he'd used them. Maybe when he was little he'd told his mother he loved her, but that was a very long time ago.

Lily's arms tightened around him, her voice muffled in his shirt. "We're going to be together always, aren't we, Trace? Forever and ever."

"Forever and ever. Pretty soon, things are going to start going our way, Lily. We aren't going to be living in motels forever. I'm going to get a job and we'll find a place to live and everything will be nice. I've just got to find a good job."

"You can do it, Trace. I know you can." She looked up at him, absolute belief in her eyes.

BUT IT WAS GOING TO TAKE more than Lily's belief in him to change the way they were living. Getting a job was easier said than done. No one wanted to hire a scruffy kid they didn't know—a kid with no identification and no useful experience. Trace picked up an occasional day's work but never anything lasting. The money kept dwindling until the time came when they didn't have enough left to stay in even the cheapest of motels.

They joined the nameless people who lived on the streets of Los Angeles, picking through garbage cans for food, sleeping in packing boxes. The Southern California spring came early so at least they didn't have to worry about the cold, but that was the only thing that went their way. No matter how bad their situation got, Lily's belief in Trace never wavered. When he wanted to give up and lie down and die, he'd look at her and know that he couldn't do it, not as long as she was depending on him to take care of her.

He shielded her as best as he could but he couldn't protect her from all the horrors of living on the streets. Derelicts, junkies and prostitutes were their neighbors wherever they spent the night. Some of them were kind, but most of them regarded two children as just that much more competition for the few resources the streets offered.

January marked Trace's sixteenth birthday, though he barely gave it a thought. At sixteen he could have easily passed for twenty, topping six feet and being broad shouldered, though the past few months of hard living had left him too thin. Most people didn't bother them.

He took odd jobs whenever and wherever he could find them, but they were few and far between and there was always Lily to worry about when he had to leave her alone. When he couldn't find a job, he stole food to keep them alive. His shame went deep but hunger went deeper still.

The best days were the times when he and Lily went to the library. It was warm and clean there and he could lose himself in a book. For a few short hours it was possible to pretend that everything was different. But they had to be careful, going at times when the librarians wouldn't wonder why Lily wasn't in school. It was only a small escape.

Things couldn't go on the way they were. Lily might have boundless faith in him but Trace knew he was reaching the end of his rope. Her faith couldn't carry him much further. Something had to break and he was afraid it was going to be him. And then who would take care of Lily?

Chapter Four

The alley was quiet, with only the occasional shuffling movement from one of the bums who slept farther back in the darkness telling Trace they weren't alone. The early June night was hot. He'd heard some of the bums complaining that it was going to be a scorcher of a summer. Three months ago the street people had been competing for the warmest doorways and alleys. Now they were competing for the places that caught the edge of a cooling breeze.

It was only an hour or two until dawn. In the hills around Los Angeles, respectable people slept in their clean beds, dreaming of new cars, better jobs and mink coats. On the streets, the few dreams that were left were of hot meals and clean clothes. Even the streets slept at this hour.

Trace was awake.

He sat next to Lily's sleeping form, staring out at nothing in particular. A street lamp lit the mouth of the alley a few feet away, throwing sharp shadows into the packing crate they'd called home for almost a week now. Trace wasn't sure he knew how to dream anymore. There'd been a time when he'd had a lot of dreams but it was getting harder and harder to remember them. The only dream he still had left was for Lily. She wasn't going to grow up on the streets. That was the one promise he'd made himself. No matter what, she was going to have a home. Now all he had to do was figure out a way to find it for her.

The way things were going lately, it would take a miracle. And his faith in miracles had been dead a long, long time.

Moving quietly so as not to disturb her, he picked up the old satchel that he'd taken when they left Oklahoma. God, that seemed years ago. He had to think hard to remember the boy he'd been then, the dreams he'd had. It had all seemed so simple. He shook his head and then had to stop, breathing deeply to control the dizziness. Lack of food. In the past three days he'd only been able to steal a few pieces of fruit and a tin of sardines. Most of that he'd given to Lily, telling her that he'd already eaten. He might have been able to steal more but he had to be so careful. If he got caught, Lily would be left alone.

When the dizziness passed, he opened the satchel and began removing its contents. It held pathetically little but it was everything they had in the world. He shook the clothing out carefully, hoping against hope that a forgotten dollar might fall out of some hidden pocket. There was nothing, and he ran his hand over the inside of the satchel, prying up the fiberboard bottom and running his fingers under it. He touched something and his heart leaped. God, let it be money. Even a dollar would buy them a box of crackers and a few pieces of fruit.

Trace held his breath as he eased the scrap of paper out of its trapped position, hardly daring to hope, unable to stop hoping. It slid free and he let his breath go in a rush, disappointment swamping him. He didn't even need to bring it out into the light to know it wasn't money. It wasn't the right size or the right feel.

It was an old envelope and he almost crumpled it up and threw it away, but something made him hesitate. Maybe it was curiosity. Maybe it was a forlorn hope that the paper might offer some salvation. Whatever the reason, he turned the envelope toward the street lamp and squinted at it, trying to make out the lines of print that ran across it. He couldn't read what was written there, but in his mind's eye he had a sudden image.

"If something goes wrong, you can go here and get help." John. He hadn't thought of the man who'd given them a ride to Denver in months, but now his image was as clear as if the driver were standing next to him in the alley. "If something goes wrong, you can go here and get help."

Trace smoothed the envelope over his knees, his fingers shaking. He'd forgotten all about it. He'd taken the address because it was easier than refusing. He'd been so sure they wouldn't need help. It was a miracle he hadn't thrown the piece of paper away. A miracle. Hadn't he just been thinking that a miracle was what he and Lily needed? Maybe this was it.

It was barely light when he roused Lily and they left the alley. She followed him without complaint. He knew she was hungry but she didn't say anything. She knew as well as he did that they didn't have any food. Determination set his jaw into a tight hard line, adding years to his age. It wasn't right that she was living like this.

They snuck into a gas station bathroom and did their best to clean up. It wasn't possible to wash away the grime of four months on the streets with a harsh paper towel and cold water but Trace did the best he could, running a comb through Lily's hair and smoothing his own into vague order. Staring into the cracked mirror, he barely recognized the face looking back at him. It wasn't the same face he'd known a year ago. But then, he wasn't the boy he'd been a year ago.

It cost them the last few cents he had in his pocket to catch a bus to Glendale, but it was too far to walk. Trace was pinning all his hopes on the scruffy envelope in his pocket. There had to be someone who'd help them at the address John had given them—someone who would at least help Lily, if not him.

The address turned out to be a liquor store and Trace felt his hope flicker. It didn't seem likely that there'd be any help here. He checked the address again, sure that he must have made a mistake, but the printing was strong and clear. Well, they were here and, God knew, they had nothing left to lose.

"Lily, I want you to wait outside for me. Don't talk to anyone and don't move from right here. Okay?"

She nodded, her eyes too big in her thin face. "What are you going to do, Trace?"

"I'm going to talk to someone about a job." That was as good an explanation as any. He didn't want to tell her any more, didn't want her to hope for something that might not exist. "You wait right here for me, okay?"

"Okay. Trace? Do you think maybe, if you can get the job, they'd give you something to eat?"

"I'm sure they will." He had to force the words out past the tightness in his throat.

A bell jingled as he pushed open the door. Inside, the store was cool and clean. A long counter filled one side of the room, and behind it were the liquor bottles. On another wall was a glass case full of beer, sodas and a few rather limp, prepackaged sandwiches. Two short aisles of food provided most of the necessary ingredients for a casual get-together. Chips and dip, crackers and cookies. Trace's stomach rumbled hungrily and he had to drag his eyes from the display of food.

He turned his attention to the man who stood behind the counter. The last faint hope drained away. There was no way this man was going to help them. Maybe John had written down the wrong address, maybe the store had changed hands or maybe he'd been playing some cruel joke, but they'd get no help from this man.

For one thing, he was talking with a customer, obviously on the best of terms, and the customer was wearing a very crisp, very official uniform. When you lived on the streets, you learned that the police were not your friends, at least not if you wanted to stay on the streets. Trace had become adept at recognizing a police car from at least a block off, giving him time to dart into concealment, terrified the officers would stop and ask why he wasn't in school, why Lily wasn't in school.

Setting aside the fact that the proprietor was on chummy terms with a cop, Trace could see just by looking at the man that there was no help to be had. Medium height but stocky enough to look shorter. Red hair cut short in a vaguely military style. His face square jawed and tough. There was no softness there, no compassion.

Anger slid into the void left by half-formed hope. Anger, despair and a desperate defiance. He'd spent their last penny to come here. They had nothing left. Nothing in the world but each other. He'd been a fool to hope. He should have learned by now that hope was a cruel emotion, leading to disappointment. Well, he'd been a fool for the last time. He was damned if they'd come all this way only to leave with empty bellies. He turned his attention to the shelves of food, vaguely aware of the jingle of the bell as the officer left.

MIKE LONIGAN shut the register and glanced at the kid who was standing between the aisles of food. It wasn't hard to see beneath the surface attempt at tidiness to the worn clothing and scuffed shoes. His elbows showed through the thin fabric of his shirt and the battered jeans were almost an inch too short.

He glanced up once, meeting Mike's eyes for an instant before turning away. That one glimpse left Mike with a haunting image. The kid had the look of a man, but the hollows in his cheeks and the despair in his eyes revealed his youth. So much emotion. Hunger, anger, frustration—they roiled inside the boy. Where the hell were the kid's parents?

Mike continued to watch him in the angled mirror that hung near the ceiling. Either the boy hadn't noticed the mirror or his hunger was too great to care. Mike knew the exact moment when the can of tuna disappeared into a pocket. It was followed by two packages of cheese and crackers. It wasn't a particularly well done job of shoplifting, Mike thought dispassionately. He'd certainly seen smoother moves. He left the register as the boy moved casually toward the door as if he just hadn't found anything he wanted.

"I usually ask people to pay for the things they take from the store." At the sound of his calm voice the boy froze, his eyes flicking from the door to Mike's stocky form as if judging the distances. He must have decided that he'd never make it. His eyes dropped to the floor.

"I don't know what you're talking about," he said sullenly.

"I'm talking about a can of tuna and two packages of crackers. They seem to have slipped into your pockets."

Those dark blue eyes looked up and then away. His lean cheeks took on a darker tint. Shame?

"Shoplifting is illegal, son. I could call the police." This time the emotion was easy to read. Total panic darkened the boy's eyes to almost black.

"You don't have to do that. I'll give the stuff back."

Mike's interest sharpened. He'd dealt with quite a few kids who shoplifted and this wasn't a typical reaction. By the time they'd reached the low this boy had obviously hit, most of the emotion had been beaten out of them. Usually they were angry, sometimes defiant, sometimes almost relieved. At least Juvenile Hall offered a chance for a hot meal.

"Why don't you tell me why you were stealing the stuff in the first place."

Silence.

"What's your name?"

"Trace." The boy shoved his hands in his pockets and pulled out the food, holding it out to Mike. "Here, take the stuff back. I'm sorry I took it." His eyes were pleading. Mike shook his head slowly.

"How long have you been on the street?" He saw the boy's fingers clench the food but his gaze dropped back to the floor and he didn't say anything.

"What about your folks? Do they know where you are?" The boy didn't say a word. He might have been deaf for all the reaction he showed. Mike felt a touch of irritation mixed with admiration. The kid had guts.

The bell jingled and the kid looked up, his eyes widening, his lean body suddenly taut. Mike tensed, his hand reaching for the gun he no longer wore. What if the boy was part of a gang? He pivoted slowly, wondering if he was going to find himself looking down the wrong end of a shotgun. But it wasn't a gang member who stood just inside the doorway. It was a little girl with enormous, deep green eyes, her clothes as tattered as the boy's, a filthy stuffed dog clutched in her arms.

"Trace?" She said the name uncertainly, her gaze going from the boy to Mike and back again as if she sensed that something was wrong. The boy pushed past Mike, setting his hand on the little girl's shoulder.

"I told you to wait outside, Lily. You weren't to move."
Fear lent an edge to his voice and the child's eyes filled with
tears.

"You were gone so long, Trace. I got worried and scared.
'Sides, you said we'd get something to eat here and I'm
hungry. So's Isaiah. Don't be mad at me."

Trace sucked in a quick breath, his hand softening on her
shoulder. "I'm not mad. I'm sorry I snapped at you. You
go on back outside and wait for me."

"Wait a second." Mike saw the boy's shoulders tense before he turned to look at him. Standing next to the child, he
seemed hardly more than a child himself, but he couldn't
have looked more ready to kill to protect her if he'd been a
man full grown. In that moment Mike realized that twenty
years as a police officer hadn't been enough to drive all the
softness out of him.

"I was just going to have lunch. Why don't the two of you
join me?" He didn't wait for an answer. He moved past
them and flipped the lock on the door, turning the Closed
sign outward before gesturing them toward the back of the
store.

"I think I've got some hamburger. How does that
sound?"

"It sounds great." Lily beamed up at him and Mike
blinked. He couldn't remember ever seeing such an utterly
exquisite child. Not pretty in a childlike way but out-and-out
beautiful. She was going to be a knockout in a few years.
Trace watched him more warily, but hunger won out over
caution and he followed Mike into the back room.

There was a tiny kitchen in one corner, wedged in among
boxes of liquor and cases of beer. Mike made lunch with
easy efficiency. His first thought was to make the meat pat-
ties as big as possible, but when the stomach had been empty
a long time, too much food could have painful results.

Within a few minutes he set modestly sized hamburgers, along with glasses of milk, in front of his unexpected guests.

Lily bit into hers with every sign of tasting her first decent food in months. Trace was more cautious, his eyes watching Mike warily. But again, hunger was a more powerful force than caution or pride, and he soon dug into the food.

During the course of the meal, Mike managed to pry a few pieces of information out of them. Lily was more forthcoming than the boy, happy to tell him anything he wanted to know. From Lily he learned that they'd come from Oklahoma and that they'd been in L.A. since before Thanksgiving. He also learned that, as far as she was concerned, the sun rose and set in the tall boy next to her. Every other sentence began with "Trace said" or "Trace did."

Trace was less generous with information. He admitted that they had no money, that they'd been on the streets for several months, but he wouldn't talk about how they'd come to be on the streets or what they were running away from. Whatever it was, they weren't going back. The look in the boy's eyes as he spoke made Mike forget how young he was.

Mike took a certain pride in his ability to judge character. He knew he was going out on a limb but he simply couldn't turn them back onto the street. They needed more than a hot meal. A lot more.

"How did you end up at my store? From what Lily says, you took a bus here this morning."

Trace hesitated a moment and then pulled a ratty envelope out of his pocket, shoving it across the tiny table toward Mike.

"The guy who gave us a lift to Denver said that we should come here if we needed help."

Mike stared at the bold printing, feeling his heart give a sharp kick.

"What was his name?" Was that his voice sounding so anxious?

"John. He didn't say a last name."

"I don't need one." Mike's rough fingers smoothed out the envelope. Maybe it wasn't too late to make up for the past, after all. Maybe he'd given up hope too soon.

"I tell you what, I'm going to close up early today. You two can come home with me and stay the night. We'll decide what to do with you in the morning."

Trace stared at him, his expression wary. "Lily and I stay together. Nobody is going to separate us."

Mike nodded. "Fine with me."

An hour later he was opening the door of a small house in a modest neighborhood above Glendale. Trace stepped inside, feeling as if he were walking into a dream. In his childhood he'd sometimes fantasized about living in a house that didn't lie in the middle of the prairie. A cozy house with green lawns and trees around it. This house could have been the one in his dreams.

"You two could both use a shower, I'd guess. There's a bathroom upstairs and one downstairs. Why don't you get cleaned up and I'll see what I've got for dinner."

"We just ate." As if on cue, Trace's stomach growled loudly. He flushed and Mike laughed, not unkindly.

"It's going to take your stomach a while to make up for lost time. It's best if you eat a few small meals instead of one or two big ones. Give your belly a chance to adjust. Come on, I'll show you the bedroom you can use and then the bathrooms. Take your time getting cleaned up."

Later that night as he lay in bed, Trace stared up at the ceiling, unable to sleep. The first decent bed he'd had in months and he was wide awake, his mind churning with possibilities. Mike Lonigan was gruff but he seemed kind. Lily slept peacefully in the twin bed across from him, Isaiah clutched firmly to her chest. Mike had suggested that the dog could use a washing and they'd see about it tomorrow.

Tomorrow. It had been so long since he'd made any plans for tomorrow beyond just surviving. Despite himself, Trace felt a shallow flicker of hope. Maybe their luck really had changed. If Mike would help him find a job... Maybe he'd even let them live here if they could pay rent.

He shut his eyes, forcing his mind to go blank. It was too soon to start hoping. He'd see what tomorrow brought before he made plans for the day after.

Chapter Five

Despite Trace's pessimism, their luck seemed to have changed at last. The envelope that had been given to them so many months ago turned out to be the key to their survival—their salvation. Mike Lonigan's stocky body was an odd package for an angel but he was little short of that.

He opened his home to the two refugees, offering them a place to stay and the first decent food they'd had in months. When they came downstairs the next morning, Trace was tense, uncertain, wondering how he could persuade this stranger to let them stay. It galled his pride that the only argument he could offer was their desperate need. For Lily he'd swallow that pride, but not without a struggle.

But somehow Mike didn't make it seem like a shameful thing that they needed a home. He made it seem like an equal trade. They needed a home, he had plenty of room. Years later, Trace still marveled at the deft touch Mike had employed. Even the prickly pride of the man-boy he was at sixteen had been soothed and he was left with the vague impression that they were doing Mike some kind of a favor by staying with him.

There were no formal arrangements made, no point where Mike asked them if they wanted to live with him permanently. They simply stayed one day and then two and then a week. At the end of two weeks, Mike found a job for Trace working in a grocery store not far from his own liquor store. The owner was a friend of Mike's and he didn't object to Lily accompanying his new employee like a small shadow.

Lily opened her heart to Mike with grave ease. She accepted his presence in her life the same way she'd accepted Trace, their running away and living on the street. She seemed to watch the world through eyes that were too old, had seen too much. With Trace and Isaiah close by, Lily's family was complete. Gradually Mike became a part of that small circle and she accorded him the same devotion she gave to Trace.

For Trace, acceptance was much slower. Mike earned his respect, even a certain amount of trust, but affection was something else again. In his limited experience, adults were seldom to be depended upon. His stepfather, his mother, even his father—none of them had shown him a reason to have faith in this newcomer in his life.

He settled into Mike's house cautiously, trying not to grow too accustomed to its comforts, trying not to depend on the stocky gruff man who'd plucked them off the streets.

Mike watched the boy he'd taken in, reading the wariness in the cool blue of his eyes, the stubborn pride in the set of his shoulders. Trace reminded him of another boy, his hair darker, his eyes a different shade but still holding so much young pride. He hadn't understood that pride and he'd paid dearly for his lack of understanding.

Mike wasn't an overtly religious man but he had a strong belief in the powers above. Perhaps he was being given a chance to rectify some of his mistakes. He couldn't change the past, but with Trace he could make up for some of the mistakes he'd made with his own son. Mistakes that had cost him a high price. Surely it was a sign that the two of them had been sent to his store in such a way.

Lily was the glue that held the three of them together. Mike knew that without her, Trace would have struck out on his own, no matter how foolish it would have been. But he wanted more for Lily than he expected for himself so he stayed. Mike understood and respected his reasons. He didn't yet know why the two of them had left home. Lily was vague on the subject. She'd only done what Trace had told her. On the one occasion Mike broached the subject with Trace, the boy's eyes grew frighteningly cold. When the time came that Trace trusted him, perhaps then he'd find out what those reasons had been.

So he waited, biding his time, careful to respect the fact that Trace was much older than his years, careful not to presume too much too soon. He tried to guide and suggest rather than order and demand and he had the satisfaction of seeing a little of the boy's wariness fade.

When fall approached, Mike introduced the subject of school with cautious steps. It didn't surprise him when Trace flatly refused to go. The boy had been through far too much to slip neatly back into a typical sixteen-year-old's life. But he was surprised that Trace supported him when it came to Lily's returning to school. When he thought about it, he realized that he shouldn't have been surprised. Trace was fiercely determined that Lily have a normal life.

So the little household shifted along together, not quite smooth yet but slowly finding a tentative balance that was comfortable for all of them. The weather cooled and a few trees halfheartedly turned rather yellow. Southern California's version of fall came and went without fanfare. The rains dampened the streets enough to bring out the summer's accumulation of oils, making driving a hazardous affair, and then they departed for another month and the sun shone down with bright good cheer.

The Thanksgiving holiday was spent as Mike always spent it, working in one of the missions, feeding the homeless. Trace and Lily worked with him. Trace dished out food, his eyes dark. A few months ago he and Lily had been sleeping in the streets with the men and women he was now serving. If it wasn't for Mike, they might have still been there. The memories were too close, too vivid, and it was a long time before he slept that night, thinking of what could have been.

After Thanksgiving, Christmas rushed toward them and the contrast was even more vivid. This year he had money in his pocket. Not a fortune but enough. They had a roof over their heads. A home, not a motel room. This year Lily was going to be the angel in the Christmas play, and Trace was ashamed of the way his eyes burned when he saw her in the simple white dress Mike's neighbor had made for her, a silver halo ringing her inky hair, her eyes wide and excited as she solemnly performed her duties onstage.

Mike threw himself into the holiday with Irish fervor. The sight of him standing at the kitchen counter, swathed in a chef's apron, his fiery red hair standing on end, flour coating every surface as he doggedly worked his way through a recipe for gingerbread men, should have been enough to send Trace into peals of laughter. But the emotion he felt wasn't amusement. He felt as if something had cracked inside, some long-held barrier. He backed away, unconsciously trying to repair the damage. If he didn't protect himself, he was going to get hurt.

But the barrier had been wearing down for months; he just hadn't noticed the cracks in his defenses. Maybe it was the holiday season. Maybe it was just a very human need to believe in someone.

A huge tree stood in one corner of the living room, far too large for the small room and yet somehow just right. Trace had no way of knowing that it was the first tree Mike had

had in nearly six years. All he knew was that the little house oozed warmth and holiday spirit and something seemed to be crumbling inside him.

Lily went to bed early on Christmas Eve in the hope that it would make Christmas morning arrive a little sooner. When Trace went up to check on her at nine she was fast asleep, Isaiah's felt eyes watching over her. On the night table Esmeralda sat, her painted blue eyes chipped and faded.

Trace hesitated at the top of the stairs, listening to the rain outside, the closest L.A. ever got to a white Christmas. Mike was in the living room with a fire in the fireplace, the lights from the tree glowing. He walked down the stairs slowly, as if pulled half against his will.

"Trace. Glad you came back down. I was just about to have some more eggnog. You want some?"

"Sure." Trace put his hands in his pockets and then pulled them out again, nervous without knowing why. He took the chilled mug from Mike and sipped, tasting the subtle bite of rum.

"Lily asleep?"

"Yeah. Out like a light." Trace sat down at the opposite end of the sofa from Mike, a half smile flickering across his lips. "I think all the waiting has really worn her out."

"My son was like that when he was little. Christmas just about killed him every year."

Trace looked at Mike, surprised. "I didn't know you had a son."

Mike's smile was tinged with regret. "Still do, as far as I know."

"You've never mentioned him."

"Michael and I parted company a few years back. He left home and I haven't seen him since."

"He ran away?"

Mike shrugged. "More or less. He was older than you are. Almost nineteen. I guess it's not really running away at that age but he's gone just the same."

"Why did he go?" The question was jerked out of him before he could control it, his need to know stronger than his need to keep his distance. Mike didn't seem offended. His wide shoulders lifted in a shrug and he stared into the fire, his eyes full of memories.

"We fought a lot. Always had, even when he was a boy. He was stubborn and so was I and we clashed head-on more times than I can remember. Then his mother was killed when he was fifteen and it seemed as if we just couldn't get along after that. It was my fault, probably. I thought keeping him on a tight rein would keep him from making mistakes. I guess I forgot that part of growing up is learning from your mistakes.

"Anyway, we quarreled about everything. A lot of it seems pretty stupid now but it seemed worth fighting over then. I don't even remember what the last fight was about. But Michael stormed out, saying he'd never be back. I didn't believe him so I let him go. A week later I got a letter from him saying he'd joined the marines. It was the last time I heard from him."

"How do you know he's alive?"

Mike's smile deepened. "Oh, I got some evidence not long ago that he's all right."

The room was silent for a long time, only the sound of the rain and soft hiss of the fire filling the quiet. It was Mike who spoke first.

"You know, you've never told me just why you felt you had to take Lily and run away from home, Trace. You don't have to tell me, of course, but sometimes it helps to talk about things. That's a lesson I learned a little late."

Trace's fingers tightened over the mug until the knuckles showed white. He wasn't going to say anything. He'd sworn to take the truth to the grave with him. It was too shameful to tell anyone.

"It was because of Lily," he said jerkily without looking at Mike. "I had to keep her safe."

"Safe from what?"

"I...she's not really my cousin, you know. At least we're not blood related. My stepfather was her uncle. When her folks were killed in a plane crash, she came to live with us. I'd never seen anything so beautiful in all my life. She didn't even look real. She didn't belong there. The house was just a shack.

"My mother tried," he added fiercely, as if Mike might have been thinking she hadn't. He looked at Mike but saw nothing but interest. There was no judgment in his eyes. After a long moment he continued. Now that he'd started, it was impossible to stop the flow of words.

"She tried but she just didn't have any strength left, and then there was Jed." The name was full of hatred.

"Your stepfather?" Mike asked the question gently, not wanting to do anything to discourage him.

Trace nodded, staring into the fire. "He was a pig. He drank and he used to beat my mother. Till I got big enough to stop him. But then there was Lily, and I couldn't let him hurt her. I just couldn't."

"Hurt her? Did he beat her?" Mike was trying to feel the way, trying to clarify the jerky picture the boy was painting.

"No." The flat word was all Trace said, but Mike waited, sensing there was more. After a long moment he started again. "It was the way he looked at her. He shouldn't have looked at her like that. She's just a little girl. I kept her in my room and I heard him go to hers and then he came and stood outside my door. So I kept her with me again and then one night I waited up with a gun.''

He stopped, his eyes focused on something only he could see. Mike waited. "Did you kill him, Trace?" *What was he going to do if the boy had killed a man?*

Trace shook his head as if coming out of a trance. "No, but I wanted to. I prayed he'd come through that door. I could have pulled the trigger without a thought. I *wanted* to see him die." He glanced at Mike and the look in his eyes made it clear that he was telling no less than the truth. "So I took Lily and ran."

"What about your mother?" Mike asked gently.

"She couldn't do anything," Trace said in a flat way that made it impossible to argue. "She wanted to. I know she wanted to but she just didn't have the strength. You can't blame a person for that, can you? She did the best she could." His voice cracked with emotion and Mike reached out hesitantly, uncertain if he had the right to offer comfort but knowing he had to try.

"You took on a lot of responsibility."

"There wasn't anyone else."

Mike set his hand on the boy's arm, feeling the rigid muscles, the tension that locked them tight. "I'm sure your mother did the best she could, son. Just as you did the best you could."

It might have been the word *son*. It might have been the tone of his voice. Or it might have been that Trace had simply had as much as he could handle. He'd been strong for so long. He couldn't remember a time when he'd been able to lean on someone else completely. All his life he'd been protecting someone, first his mother and then Lily. He could feel himself dissolving inside and he knew he should get up and leave before he made a fool of himself. But something held him where he was, something even stronger than pride.

Need. He needed, desperately, to know that he wasn't alone anymore.

"I—" His voice cracked and he fought to get it under control, setting down the mug and wiping his fingers on his jeans. "I should get to bed." His voice sounded strange, scratchy and hoarse.

Mike's hand tightened on his arm, a gentle pressure that seemed to offer something Trace couldn't even define.

"You know, it's not a bad thing to need other people, son. Everybody needs a little help now and again."

There it was again. Son. No one had ever called him that. Son. He wished suddenly, quite desperately, that he *was* this man's son. That he had a right to that title. He shook his head, aware of a fierce burning in his throat.

"I don't—I can't—" He couldn't get the words out. He looked up, meeting Mike's eyes, and the last of the long-held barriers collapsed. There was compassion in the older man's expression, but there was also something else he was afraid to put a name to. Love?

"I—" Mike's image wavered in front of him. Trace drew a deep breath, fighting for control, but Mike had already seen the moisture in the boy's eyes and he wasn't going to let him throw up those barriers again. His hand settled gently on Trace's shoulder and he felt the shudder that ran through the lanky body in the instant before that long-held control crumpled and his breath exploded on a sob.

Mike held him, his arms strong around Trace's shaking body. His own face was tight and hard, thinking of what the boy had gone through in his short life. Too much responsibility much too soon. His stepfather should have been shot.

Trace drew a deep breath, his shoulders stiffening as he sat up. He wiped his eyes self-consciously, his face flushed, his expression uneasy.

"I'm sorry. I don't know what happened," he mumbled.

"I'd say you reached the end of your rope. Nothing to be ashamed of in that."

"Men don't cry."

"One of the biggest lies around." Mike reached for a pipe and began to tamp it full of tobacco. "Men hurt the same as women."

Trace looked uneasy. "You don't think I'm a...a sissy or something?"

Mike's snort of laughter held an undercurrent of some emotion Trace couldn't identify. He continued to tamp tobacco into the pipe, taking neat little pinches, his movements calm.

"I think you're about as far from a sissy as it's possible to get. You've taken on responsibilities men twice your age would have hesitated to tackle. You got Lily out of a bad situation and you kept her safe. You've got guts. I tell you what, when I was on the force, I'd have been proud to have you for a partner."

Trace flushed, his shoulders straightening. He'd known Mike Lonigan long enough to know that he couldn't have been paid a higher compliment.

Mike lit his pipe and the sharp woodsy scent of the tobacco drifted in the air. The fire hissed as rain found its way down the chimney and evaporated in the flames. They sat in silence for a long time, listening to the rain and watching the sparkle of lights on the Christmas tree.

Mike couldn't have said how much time had passed when he looked over to find that Trace had fallen asleep, his head propped in the corner of the sofa, his long body twisted in an impossible angle.

If he narrowed his eyes, Mike could almost imagine it was Michael. There'd been some good times between the two of them. But not enough, not near enough. He'd pushed too hard and listened too seldom. And he'd paid for it.

He looked at the Christmas tree, narrowing his eyes against a burning sensation. He hadn't had a tree since Michael left home. The holidays had been just a time to get through since then. He'd missed them, missed the excitement, the fun. He might have taken two kids off the street but they'd given him far more than he could ever give them. Life. He felt alive again. He had something to look forward to. He wanted to see Lily grow up, wanted to see Trace fulfill all the potential he saw in the boy.

But he'd learned his lesson too late to salvage his relationship with his own son. He wasn't going to push Trace the way he'd pushed Michael. He'd let the boy make his own choices, his own decisions. Not everyone was given a second chance. He'd been blessed and he was going to handle this blessing with care.

He nodded, the pipe clamped between his teeth. As for the three of them, they were going to be the salvation of one another. He had the feeling life was going to go nowhere but up from here on out.

Dear Mom, I hope you are well. Lily and I are just fine. The weather here has been warm for the last week or so but it's been a wet winter overall. I guess the farmers can use the rain.

Trace stopped, his fingers tightening on the pen, his brows hooking into a frown. So far the letter sounded as if he were writing to a total stranger. But then, wasn't that exactly what Addie was? He hadn't seen her in eight years. But she was his mother.

Thanks for the birthday card. I'll try to send you a picture when I get a chance, though I don't look much different at twenty-four than I did when I left home.

Lily is the one who's changed. She's almost seventeen now and very beautiful. She doesn't date much, which is probably just as well. Mike is very protective of her.

Mike wasn't the only one. Trace reached for his coffee, nursing it between his palms while he stared at the photo of Lily that sat on one corner of the table that served as both desk and dining room in the small apartment. It was just a school picture, one of hundreds the photographer had taken that day, but the beauty of the subject lifted it out of the ordinary.

Lily's eyes looked out at him, a deep green that seemed to hold so many secrets. He picked up the photo. There was a spring dance at her school the end of the week. Lily had modeled her dress for him when he saw her last weekend and Mike wasn't the only one who'd been struck by the way she seemed to have grown up overnight.

It wasn't a comfortable realization. It was safer to think of her as a little girl. Safer? He shook his head, setting the photo down.

I'll graduate from the academy next month. I think Mike is more excited than I am. I guess he always hoped that his own son would go into police work and I'm a good substitute.

Don't believe everything you see on television about the dangers of being a cop in L.A. It's not as bad as it looks.

Well, I've got a million things to do so I'm going to sign off now. Take care and write soon.

Love, Trace

He set the pen down, feeling as if he'd accomplished a difficult assignment. As the years passed, it became harder and harder to write to his mother, and the letters grew fewer. He'd never understand why she chose to stay where she was. It was almost five years now since he'd written to suggest that she come to L.A. Mike would help her find a job. And she'd written back to say that she couldn't come because Jed was ill and needed her to take care of him.

Something in Trace had broken then. He still didn't fully understand the rage he'd felt, but some final tie to his childhood had been severed forever. At every critical moment in life, Addie chose Jed. She chose a life with a man who had beaten her and degraded her. Trace didn't understand it and he'd stopped trying. He never again suggested that she move to California.

He finished the last of his coffee, his glance settling on Lily's photo again. Those green eyes always seemed to hold so many secrets. He remembered the way she'd looked in her white dress, her thick black hair draped in a rich fall across one shoulder, those eyes looking at him in a way that was half a question, half a challenge.

His body tightened in a shockingly familiar way and he stood up abruptly, a short violent curse exploding out of him. He'd been concentrating too hard at the academy. Lily was just a kid, no matter what her eyes seemed to say. He poured another cup of coffee, scalding his tongue on the dark liquid as if punishing himself for his thoughts.

They'd been through a lot together. It was understandable that she was on his mind—in a way that was no longer childlike. Wasn't that supposed to be a normal part of a young girl growing up? She was aware of him as a man, not just a pseudo brother. There was nothing wrong with that.

They'd get through this stage, just as they'd gotten through everything else—together.

Book Two

Chapter Six

Seven Years Later

Dampness fell sporadically, more an omnipresent moisture than actual rain. It dampened the eucalyptus leaves and then dripped silently to the ground beneath. Most of the people around the open grave huddled under huge umbrellas.

Trace wasn't aware of the dampness. The misty drizzle was just one more touch of unreality in a day that was already surreal. He stood at attention, staring straight ahead. The collar of his uniform felt too tight, making it difficult to breathe. He blinked against the ache in his eyes, narrowing them under the brim of his cap. There seemed to be a hard lump where his heart should be.

He couldn't look at the dark casket, the wood shiny and wet. He couldn't look at the open grave where the casket would soon rest. That might make it real. None of this could be real. In a minute he'd wake up and find out that Mike wasn't really dead, that this wasn't his funeral. But he didn't really believe that was going to happen.

He didn't have to turn his head to see the men who flanked him, all of them in dress uniform, standing at attention out of respect to a departed colleague. It didn't matter that Mike had left the force nearly twenty years ago. He'd stayed active as a volunteer, and he'd had a lot of friends on the force.

The formality of the uniformed men only added to the surrealistic feel. He just couldn't make it seem real. Not the mourners, not the minister's voice droning on unheard, not the open grave or the looming casket. None of it felt real. Especially not Lily.

He looked across the grave to where she stood, surrounded by neighbors and friends who'd come to pay their last respects to Mike. It was the first time he'd seen her in almost two years. If he'd ever thought that her beauty was more his imagination than reality, the truth stood before him.

Wearing a simple dress covered with a thin black coat, she looked like a painting of a medieval Madonna. She was all black and white. Black coat, black hair, her face without a hint of color. As if sensing him looking at her, she lifted her eyes to his. Even across the few feet that separated them, he could see the pain swimming in her green eyes. He glanced away. Her pain made everything too real.

He realized that the minister had stopped talking. No one moved as the casket was slowly lowered into the grave. Trace watched it disappear, still without allowing himself to believe in the reality of what was happening. Lily stepped forward, bending to scoop up a handful of dirt, holding it tightly for a moment as if trying to fill it with love, and then she opened her fist. The damp soil hit the wood below with a faint thud, like the first beat of a death knell.

Feeling as if he were wading through quicksand, Trace moved around the grave until he stood next to her. He stared down at the shiny wood, noticing the smattering of soil that was Lily's offering. Bending, he filled his hand with moist earth. It brought to mind an image of Mike at work in his garden. *Soil's the only lasting thing in this world, Trace. It'll be here long after you and I are gone and forgotten.*

A damp musty smell rose from the soil he held, full of all the potential for life, now a witness to death. His eyes burned as he lifted his hand over the grave and opened his fingers. The soil sprinkled downward, mixing with what Lily had put there, a final offering to a man they'd both loved.

Beside him, Lily raised her hand to her mouth, stifling a sob. Trace put his arm around her shoulders, pulling her close to lean against him. They stared at the casket a moment longer, reluctant to break this last link. The minister murmured a final prayer, his voice solemn.

The minister rode with them in the car to Mike's house. Mike hadn't been much of a church-goer but he and the minister had been personal friends. No one said anything during the short ride. There just didn't seem to be anything to say.

Looking back later, Trace remembered the afternoon as a series of vignettes, separate from one another, yet forming a coherent picture of loss. The house was full of people yet it felt empty. Mike's stocky presence was gone, leaving a gap that couldn't be filled by the friends who came to offer their condolences.

Lily moved among the guests, her slim figure wraithlike in the plain dark dress, her hair drawn back from her face. Trace watched for her, his eyes seeking her out, needing to know she was there. There was a bruised look to her eyes. Pinched lines around her mouth told of her grief more eloquently than words ever could.

People talked, at first in hushed tones, gradually in normal voices. An occasional spurt of laughter punctuated some of the more memorable stories of Mike's adventures. It was just as it should be. There was nothing Mike would have hated more than everyone standing around crying.

Trace forced himself to smile at the appropriate moments but his grief went too deep to allow room for nostalgia. He found himself glancing at the door, half expecting to see Mike standing there, his face split by a wide grin, telling them that he'd only been kidding.

People began to drift away as the short winter daylight faded. Voices were subdued again. For these few hours, it had almost been as if Mike were still with them. But leaving his home now, they knew he was gone from them forever.

Trace shook hands and murmured his thanks until he felt like a mechanical doll. When the door shut behind the last guest, he slumped back against it, drained. A quiet noise in the living room reminded him that he wasn't alone.

Lily. What was he going to say to her? She'd left for England right out of college, taking a job tutoring an American family's children. Two years. It was a long time. He lifted himself away from the door and moved into the living room. Lily was gathering dishes into a stack, her movements sluggish, reflecting her exhaustion. Trace remembered that she'd flown in from England only this morning. God knew what time her body thought it was.

"Leave those."

She jumped at the sound of his voice, glancing up at him and then looking away. "I'll just put them in the kitchen."

"They'll keep where they are until morning. You look beat."

"I'd rather get them out of the way." She added another plate to the stack. With a sigh, Trace moved forward, gathering cups and glasses as he went, stacking them precariously high before following Lily into the kitchen. They worked without speaking.

"Are you hungry?" Lily asked. "A lot of people brought food."

"No, thanks. Why don't you sit down and I'll make some tea. You still drink tea?"

Lily shut the refrigerator door and gave him a half smile. "Yes. Do you still think it tastes like bathwater?"

"Yes, but I don't have the energy for anything stronger right now." Neither of them seemed to have anything to say while the water boiled and the tea steeped. Trace carried a tray into the living room and set it on the floor next to the sofa. While Lily poured tea into sturdy mugs, he built a fire. The cheerful crackle of burning logs helped to offset the thick silence that seemed to fill the house.

"So, how was England?"

"It was nice. I enjoyed tutoring the Fairfield children. They were a handful but they were nice kids."

"Did you get to see everything you wanted to see? I know when you left you had plans to see every square inch of Europe."

"I didn't manage quite that much but I did get to travel a bit."

"Good. I'm glad you didn't spend all your time trapped in a classroom."

"No, I didn't."

Silence descended again. Europe wasn't what was in the forefront of either of their minds but it was safer than what they really wanted to talk about.

"So, how's life as a cop? I hear you're up for a promotion." She tried to sound cheerful but her words rang hollow.

"Yeah. I'll believe it when it happens."

"You didn't write very much."

He shrugged uncomfortably. "I'm not much good with letters." Besides, what would he have written? He couldn't have told her how he really felt. He wasn't even sure himself. He hadn't known since the summer she turned eighteen, but that wasn't something he could think about now. So he'd limited his letters to an occasional note and told himself it was for the best. And he'd lived in dread of the day she'd write to say that she'd met a wonderful man she wanted to marry.

"Mike always keeps me up-to-date on what you're doing." She stopped abruptly, realizing what she'd said. "I guess you'll have to do your own writing from now on, won't you?"

"I guess so." Trace stared into the fire, his jaw tight. Mike's absence was suddenly a presence in the room. It wasn't possible to ignore reality any longer.

"Did you let his son know?"

Trace shrugged, swallowing down the hot tea in a gulp before getting up to find the bottle of Scotch Mike had always kept underneath the bookshelves. He poured himself a healthy dose before turning to look at Lily again.

"I sent a telegram to the last address I could find but I don't know if he got it. It was somewhere in the Middle East, some Podunk country with an unpronounceable name."

"Had they spoken? Mike said one time that he was thinking of writing Michael."

"I don't think he did. I don't know exactly what happened between them but Michael hasn't been home in close to twenty years."

Trace paused, taking a quick swallow of Scotch, hoping it would burn away some of the ache in his chest. "He should have come home."

Lily nodded. "Maybe he thought there'd be more time." She leaned her head back, staring into the fire, her expression pensive.

Trace watched her, wondering how it was possible that she grew more beautiful with each passing year. Her face was like a fine porcelain sculpture, lighted by the deep green of her eyes and the soft coral of her mouth. With her hair caught back, the delicate angles and planes were exposed in a way that not many women would have dared.

His eyes traced the line of her throat and touched on the soft swell of her breasts before he could drag his gaze away. For just a moment he could taste her, the way her mouth had softened under his, the way her body had molded so perfectly to him. Six years hadn't dulled the memory. Six years hadn't altered the need.

"What happened, Trace? What really happened to Mike?"

Trace's fingers tightened over the glass. "I told you when I called you in England."

"All you said was that he was shot."

"Isn't that enough?" He finished off the Scotch and poured himself another one, grateful for the excuse to turn his back to her.

"I need to know what really happened."

"Just leave it alone. You know enough." If she heard the tightness in his voice she chose to ignore it.

"I want to know the whole truth. I want to know everything, Trace."

"Fine!" He spun around, splashing Scotch onto his hand with the sudden movement. "Fine. You want to know everything? What shall I start with? You want to know how it felt to walk in and see Mike lying on the floor in a pool of his own blood, his eyes open and staring? You want to know how many times he was shot and how long it took him to die and how much pain they think he was in? Is that what you want to know?"

He stopped, choking the words off. He took in a deep breath, regaining his control, fighting down the anger that wanted to break loose and smash something just for the satisfaction of hearing it break. The look in Lily's eyes was all he needed to tell him how close he was to doing it. She sat stiffly in her chair, her eyes on him, wide and holding a hint of fear. It was the fear that slammed his control back into place. He never wanted to see a woman look at him with fear. Not any woman but especially not Lily. It reminded him of too many things in his childhood that he didn't want to remember.

"I'm sorry. God, I'm sorry." He sank into his chair, elbows on knees, his shoulders hunched. The scotch glass dangled loosely from his fingers. He stared at the floor between his feet. Pain throbbed in his temples, pounding in rhythm with his pulse.

"It's okay. I shouldn't have asked." Lily's soft voice stroked across him.

"No, you've got a right to ask. I shouldn't have blown up like that. It's been a rough few days." He leaned back in the chair, shutting his eyes and pinching the bridge of his nose.

"Did you find him?"

The quiet question brought flashing images playing across his closed eyelids as if they were a movie screen. The ache in his head intensified and he opened his eyes. Lily sat so close, her eyes full of sympathy and grief. He wanted to lay his aching head on her breast and let the contact soothe away the pain, but he couldn't do that. He sighed and swallowed the last few drops of Scotch.

"I found him. The killer set off the alarm at the store on his way out. Mike always had it wired so that it rang here and at the police station. I beat the police there but he was already dead."

He twisted the empty glass aimlessly between his fingers, watching the way the firelight caught in the heavy glass, reflecting gold and red colors back as if lit with a fire of its own.

"Trace, I know it hurts but I'd really like to know what happened."

"Why? Isn't it enough that he's dead?"

"Ever since you called, I've been imagining what happened in my mind. You can't tell me anything worse than what my imagination has already come up with."

He didn't say anything for a long time, weighing her words against his memories. He'd been protecting Lily for so long. It was hard to let go of those old instincts. He wanted to shield her from anything harsh or unpleasant. Looking at her now, he knew it was time to put aside the image of the little girl she'd been. That little girl had needed his protection but she was gone. The woman who sat across from him deserved to be treated as an adult.

"Mike's car was out of commission," he started abruptly. "I had the day off so I loaned him the 'Vette. I had some work I wanted to do on my motorcycle and Mike was letting me use the garage here. The manager of my apartment building frowns on having parts strewn all over the garage."

He stopped, staring at the empty glass, but he was seeing other things. "I was making coffee when the alarm went off. Scared the life out of me. I hadn't started on the bike yet so I took it and made it down the hill in record time. I don't even remember what I was thinking. I knew Mike must have been at the store. I do remember thinking that maybe he'd set it off himself. I thought how embarrassed he'd be to have me and the cops all rushing over there only to find out it had been his mistake.

"I wasn't all that worried. Concerned, but not worried. Even if it *was* a burglar, Mike could take care of himself. He had a gun under the register, and besides, he could talk himself out of anything. It couldn't have been more than five or six minutes after the alarm went off before I got to the store. I'd grabbed my gun on the way out of the house and I took it out just in case. I called Mike's name but he didn't answer. The door was open and the alarm was screaming loud enough to wake the dead but Mike didn't answer.

"I guess that was when I began to think that maybe something was wrong. I worked my way to the door, trying to keep out of sight, but there wasn't any real need. There wasn't any need at all."

His eyes were a dark tortured blue. He drew his mouth in tight, chewing on the inner skin of his lip, looking at things only he could see.

"Mike was lying in front of the counter. There wasn't anyone else in the store. I could see he was dead. He had to be. All that blood. But I couldn't believe it. I tried C.P.R. but it was too late. I didn't hear the units responding to the alarm. They finally pulled me away from him. I had blood all over my hands. Mike's blood."

He stood up, thrusting his fingers through his hair, his lean frame tense with memories. He didn't look at Lily. He was beyond worrying about what this might be doing to her, beyond stopping. He hadn't talked to anyone about the events of that morning. Now that the floodgates were open, they couldn't be closed.

"He must have just opened up the store. Whoever it was came in behind him and opened fire with a .357. The impact of the slugs spun him around. They emptied the chamber into him."

Lily pressed her hand to her mouth, her fingers shaking. "Did he . . . it must have killed him instantly."

"It should have. God knows it should have. The coroner said he should have been dead by the time the fourth bullet hit him but he lived at least a minute or two. Somehow he managed to get to his wallet."

"His wallet? Why would he want his wallet?"

Trace shrugged. "I don't know. There wasn't anything unusual in it. A few pictures, driver's license, about thirty dollars. Nothing special."

"Do you have any idea who did it?"

"Nothing so far. Nothing was stolen. No fingerprints. No motive. At this point it looks like it was just random violence. Dammit!" He picked up the glass, his knuckles white around it for an instant before he hurled it into the fire. It shattered against the back of the fireplace with a crash.

The small act of violence did little to ease his pain. He braced his arm along the mantel, leaning his forehead against it and staring into the fire, watching the fragments of glass fill with red flames. It was a long time before he looked at Lily again.

She was sitting very still, her hands clasped together in her lap. Her face was composed, her eyes on the fire. The flickering light caught on the shiny track of a solitary tear that slid slowly down her cheek.

"I think I'll go to bed now. It's been a long day." She didn't look at him as she stood up. Trace watched her leave the room, feeling the weight of her pain as if it were his own.

Too much lay between them. He wondered if she still thought of that hot summer day when everything had changed. Or had she put it out of her mind? He wanted to go to her, put his arms around her and tell her that everything was going to be all right—that he'd make it right. Only he couldn't make it right this time. He couldn't take her and run away from this hurt the way he had when they were children. This was a hurt they both carried inside. He listened to Lily climb the stairs, knowing she was going to cry herself to sleep, helpless to comfort her.

There was nothing he could do or say that was going to change the fact that Mike was gone. He wasn't going to come striding into the room, demanding to know what

Trace was doing standing around lollygagging. He'd taken two children off the streets and treated them as if they were his own. He'd provided them with more than shelter, he'd given them a real home, the first either of them had known. He'd laughed, scolded, disciplined when necessary and kept them both safe and secure.

Because of Mike, Trace had ended up a cop instead of a criminal. Lily had been able to go to college and they'd both had the security of a home, someone to love them and care about what they did with their lives. In a few moments of violence, it was all gone. Shattered.

Trace's head dropped to his arm again. The heat of the fire dried the slow painful tears before they had a chance to fall, but nothing could ease the ache in his chest.

Chapter Seven

The clouds drifted away some time during the night, leaving the day to dawn with the promise of blue skies and warm weather. The beaches would be crowded with tourists and natives eager to take advantage of the sunshine. It promised to be the kind of day that made visitors swear they'd never go home and made Angelenos feel very smug.

Trace barely noticed the weather, other than to note that it wasn't raining. As soon as he woke, he was aware of the change in his life. Mike was gone and Lily was back. The two balanced uneasily in his emotions. Grief for Mike mixed with the joy of having Lily in his life again, if only for a little while.

He dressed in jeans and a chambray shirt, rolling the sleeves up to bare his forearms. The scent of coffee reached him as he slipped on running shoes. He inhaled deeply, feeling a faint twinge of anticipation for the first time in days.

Lily was downstairs, making coffee. His sorrow over Mike was strong but his life couldn't be all wrong when Lily was in it. He'd missed her. More than he'd admitted to himself. He'd missed her for a long time now.

He rarely allowed himself to think of that hot summer afternoon when she'd come to him and told him she loved him. He knew it was only a girl's infatuation. He'd known it at the time, which was why he'd sent her away and tried to put it out of his mind. But it crept up on him sometimes, catching him unawares, making him remember how soft her mouth had been, how right she'd felt in his arms.

For the first time, he deliberately conjured up that day, trying to picture every detail just as it had been the summer Lily turned eighteen. One of the hottest summers on record.

TRACE POKED tentatively at the contents of the air conditioner. Wires and parts stared back at him enigmatically. There had to be a reason why it wasn't working but he couldn't see what it was. Not that that was surprising. He'd never claimed to be a mechanical genius.

He leaned back in his chair, tilting it up on two legs as he reached for a beer. The icy liquid flowed down his throat, giving a temporary illusion of comfort. The moment he set it down again, the heat settled in like a living presence. It was the end of August and Los Angeles was breaking records for temperatures. Ten days in a row the temperature had soared to one hundred or more. It was all anybody thought about, all anybody talked about.

Crime soared along with the mercury. Heat always brought out the crazies. He'd worked eight days straight, patrolling the streets, trying to control his temper when the people he was dealing with had long since lost theirs. It was his first day off in all that time and the air conditioner had decided to call it quits.

He took another swallow of beer and stared at the offending appliance. Why couldn't it have waited another week or two? The weather was bound to have cooled off some by then.

When the doorbell rang, it was a welcome distraction. He stood up, stretching to his full six feet two inches, running his hand over the mat of hair on his bare chest. It was too hot for clothes, too hot to breathe. He crossed the small living room, weaving his way around the coffee table and chair that took up any room left by the sofa. Maybe it was one of the guys. Some one-on-one on the basketball court sounded good. If he was going to sweat, he might as well have fun doing it.

"Lily." He stood in the open doorway, wishing he'd taken time to throw on a shirt, wishing he was wearing something more than a pair of ragged cutoffs, wishing the apartment wasn't so classically bachelor untidy.

"Hi." She looked up at him, her eyes holding a trace of uncertainty. "Is this a bad time?"

"No, it's not a bad time. Unless you count the fact that the air conditioner has decided to die on me. The place is like an oven. Not to mention I haven't cleaned in weeks." He shut the door behind her and watched her walk into the scruffy room. She was wearing a scarlet sundress that curved low across her back, and Trace looked away, ashamed of the way his pulse quickened at the sight of her smooth skin. This was Lily, for crying out loud.

"You want a soda or a glass of milk or something?"

She turned to look at him, raising one delicate brow. "Milk? I'm eighteen now, Trace. I'm a little old for you to be offering me milk."

"Sorry." He shrugged, grinning. "I guess I'm inclined to forget." Actually, looking at her now he found it impossible to forget. He shoved the thought away. "How about a Coke?"

"Sure." He moved to the refrigerator, thankful for something to do. "Here you go. At least the refrigerator's still working."

She took the icy can from him and tilted her head to take a drink. Trace's eyes followed the movement of her throat as she swallowed, noticing the delicate indentation at the base of her neck. From there it was a short inevitable journey to where the sundress crossed over her breasts, hinting at soft curves, revealing shadowy hollows. He jerked his eyes away and stared at the broken air conditioner. It was the heat.

He reached for his beer, downing the rest of the cool liquid in a gulp before meeting Lily's eyes again. She looked at him, that dark green gaze seeming to see right into his soul. As always, her beauty struck him. Her skin was too pale, her hair too black and those eyes... A man could drown in her eyes. Not him, of course. But some other man, someday. In the future. A long way in the future. A long, long way.

"So, are you looking forward to college? You leave next week, don't you?"

"I'm supposed to." She leaned against the table, her eyes on the bright red can she held.

"*Supposed* to? Don't tell me you're having second thoughts. I thought you were really looking forward to this."

She glanced up at him and then looked down again. "I don't want to go. I want to stay here with you."

Trace's finger slipped on the top of the new can of beer, jabbing the tab under his fingernail. He noticed the pain distantly. The room was still for a long moment, only the hum of traffic on the street outside breaking the thick silence. He laughed uneasily.

"I guess it's understandable that you'd be a little nervous. I mean, it's going to be a big change. Living in a dorm isn't going to be like living with Mike, but you'll be home for the holidays and next summer will be here before you know it. College is a great experience. A lot of guys I work with went to college and they all think—''

"I love you, Trace." The simple sentence cut off his rambling dialogue as effectively as a hatchet slicing through butter. Her eyes lifted to meet his and what they held made his heart stop for an instant before it began to pound in a heavy rhythm. He looked away, not wanting to see.

"Of course you love me. I love you, too. I mean, we've been through a lot together. It's only natural—'' He broke off as her palms came to rest against his chest. Such a short step she'd taken but she'd crossed a barrier he hadn't even admitted existed. The beer can slipped from his hand, landing on the floor with a thud. He didn't notice it.

"Trace, I love you. Not like a little girl. This is something more, something deeper."

He reached up to smooth back a heavy fall of black hair, aware of the fact that his hand was not quite steady. "Lily, you're only eighteen. That may seem like a lot to you now but it's not."

"Kiss me, Trace. Kiss me and tell me you don't love me."

Trace felt as if he were suffocating. She was standing so close. He could catch the scent of her perfume, soft and warm, like her skin. He hadn't even been aware that he was touching her until he saw his hand smoothing her shoulder, his thumb finding the pulse at the base of her throat.

"Lily, this is crazy."

"It's only crazy if you don't kiss me."

Her mouth looked so soft, so warm. He was hardly conscious of his actions as he bent toward her. She met him halfway, rising up on her toes, balancing herself against his bare chest. He'd only kiss her to prove how wrong she was. It was just to prove a point. That was all.

But somehow, with the feel of her mouth under his, he couldn't seem to remember the point. Her mouth felt soft and warm and right. So right. He groaned low in his throat, one hand coming up to cup her chin, holding her still for his kiss, the other arm sweeping around her lower back, lifting her into his body. The soft cotton of her dress wrapped itself around his legs, pulling him closer still. Her hands lost themselves in the thick blond hair at the base of his skull.

He lifted his head a fraction of an inch, struggling for some control, but her lashes rose and he stared into the smoky green of her eyes. Control was a fragile thing at best and it couldn't withstand the need—the love—he saw there.

"Oh, God." The words were half a prayer, muffled against her mouth as his arms tightened around her until not even a shadow could have slipped between them.

He couldn't have said how long they stood there, aware of nothing but each other. The sweltering heat of the August afternoon faded in comparison to the heat they were generating.

It wasn't until he realized he was lowering her onto the sofa that Trace came to his senses. He pulled her upright, staring down into her eyes. He'd never wanted anything as much as he wanted to ignore the voice of conscience and drown in the wide pools of her eyes. He wanted her like he'd never wanted a woman in his life. His body ached with wanting. But there was more to it than that.

He loved her.

And because he loved her, this couldn't go any further. This was Lily, not some woman he'd met in a bar. She deserved more. So much more. More than a tumble on a worn sofa. More than a sweltering afternoon in a stuffy apartment. More than him. He could never, ever be what she needed.

"Trace?" Her voice held questions and it held desire. It took all his willpower to slide his arms away from her and turn his back, fighting for control. His body pulsed with hunger and he flinched as if from a burning brand when she set her hand on his shoulder.

"Don't." The word came out harsh and abrupt but he didn't try to soften it. "This is crazy. It's all wrong."

"How can it be wrong to love you?"

"You don't know what you're talking about. You're not in love with me. You're young. You're in love with the idea of love. And you're scared about going off to college. You're looking for an excuse to avoid it."

He turned to her, trying not to notice the bruised look of her mouth or the way her hair lay tangled on her shoulders, tangled by his hands.

"You sound awfully sure of what I'm feeling." Her tone was unreadable. She was staring at the floor between them and Trace couldn't judge what she was thinking.

"It's obvious. We just got a little carried away by the heat. Heat can do crazy things to a person. You wouldn't believe the way crime picks up in a heat wave. You'll see. When you get to college, there'll be all those gorgeous fraternity guys and I'll seem like an old fogy in comparison."

Her eyes swept up to meet his and he almost changed his mind when he saw the tears beading her lashes. He steeled himself against the pain in her eyes. This was what was best for her.

"You're wrong, Trace. So wrong." A single tear slid down her cheek and Trace felt as if it were burning acid etching into his soul. He reached out, catching the droplet on his fingertip, his palm cupping her cheek.

"This is for the best, Lily. You may hate me now but someday you'll understand."

She squeezed her eyes shut, taking a deep breath before looking at him again. "I could never hate you. No matter what. I couldn't hate you. You're the one who doesn't understand.''

He stared into her eyes, fighting the uneasy feeling that she was right. Fighting the desperate need to hold her again, to make her his forever. His hand dropped away from her face as she turned, her skirt drifting around her.

Trace watched her walk to the door, feeling as if he'd fallen down a rabbit hole. Somewhere he'd missed something, but he couldn't put his finger on what it was. Lily turned at the door, her face pale but composed.

"Sorry if I made a fool of myself." She was gone before he could say anything. The door closed behind her with a gentle click.

Trace stared at the blank panel for a long time, searching for answers to questions he couldn't quite ask. He'd done the right thing. He didn't doubt that he'd done the right thing. No matter what his feelings were, he wasn't the right person for Lily. Besides, it was just a temporary aberration. He wasn't really in love with her. It wasn't possible.

He bent slowly and picked up the dropped can of beer, hooking his finger around the tab. Yes, he'd definitely done the right thing.

But if it was the right thing, why did it feel so wrong? The shaken beer exploded over him as if in silent commentary.

TRACE SHOOK HIMSELF, coming back to the present. The scent of coffee was still in the air but he could almost smell the heat of an August afternoon. They'd never spoken of that afternoon. For a long time he'd avoided her, but when they saw each other again, there was nothing in Lily's manner that led him to believe she ever thought about it. It might never have happened if it hadn't been for the memories, too vivid to be anything but real.

As he walked downstairs, he reminded himself that nothing had really changed. True, Lily wasn't the near child she'd been six years ago, but that was all that was different. She still deserved someone who could give her far more than he could ever offer.

The kitchen was bright with sunshine spilling in through the window over the sink. In jeans and a pale gold shirt, Lily looked as ethereal as a shaft of sunlight. She turned away from the stove as Trace came into the room, her smile a little ragged around the edges, her eyes red rimmed with exhaustion or tears, Trace couldn't be sure which.

"Good morning. I hope you still like French toast. I found some bread and eggs but not much else."

"French toast sounds great." His stomach twisted sluggishly at the thought of food but he ignored it. Life had to start getting back to normal, no matter how hard it was. Breakfast was as good a place to begin as any.

"I thought I might do some shopping today, get some food in the house. You'll be staying here, won't you, at least for a little while?"

Trace hesitated only a moment. His common sense told him he was going to get hurt. But he couldn't look into those eyes and tell her no.

"Sure. There's nothing at my apartment that can't survive without my presence for a while." The relief in her face was worth any future price he might have to pay.

"I'm glad. I wasn't really too anxious to stay here alone."

"I know what you mean." He leaned back as she set a plate of gently steaming French toast in front of him. "This looks wonderful. Did they teach you to cook in England? I thought all they ate in England was boiled vegetables and overdone meat."

Lily smiled at his gentle gibe. "That's a false rumor. There's really some quite wonderful food there if you know where to look. The only thing I had a hard time getting used to was that I always had to beg for ice in my drinks and then I'd be lucky to get one measly ice cube, which melted before the glass hit the table."

"If that's your only complaint, it can't have been too bad."

"No, it was a good experience. I really learned a lot and I enjoyed myself." She took a sip of hot coffee and jotted some notes on the shopping list next to her plate. "Is there anything in particular you want me to get at the store? It looks like we need everything."

"Just get whatever you want. I haven't been much in the mood for eating or shopping since—for the past few days." For just a few moments they'd almost managed to forget what had happened. Trace toyed with his food, his appetite gone. He glanced at Lily. Her eyes were lowered, watching the aimless movements of her coffee cup as she twisted it around and around between her hands. Her mouth was held tight, as if that were the only way to prevent it from quivering.

Damn his clumsy tongue. But it was too late now. There'd been a short time when they'd managed to pretend they didn't have such a tragic reason for being here. The fragile mood was gone now, not to be regained. He stood up, scraping the remains of his breakfast into the garbage disposal.

"Thanks. It was great French toast."

"I'm glad you enjoyed it." She didn't mention the fact that he'd barely eaten two bites. What they both needed right now was the illusion of life being normal, no matter how fragile that illusion was.

The day drifted by without reality. No one stopped by, the phone didn't ring. They were living next to one of the biggest cities in the country but there was a feeling of isolation about the day, as if, despite the millions of people nearby, they were all alone, set apart by their shared grief.

Trace worked aimlessly in the garage, cleaning things that didn't need to be cleaned, sharpening tools that didn't need to be sharpened. Lily dusted and vacuumed, filling her time with mindless tasks that served to occupy her hands, if not still her thoughts. They spoke occasionally on the most mundane of topics. But for the most part they avoided each other as much as they avoided their own thoughts.

Lunch was eaten in virtual silence, each picking at the pasta salad Lily made. It had been prepared more in an effort to keep them from thinking than because either of them was hungry. The afternoon was more of the same. Time drifted by with little meaning or purpose.

Everywhere Trace turned he was reminded of his loss. The house was full of memories, all of them painful at the moment. If it hadn't been for Lily, he wouldn't have stayed here. Mike's death was too new, too hurtful. But Lily was here and this was where he'd stay. He couldn't leave her alone. Honesty compelled him to admit that, no matter what the circumstances, he wanted to be near her.

Late in the afternoon the Santa Ana winds started to blow through the foothills, gusting across the canyons. Trace was grateful for something definite to do. He tied down trash can lids and moved potted plants to sheltered places. What he needed was something solid to sink his teeth into. Something he could take action on, something with a purpose. His mouth twisted. Something like a good hurricane would be nice.

As the sun set, the winds seemed to pick up force, or perhaps it was only the darkness that made them seem to howl louder. Occasionally the little house shuddered under the impact of a particularly strong gust, but it had withstood thirty years of winds; it wasn't too disturbed by this latest gale.

Dinner was even more silent than lunch. They'd run out of small talk and neither had the inclination for anything more. The winds blew steadily. The subdued roar seemed to emphasize the silence within the house. After the quiet meal, Trace offered to do the dishes, but Lily insisted that she could do them herself. He would have protested but the look in her eyes told him that she really wanted to be alone.

He wandered into the living room and turned on the television. Slumped back in a chair, he stared at the bright screen without seeing it. He could hear Lily in the kitchen, the quiet clink of dishes, the rush of running water. Under other circumstances he couldn't imagine a more pleasantly domestic scene. Sort of like *Life with Father*.

He had no idea how long he'd been sitting there when he became aware of the silence beyond the range of the television. The news poured out, unheard, unwatched. The wind still battered at the windows like an angry child wanting to get in, but other than that, he couldn't hear a sound. Up until a little while ago he'd heard the occasional clink of a plate or glass, a cupboard door shutting, all indications that he wasn't alone in the house.

But now there was only silence. Maybe Lily was having a cup of tea. Just because she wasn't making noise didn't mean something was wrong. It was foolish to feel so uneasy just because of a few minutes of quiet. Any minute now he'd hear a noise or she'd come in and tell him she was going to bed. Any minute now. But he wasn't going to wait. He stood up and shut off the television, his head cocked as he listened. For a moment, all he could hear was the roar of the wind, but then there was another sound, softer, more mournful.

She was crying.

He moved into the kitchen, his footsteps silent on the wooden floors. Maybe he shouldn't intrude on her grief. But he couldn't just walk away and leave her alone any more than he could have walked away when they were children. She was part of him, the bright half of his soul, and he couldn't ignore her pain.

Lily was hunched over the counter, her shoulders shaking with sobs. Her hands were cupped together and Trace's first thought was that she might have hurt herself. Two long strides carried him across the room to her side.

"Lily? Are you hurt?"

His anxious question brought her head up. Tears streamed down her pale cheeks, her mouth trembled with pain.

"Trace." His name came out on a sob and she held her hands out without speaking. Trace looked down, seeking some sign of injury. She hadn't hurt herself but what she held made his throat tighten in sudden painful memory. Cupped between her hands was a pipe. Nothing fancy, just a plain briar pipe, the stem slightly chewed.

"I...found it while I was...putting away the dishes." Sobs broke the sentence into choppy lengths.

The pipe blurred as he took it from her, weighing it in his hand, remembering the way Mike would clench his teeth around the stem while he worked on a crossword puzzle. If he closed his eyes he could almost smell the warm aroma of tobacco.

"Oh, Trace, I'm going to miss him."

"I know, honey, I know." He put his arm around her shoulders, pulling her close. She leaned into him, her tears dampening his shirt, her sobs tearing at his heart. He set the pipe on the counter and ran his hand over her hair, a mindless rhythmic movement meant to soothe and comfort.

She sobbed against him, the cleansing flood of tears washing away some of the hurt. Trace held her, wishing he could absorb her pain. But her hurt was her own and all he could do was let her know she wasn't alone. He rested his cheek on the softness of her dark hair, closing his eyes tight, feeling tears burn beneath his eyelids.

"It's going to be all right. I'm here, love. I'm here."

After a long time her sobs eased to an occasional broken breath. When she pushed against his chest, Trace's arms loosened slowly. Holding her was an exquisite agony but one he was reluctant to relinquish.

"I must look awful." She wiped self-consciously at her eyes, sniffing. Trace leaned over and pulled a handful of tissues out of the box on the counter and handed them to her.

"You look beautiful, as always."

Lily dried her eyes and blew her nose before giving him a skeptical look. "Thanks." She glanced down, her fingers tearing at a tissue. "I'm sorry I fell apart like that."

"You're entitled." He brushed a lock of hair back from her face, aware of the silky feel of it in his fingers.

"I promised myself I was going to be strong."

"Crying doesn't make you any less strong."

She tilted her head back to look up at him, her eyes bright green. "Did you cry?"

"Sure," he lied without hesitation. "Howled like a baby."

Lily studied him for a long moment with that look in her eyes that always made him feel as if she were seeing things he couldn't see. She shook her head. "I don't think so. I don't think you've let yourself cry in a long time—not since I've known you. You didn't cry when we left home and you never cried all those awful months."

He shrugged. "I guess if I was a sensitive kind of a guy, tears would come easier." But he remembered a Christmas Eve when tears had eased some of his pain.

"It doesn't take tears to make a man sensitive."

Trace looked away, afraid of what he might see in her eyes. He shouldn't have let himself remember that hot summer day. The memories were too close, too vivid. The room was quiet for a moment and then he glanced back at her. She reached out, fingering the pipe.

"I'm going to miss him an awful lot."

"I know. He was a great guy."

"Do you ever wonder where we'd be without him?"

"Sure. I'd be in prison and you'd have been left on the streets alone."

Her lower lip quivered and her eyes filled with fresh tears. "It hurts, Trace. It hurts so much."

"I know, baby, I know. Don't cry anymore." He responded to the pain in her eyes instinctively, reaching up to cup her face in gentle hands. A single tear slid down her cheek.

"I'm sorry." The apology came out as a choked whisper and Trace felt his heart break. She looked so small and vulnerable. He'd been protecting her for so long. It hurt that he couldn't protect her from this pain.

"Don't, baby. Don't cry anymore. I'm here. I'll always be here." The words were whispered against her cheek as he kissed the solitary tear away. His mouth touched the corner of her mouth and time froze. For an endless second neither of them moved. Trace would never know who moved first. Did he shift or was it she? In the end it didn't matter. What mattered was that their lips met and suddenly there was nothing else in the world but them.

He'd almost managed to convince himself that her mouth wasn't as sweet as he'd remembered from those few stolen kisses. He'd told himself that it wasn't possible that a woman's mouth could mold to his so perfectly. He'd told himself that, but he hadn't believed it.

Lily's mouth softened and opened beneath his like a flower responding to a spring shower. The kiss had started out as a comfort, but the quality shifted too quickly for Trace to stop it. It wasn't possible to want to stop it. She felt so right in his arms. Grief sharpened the edges of their need. Death had walked through their lives, leaving wreckage behind. Each felt a deep need to affirm life, to hold on tight to each moment, aware of life's fleeting qualities.

His tongue explored the warm sweetness of her mouth, his arms pulling her close until not even air could have fit between their bodies. Lily's hands slid up his chest to his shoulders, clinging to him.

Sanity returned to Trace's mind and he drew back, staring down into her eyes. "This is crazy. I shouldn't be doing this."

"Yes, *we* should." The delicate emphasis made it clear that this was a step she was taking by choice. "Please, Trace. This is right. Feel how right it is."

He didn't move, trying desperately to remember all the reasons why this was wrong. This was Lily. He had no right to want her like this. No right to touch her. But it was impossible to think when her fingers were busy sliding the buttons of his shirt loose, one by one, her fingertips brushing against his chest with each move.

He closed his eyes, his hands coming up to catch her shoulders, intending to push her away. This had to be stopped now before something happened that they'd both regret. But her hands were against his chest, her fingers kneading his strong muscles.

"Lily." He couldn't have said whether the name was a protest or a prayer. His hands tightened on her shoulders but he didn't push her away.

"This is right, Trace. I know it's right." She leaned into his hold and his arms bent weakly, allowing her closer. He shuddered as her breath ghosted over his skin and then her mouth touched his collarbone.

"Love me, Trace. Please love me." Her hand slid up into his hair and she raised herself on her toes, pressing herself against his rigid body. "I need you."

Trace opened his eyes, looking down into her face. He was lost. He knew and she knew it. It was wrong. He knew it was wrong but he couldn't seem to remember why. He couldn't think of anything but the way she felt, the way she looked, the scent of her.

"Crazy." But the word was smothered against her mouth. Lily's arms circled his neck as he bent to scoop her into his arms. He carried her upstairs to his bedroom and kicked the door shut behind them. The room was dim, lit only by the bright moonlight that spilled in through the open curtains.

He set Lily down next to the bed, letting her slide against his body, feeling the teasing pressure from the top of his head to the soles of his feet. Her hair cascaded over his hands, a silken black waterfall that seemed to bind him to her. His mouth traced the length of her throat, his tongue settling on the pulse that beat so heavily at its base.

He'd been waiting for this for so long. All his life, it seemed. Lily pressed against him, feeling the boldness of his arousal along her hip. Her eyes widened for an instant, their expression impossible to read in the moonlight. His hand found her breast and her eyes closed, her slim body shuddering in his hold. Trace eased his leg between her thighs, pressing upward with gentle insistence. A soft whimper escaped her, her head falling back against his arm.

Arousal pounded in his veins, hot and demanding. He'd wanted for so long, needed for so many years. His hands were impatient with her shirt, tugging it off over her head, begrudging even those few seconds when they had to be apart. Her bra slid away, baring high firm breasts to his eyes, to his touch. He lifted her off the ground, an arm under her buttocks bracing her.

"Trace." His name escaped her on a gasp of startled pleasure as his tongue teased gently at one taut nipple. He held her there, taking his time as he painted each breast with delicate strokes before drawing a firm peak into his mouth to suckle hungrily. Her skin was hot and flushed as if with fever when he finally let her slide the length of his body. Her knees buckled and she would have slipped to the floor if he hadn't kept hold of her.

Trace looked down at her dazed expression and felt a purely male satisfaction. He'd brought that look of mingled need and wonder to her face. And then it was his turn to shudder as her trembling fingers slid the remaining buttons from buttonholes, tugging at his shirt until he shrugged it off, leaving them both bare to the waist.

Lily stretched up on her toes, linking her arms around his neck, her eyes meeting his as she leaned into him. Trace flushed, his eyes closing at the first sweet pressure of her breasts against his skin. His hands spanned her smooth back, drawing her closer, savoring the gentle torture. Lily's fingers slid into the thick hair at the base of his skull and his eyes flicked open to stare down into hers.

She wanted him. The knowledge washed over him like a sweet benediction, filling all the dark corners of his soul with warm light. She truly wanted him. For now, for a little while, he let that knowledge drown out the small voice that was trying to tell him that this was wrong. Lily wanted him. He didn't want to know anything else.

His mouth caught hers, his tongue slipping inside and then withdrawing, only to plunge forward again. She moaned, her hands clenching in his hair, her mouth welcoming his invasion. His breathing was harsh when he dragged his mouth from hers. He kissed his way down her throat, sinking to his knees in front of her, his lips and tongue worshiping her breasts. The snap on her jeans gave way beneath his fingers and he slid his hands inside the worn denim, cupping her bottom through the thin fabric of her panties.

Lily whimpered low in her throat, her hands clinging to his shoulders, his hold the only thing that kept her from sinking bonelessly to the floor. The jeans slid downward and she braced herself against him as she stepped out of them, her knees shaking. He knelt there a moment longer, his face pressed to the firm plane of her stomach, her hands tangled in his hair.

He rose slowly to his feet, lowering her to the bed with the motion. She lay beneath him, her slender body clad only in silk and moonlight. The white-gold light gilded her form, casting shadows and lighting curves. She was the embodiment of all his dreams.

Trace's hands were shaking as he unsnapped his own jeans. The rasp of a zipper sounded loud in the quiet room. The heavy denim rustled as he tugged the jeans off, tossing them aside. He stood before her as if awaiting some judgment. He could feel her eyes on him, tracing over broad shoulders and hair-matted chest, a taut stomach and narrow hips. Her gaze paused there and he felt the look as if it were a touch. There was a frozen moment when neither of them moved, and then Lily lifted her arms to him.

The bed creaked beneath his weight. Her soft moan of pleasure was swallowed up in his kiss. Their bodies slid together, softness and strength. Her panties slipped away, leaving her as vulnerable as he—more so perhaps, as woman is always more vulnerable than man.

His hands stroked her, learning every warm curve. Lily's hands explored his body. Sweet torture. He wanted it never to end; he wanted to end it right away. His fingers threaded through the triangle of dark curls that lay at the top of her thighs, finding the moist heart of her, and she shuddered beneath him. Her hand slid across his hip and closed around his arousal with delicate demand and it was his turn to shudder.

"Trace, now. Please, now." Her words pierced the last of his control and he rolled to pin her beneath him, his hips nestling between her waiting thighs.

He rested his weight on his elbows, winding his hands in the heavy length of her hair, staring down into her face as he arched forward, finding her waiting warmth with his hard strength. Her eyes widened in the moonlight, staring up at him. Her lashes flickered uncertainly and he froze, staring down at her.

"Lily." The name was not quite a question, only half a protest. He might never have felt it before but there was no mistaking the thin barrier that halted him now. Her hands tightened on his shoulders.

"Don't stop. Please, Trace. I want this. I want you. Don't stop now." The words tumbled over themselves.

"As if I could, sweetheart. As if I could." He bent, his mouth closing over hers as his hips arched heavily forward. He tasted her quick sharp gasp of discomfort as if it were his own, but then it was over. He lay still, reining in his own pounding need, giving her body time to adjust to his.

He started to move, slowly at first, a shallow thrusting movement. Lily echoed the movement. Trace thought he would surely die of pleasure. Her body fit his so perfectly, as if they'd been made for each other. The pleasure built.

Her soft whimpers slid over his skin like hot caresses. She twisted beneath him, demanding things she couldn't name, feeling needs she couldn't control. And he answered those demands, those needs. They moved together like two halves of a whole—heat and friction, shadow and light.

The explosion, when it came, was like nothing he'd ever known before. Lily arched, her body taut with pleasure, his name on her lips a soft cry of fulfillment. Trace shuddered in her arms, burying his face in the pillow as waves of sensation racked his body, leaving him at once weak as a kitten and filled with strength.

The slide back to earth was slow and gentle. Lily murmured a protest as he lifted himself from her and moved to the side.

"Don't go."

"I'm not going far." He slid an arm beneath her, drawing her close, pillowing her head on his shoulder. She lay against him, her body lax and satiated.

Long moments slipped by. Neither of them spoke. There didn't seem to be any need. In all his life Trace had never felt so right, so complete. For the first time in his memory, he felt as if he belonged somewhere, really belonged. With Lily's body cuddled so close to his and the scent of her filling his head, he felt as if he'd come home.

In the back of his mind he knew the feeling couldn't last. Reality would intrude sooner or later. He'd have to think about right and wrong and the future. But for this short space in time, he wasn't going to think about any of that. He wasn't going to think about anything beyond how totally right he felt at this moment.

He stroked Lily's shoulder, marveling at the smoothness of her skin. "Are you all right?"

She stirred, rubbing her cheek against him like a well-fed kitten. "I've never been more right in my life."

"Why didn't you tell me this was your first time?"

"You didn't ask." She tilted her head back and he caught the gleam of her smile in the darkness.

"Brat." But it was a loving complaint. He was quiet, his hand moving softly on her. "Why?"

"Why what?"

"Why now and why me?"

She was quiet so long that he began to think she wasn't going to answer him.

"Now because I need you. We needed each other. I wanted to feel alive again and I wanted to be close to you. And it had to be you. Always. It couldn't ever be anyone else."

Her quiet words fell like warm rain on his soul. He caught her close, burying his face in her hair. Emotion welled up in him and was tamped back down. It wasn't possible. She might think it now, but he knew that their lives had to follow different paths. Dreams only came true in fairy tales—and this was real life. But for just a little while, he wanted to pretend that maybe some dreams *could* come true.

"Trace."

"Hush." He stopped her before she could say something to shatter the dream. "It's late. Go to sleep."

She hesitated for a moment and then relaxed against him. After a while her even breathing told him that she slept. Trace couldn't see a clock from where he lay but he knew it must be late. He eased his arm out from under Lily and sat up on the side of the bed. The lights were still on downstairs and he couldn't remember whether he'd turned the television off or not.

Not that it really mattered whether the lights or the television stayed on all night, but he wasn't going to go to sleep just yet anyway. It took only a few minutes to turn off lights and make sure the door was locked. The wind still battered at the small house and Trace stood in the darkness listening to it for a long time before he climbed the stairs to his bedroom.

Lily stirred as he slid back into bed, gravitating to him as if to a magnet. She cuddled up against his body, curving herself to him as if made to be there. Trace stared up at the dark ceiling, listening to the wind lash outside and wondering if he'd ever know another moment of such supreme peace.

Chapter Eight

Trace came awake suddenly, aware that something wasn't right. Lily slept peacefully beside him, one arm thrown across his chest, her face buried in the pillow. The wind still roared outside, coming in gusts but never really stopping, and he could almost believe that it was some sound borne of the wind that had wakened him. But that wasn't it.

There was someone else in the house. He knew it as surely as if he could see the person standing right in front of him. He lifted Lily's arm and slipped out from beneath it, aware of her mumbled complaint before she relaxed back into sleep. He slid off the bed, reaching for his jeans with one hand and his gun with the other.

He crossed to the door, automatically avoiding the floorboard that squeaked. The door eased open with a faint click and he moved into the hallway, his bare feet silent on the hardwood floor. Flattening himself against the wall, the gun held ready, he slipped down the staircase, a shadow among shadows. Any small noise he might have made was swallowed in the ever-present howl of the wind.

Despite himself, he thought of Mike suddenly, lying in a pool of his own blood, all the life drained out of him. Trace shook the image away. Mike's death had nothing to do with this. Someone had broken into the house and he had to find out who. But there was still a coppery taste in his mouth and his heart beat a little too fast.

The hallway was dark and empty. Trace hesitated there, straining his ears for some sound, a clue as to the location of the intruder. It came in the form of a faint thud and then a quiet curse from the direction of the living room. Trace slid into the doorway, careful not to silhouette himself in the opening. His eyes, already adjusted to the darkness, picked out a vague shape.

"Don't move. Put your hands up and stand very still." His voice echoed in a sudden lull in the wind. He cocked the gun for emphasis, his hands steady. The figure, only dimly seen, froze. For the space of several slow heartbeats, the tableau remained.

"I was just going to turn on a light." The voice was low and husky.

Trace hesitated a moment. A light would do him as much good as the other.

"Go ahead but be careful. A forty-five leaves a very nasty hole."

"I'm aware of that." A small lamp snapped on and Trace narrowed his eyes against the sudden light, keeping the gun trained on the intruder. The man straightened away from the lamp, his expression calm. It was hardly the look to be expected from someone who'd just been caught breaking and entering.

He was a tall man, almost matching Trace's own six-two. Trace guessed his age to be somewhere around forty or so, give or take a few years. His hair was dark and his upper lip was concealed by a thick dark mustache. There was a niggling sense of familiarity about the man, though Trace had never seen him before.

"I suggest you hold real still while I call the police." He shifted toward the phone.

"Time was when this *was* the police. Or at least part of them."

Trace stared at him, nagged by that vague familiarity. "Who are you?"

"John Lonigan, Mike's son. Who are you?"

Trace studied him for a long moment before easing the hammer back into place. He didn't lower the barrel.

"Mike's son was named for him."

The intruder shrugged. "John Michael Lonigan. Nobody but Dad ever called me Michael."

"How did you get in?"

Michael Lonigan—if that was who he really was—held up a key. "Dad never changed the locks."

Trace looked at him, his eyes narrowed in thought. Maybe that nagging sense of familiarity was caused by some resemblance to Mike, though it wasn't readily apparent. Mike's shorter-than-average red-haired figure bore little resemblance to the man standing before him. Still, Trace was inclined to believe the guy.

"Do you have some identification?"

"Sure. I've got my passport." He cocked one eyebrow at the gun. "You going to shoot me if I reach for it?"

"Not if that's all you pull out of your pocket." Trace moved forward as the other man drew a folder from inside his jacket. The photo matched and the identification did indeed state that he was one John Michael Lonigan, American citizen. Trace flipped it shut and started to hand it back but the movement was never completed. A floorboard creaked behind him and the passport hit the floor with a splat. In the split second it took him to half turn and bring the gun up, Trace had time to wonder why it hadn't occurred to him that the man might have an accomplice. If he was about to die, what was going to happen to Lily, still sleeping upstairs?

Over the barrel of the .45, he met Lily's startled eyes. She was standing in the doorway, his shirt covering her almost to the knees, her hair spilling down her back. One hand pressed against the base of her throat, and her wide eyes shifted from him to the gun he held.

Trace lowered the gun, his thumb easing down the hammer he'd automatically drawn back. In some distant part of his mind he wondered if anyone else could see that his hands were shaking.

"Dammit, Lily! You should have said something to let me know you were there. I could have shot you."

She smiled weakly, pressing one hand to her chest. "Sorry. But I knew you wouldn't shoot if you didn't know what you were shooting at." Her utter confidence in him left Trace speechless. She looked past him to where John Lonigan was standing. "What's going on? Who is that man?"

Trace turned, running a hand through his rumpled hair. "He says he's Mike's son. His passport agrees." He scooped the passport off the floor and handed it to John. "This is Lily. I'm Trace."

"Trace and Lily." John's eyes widened for a moment before he took the passport. "You live here?"

"We have for the past fifteen years or so. You'd have known that if you'd ever come home." Trace didn't try to conceal his feelings.

John nodded. "You're right. I should have been home a lot sooner. You must have been the one who sent me the telegram about Dad. Thanks."

"It was a case of too little, too late, don't you think?"

Lily frowned at Trace, obviously trying to discourage his hostility, and then smiled at John. "It's nice to meet you."

"The pleasure is mine, believe me." John took her hand, his palm engulfing hers. His eyes flicked downward, taking in the man's shirt and slim bare legs before sweeping upward to the tousled black hair that lay about her shoulders.

There was nothing offensive in the look, Trace noticed, so why did he want to punch the other man in the jaw? It was blatantly obvious that he and Lily had just climbed out of the same bed. If Lily realized what John must be thinking, it didn't seem to bother her.

"I gather you and Trace have already met?"

"Not formally, although a forty-five is a hell of an introduction."

He smiled and Trace was struck by that familiarity again. He dismissed it and slid the safety on his gun before holding out his hand. They shook hands, each measuring the other. Trace saw a man past his first youth but with eyes that seemed much older. He was solidly built, and in his jeans and denim jacket he made Trace think of cigarette commercials.

"Sorry I startled you. The place was dark and I assumed it was empty."

"No problem." A gust of wind hit the house with a giant fist and no one said anything for a moment, as if in respect for nature's fury. "You must have a lot of questions."

"Quite a few," John agreed.

Trace ran his hand over his bare chest, looking down at his own half-dressed condition before glancing at Lily. She was modestly covered but he had to admit that he'd feel better if she had on something a little more conventional. She looked altogether too tousled.

"Look, why don't you let us get some clothes on and then I'll make some coffee and we can talk."

"Why don't I make the coffee? If the kitchen hasn't been moved, I suspect I can find my way around it well enough to manage that."

"Fine. We'll be down in a couple of minutes." Neither of them spoke on their way upstairs, though Trace didn't doubt that Lily was as aware of him as he was of her. He walked a little behind her, watching the way his shirt clung to her slender body, hinting more than revealing. But he didn't need more than a hint to remember the way she'd felt in his arms.

His bedroom door shut behind them. Trace flipped on the light before crossing to his holster and sliding the gun back into place.

"I'm sorry I startled you," Lily said quietly.

Trace turned to look at her, trying not to notice how beautiful she was. "No harm done, but you shouldn't sneak up on a man holding a gun."

"I didn't know you were holding a gun." She sat down on the edge of the bed. The movement tugged the hem of the shirt up, exposing a length of thigh. Trace looked away. He went to the closet and pulled out another shirt, shrugging into it with his back to her.

Did she have any idea what she was doing to him? Any idea how much he wanted her? Seeing her sitting on the rumpled covers, her hair like black silk against his shirt, it was all he could do to resist the urge to tumble her back onto the bed and make love to her, ignoring the fact that he shouldn't have made love to her in the first place, ignoring the fact that Mike's son was waiting downstairs for them. Ignoring everything but the hunger that gnawed at his gut.

"Trace? What's wrong?"

"Nothing. I just think we should get downstairs. John is waiting for us." He flinched as her hand touched his shoulder. The light contact was almost painful and he moved away casually, picking up his running shoes as if all he had on his mind was getting dressed.

Lily said nothing and her silence compelled him to look at her. She was watching him, her face still, but he'd known her too long, loved her too much not to see the hurt in her eyes. He dropped the tennis shoes on a chair and ran his fingers through his hair, trying to find the words to say what should be said.

"Are you sorry we made love?" Her chin was tilted; there was pride in every line of her body.

He should tell her that he was sorry. That would probably be the end of it. She'd realize how wrong he was for her and she'd go about finding someone who was right. She'd be hurt for a while but it would be a clean break. She watched him, her eyes waiting.

"No. God, no." He reached out, taking hold of her shoulders and pulling her against him. She buried her face against his bare chest, her breath leaving her on a sound that was close to a sob. Her arms circled his waist beneath the open shirt, holding him as if she were afraid to let him go. Trace bent down, laying his face against her hair, drawing in a deep breath and filling his senses with the scent of her.

"I was afraid you were going to tell me you were sorry." Her voice quivered with an edge of pain and Trace felt his heart clench. She was still hurting from Mike's death. He couldn't hurt her anymore, no matter how good the reasons.

"I couldn't be sorry. Not ever." He cupped the back of her head, tilting her face up to his, and kissed the dampness from her eyes. She lifted her arms to circle his neck, pressing close to him as if he were the only secure thing in her world right now.

He held her for a long time, feeling the sweet pain of having her in his arms, knowing it wouldn't—couldn't last.

"We ought to get downstairs before John decides we've died up here," Trace told her at last. Lily's arms loosened and he had to resist the urge to grab her close again. Instead, he let her step back. She ran her fingers through her hair, smoothing it behind her ears.

"I guess I look like a mess."

Trace's eyes darkened as he gazed at her. Was she really so unaware of how she looked? She stood there, wearing his shirt, her legs long and sexy beneath its curved hem. Her hair was a tangled black mane that seemed made for a man's hands. And her face— How could he describe her face? She was an angel, she was a dream, she was everything any man could want.

The surge of possessiveness caught him off guard and he leaned forward, burying his hands in her hair, tilting her face up to his. He had only a glimpse of the startled green of her eyes before his mouth settled firmly over hers. Her lips softened for him, inviting him inside. It was an invitation he didn't even try to resist, and for a few minutes the room was silent, only the wind outside filling the stillness.

Trace dragged his mouth away from hers at last, his eyes gleaming with a purely male satisfaction. She looked like a woman who'd been well and thoroughly loved. The thought gave him an inordinate amount of satisfaction.

"You look fine. Put some clothes on and let's get downstairs before he sends a search party after us."

A few minutes later they entered the kitchen. The wind roared outside but the kitchen felt warm and cozy in the early morning hours. Curtains shut out the darkness and the rich scent of coffee filled the air. John looked up as they entered, his eyes skimming over them both as if seeing more than just the surface. Trace had the odd feeling that the other man could have told him what had occurred upstairs with fair accuracy. It was not a comfortable thought.

"I hope you don't mind." He gestured to the plate in front of him. "I made myself a sandwich. The food on the plane was pretty bad and I didn't take time to get anything else before I came here.''

"Help yourself." Trace crossed to the counter and got down three mugs. Behind him he heard the scrape of a chair as Lily seated herself at the table. He poured coffee and set it on the table, turning a chair around and straddling it. John was just finishing a thick ham sandwich and he reached for the coffee, taking a long swallow of the steaming liquid before leaning back in his chair.

"Do you mind if I smoke?"

"Go ahead," Trace told him.

John reached for his cigarettes, catching Lily's disapproving look and giving her an apologetic smile. "I know it's a bad habit. I keep threatening to quit."

"It's very bad for you."

"I know." He lit a cigarette and drew smoke into his lungs. "I'm going to quit. Tomorrow."

Lily smiled reluctantly and Trace didn't have any trouble recognizing the look of male appreciation in the other man's eyes.

"So, I gather you must have received my telegram." He didn't care if his words were abrupt. John wasn't looking at Lily anymore.

"I got it," he said quietly. The memory obviously held some pain. "I'd have been here sooner but I was in the Middle East and it took a while for the telegram to reach me."

"You missed the funeral," Lily told him.

"Dad wasn't much for ceremony. I don't suppose he'd mind that much that I didn't make it home for his funeral." He stopped and stared down at his coffee. "Stupid. The first time I make it home in nearly twenty years and it's for his funeral." His mouth twisted in a half-bitter smile.

"I'm sure Mike understood." Lily reached out to cover his hand with her much smaller one.

John swallowed the last of his coffee and set the cup on the table with a thump. "I was going to make it home this past Christmas. Then something came up and I figured I'd try for the summer. I guess I just ran out of time."

He didn't add anything to that. Neither Trace nor Lily spoke, allowing him a few moments of quiet grief. Lily's eyes met Trace's, full of compassion. Trace swallowed a jealous twinge, knowing he was being foolish.

"How did it happen?" The abrupt question drew his attention back to John. "All the telegram said was that he was dead. I managed to get enough information to know he was shot but I don't know much beyond that."

"How did you manage even that much?" Lily asked. "You must have been traveling pretty steady to get here so soon."

"I've got sources I can call on. When you've traveled as much as I have, you learn who to call when you need something."

Trace felt there was more to it than that, but now was not the time to pursue the question.

"So what happened to Dad?" John asked.

Trace lifted his shoulders in a shrug, twisting the coffee cup between his palms, his eyes on the aimless movement. "Mike went to open up the store. Someone came in behind him and emptied a three fifty-seven into him." The flat words painted a picture more horrifying than any elaborate descriptions could have done.

"My God." John's face was pale, his eyes staring at nothing in particular. "Did he die quickly?" It was the same question Lily had asked and Trace wanted to be able to tell him that Mike hadn't even known what hit him.

"Fairly quick."

"You found him?"

"Yeah." Trace blanked his mind from the memory of Mike's body lying sprawled on the floor.

"It must have been hell."

"It wasn't much fun." Trace finished his coffee.

"Do they know who did it?" There was a tightness in John's voice that Trace could relate to.

"No. Nothing was stolen and there are no fingerprints. At this point it looks like random violence. Maybe some junkie whacked out on drugs. Could have been gang related, though we haven't been having much trouble with gangs in that area. Could have been almost anybody. We don't have a motive and we don't have much by way of clues."

He stopped but no one said anything. There didn't seem to be much to say and they sat there in silence, all of them wrapped in thoughts of their loss. Trace looked at John, wondering what he must be thinking, what he must be feeling. Twenty years away from home. There was little to be read in his face. His eyes were shuttered, revealing nothing. Trace had the feeling that this was a man who didn't reveal anything he didn't choose to.

The wind, which had died down while they talked, suddenly hit the house with a powerful gust. The lights flickered, going out for an instant before coming back on. The quick flash of darkness brought them back to the present.

"Looks like we might lose the lights after all," Trace said as he stood up. He rinsed his cup and set it on the counter.

"I'd forgotten what the Santa Anas could be like. In my memories, Southern California was always the land of endless sunshine and perfect weather. You tend to forget the less pleasant aspects of it."

"Have you traveled a lot?" The interest in Lily's voice reminded Trace of how little he'd traveled, how little he'd seen.

"I've traveled quite a bit."

Trace had never been so glad to have the electricity go out. It had the immediate effect of ending the conversation.

"Hang on. I got lamps out earlier." He felt his way along the counter to the lamps and turned the knob on the first one. There was a click and then a pop as the electronic lighter hit the butane. Harsh crisp light flooded the kitchen as he lit another lamp.

"Well, at least it waited until we finished our coffee," Lily said philosophically.

"True." John looked at his watch. "It's going to be light in just a couple of hours. I don't know about you guys, but I could use a little sleep."

"Me, too." Lily put her hand over her mouth to stifle a yawn. Trace was suddenly aware of the exhaustion that hovered just out of reach, as if waiting for him to relax before it pounced. He lifted his shoulders but the feeling didn't go away.

"If you don't mind, I thought I'd sack out on the sofa. I can find a place to stay in the morning." John glanced up at the roof as another gust of wind tore at the house. "That is if we don't all blow out to sea before then."

"Don't be silly, John. This is your house as much as ours, more really. There's no reason for you to find another place to stay or for you to sleep on the sofa," Lily told him in a tone that brooked no argument.

John glanced at Trace, one brow raised in a question. Trace nodded. "She's right. I can clear out of my room and sleep in Mike's."

"No, I'll sleep in Dad's room. It probably has less vivid memories for me than it does for you." No one mentioned the fact that Trace and Lily had obviously been sharing a room earlier, which would leave two empty bedrooms in the house. If it occurred to John, he had the tact not to say anything.

He picked up one of the lamps, lifting it in a vague salute. "I'll see you tomorrow." He strode from the kitchen, his footsteps quiet despite the boots he was wearing. A man accustomed to moving in silence. Trace noticed the habit absently. He was more concerned with the fact that he and Lily were alone.

Neither of them spoke until they heard the thud of an upstairs door closing. The lantern cast vivid patterns of light and shadow, making the familiar kitchen look strange and otherworldly.

"I suppose we should get to bed," Trace said casually.

"I suppose so. It's pretty late."

They left the kitchen together. Trace automatically shut off light switches as they went. Not that it mattered. He was carrying the only functioning light with him. The lantern swung in his hand, making the stairs seem to shift, growing and shrinking as they climbed them.

At the top of the stairs they stopped. Trace reached out to turn the lantern down until it cast a soft glow over the hallway. Neither of them looked at the other. To the right lay Trace's bedroom.

"I don't want to be alone tonight." Lily didn't look at him as she spoke. She kept her eyes on the floor, her voice hardly above a whisper.

Trace felt a sharp pain in his chest. She sounded so uncertain, so lost. Remorse washed over him. He was being selfish, only concerned with what he was feeling, his own fears and uncertainties. What about what Lily was thinking and feeling?

She'd taken a frightening step tonight, giving herself to a man for the first time, and he was making her feel like an unwanted package left on his doorstep.

Harlequin's

Best Ever "Get Acquainted" Offer

Look what we'd give to hear from you

GET ALL YOU ARE ENTITLED TO—AFFIX STICKER TO RETURN CARD—MAIL TODAY

This is our most fabulous offer ever... AND THERE'S STILL MORE INSIDE. Let's get acquainted. Let's become friends—

Look what we've got for you:

"I had no intention of leaving you alone." She looked up at him, relief and surprise in her eyes, and Trace's guilt increased.

"I thought—" His finger over her mouth stopped her.

"Don't think. I may be a jerk but I'm not a fool. And I'd have to be a fool to sleep alone tonight."

DOWN THE HALL John heard a door shut. One door. He half smiled to himself. So he hadn't been wrong about the tension between the two of them. He turned back to the window, leaning his shoulder against the wall and staring out at the wind-ravaged darkness. The surrounding neighborhood was dark but he could see down into the valley below where lights sparkled like discarded jewels.

The view hadn't changed much since he was a kid, at least not the night view. He could remember looking out at this same scene when he was small and his father had held him up so that he could see.

His father. He closed his eyes a moment before opening them again to stare blindly out the window. The pain surprised him. It had been nearly twenty years since he left this house, vowing never to return. And he hadn't, not once in all those years. Youthful pride and anger had long since given way to a life that just never seemed to allow him to come home.

No, that wasn't entirely true. It had been easier not to come home. There always seemed to be plenty of time to mend the last few fences between him and his father. The rage and frustration that had driven him to leave had faded long ago but there'd still been just enough of the rebellious boy in him to make coming home difficult.

He let the curtain drop, shutting out the windy darkness as he turned away from the window. He looked around the room with eyes that were twenty years older than the last

time he'd seen it. Like the view, it hadn't changed a whole
lot. It was the same oak furniture that his father had
screamed bloody murder over when his mother bought it.
The carpet had to be different, but it was the same dark
shade he remembered. In the crisp light of the butane lantern everything looked strange. Too bright, the shadows too
dark.

He wandered across the room to the dresser, flipping open
the lid of a small mahogany box that sat there. Memory
stirred and he remembered giving Mike the box. He'd been
twelve, still young enough to think his father was perfect.
The box had been a project in shop class and he'd been so
proud of it. And his dad had kept it all these years.

John shut the lid quietly and turned his attention to the
photos that stood along the back of the dresser. The first
one he picked up was one he remembered vividly. It was
taken before the last football game he'd played in high
school. He could smile now at the self-consciously fierce
look the boy in the photo was giving the camera, but he remembered how important that game had seemed at the
time. Life and death.

He set the picture down and lifted the next one. This one
must be a graduation photo of Lily. She looked out at the
camera with total calm, not in the least intimidated by the
lens. He studied the picture, comparing it to the woman
who'd come downstairs wearing a man's shirt and nothing
else. She looked a little older than the girl in the photo, even
more beautiful if that was possible. The self-possession was
the same, a measuring look in those expressive eyes, as if she
were seeing much more than you wanted her to.

Lily was in the last photo, too, a little younger, maybe
sixteen or seventeen. Trace was with her. It was a candid
shot. They were both wearing jeans and casual shirts and
John recognized the front of the house behind them. It

might have been nothing more than just another informal family portrait if it hadn't been for their expressions. Trace had his arms around Lily's waist, her back against his chest. It wasn't hard to guess that Mike had posed them that way but neither of them was looking at the camera. Lily had leaned sideways to gaze up at Trace and he was looking down at her. It wasn't the position that caught the viewer's attention. It was their expressions. Trace was looking at Lily as if she were the most precious thing on earth, and Lily looked at him as if the sun rose and set because of him.

John set the picture down, feeling a funny little ache in his chest. He'd known; all those years ago, he'd known. Two scruffy kids and a battered suitcase. Nothing special, and yet there'd been something about them. They hadn't recognized him. Fifteen years was a long time and they'd been just children back then. No, Trace might have been a child in age but he'd been well on his way to manhood. Odd, he hadn't known what they were running from—he still didn't know—but he hadn't doubted that they had good reason.

He turned away from the photos and looked at the bed. He'd said that he'd take this room because it held less vivid memories for him, but that wasn't strictly the truth. The memories were there, just as real as ever. He crossed to the duffel bag that held just about everything he owned in the world and pulled out a sleeping bag, rolling it out on the carpet near the door.

He'd wanted to stay here because of the memories, a chance to say goodbye maybe. But goodbye was turning out to be a little harder than he'd expected. There were too many things left to say, too many explanations that couldn't be given.

He slid into the sleeping bag and reached out to turn off the light, plunging the room into darkness. John closed his eyes, willing himself to sleep. The wind howled outside, isolating the little house. But it didn't take a wind to make a man feel alone. Sometimes he carried that feeling inside himself.

Chapter Nine

John paused at the top of the stairs, taking a deep appreciative sniff. The smoky rich scent of coffee wafted upward, greeting the day with more enthusiasm than he'd managed to muster so far. Sleep had been elusive, teasing him with the promise of rest but never delivering. It hadn't been because he was sleeping on the floor. God knew he'd slept in worse places in his time. No, it hadn't been the physical conditions. His mind had simply refused to shut down long enough to allow him to fall asleep. Too much to think about, too many decisions that needed to be made.

He shook his head and breathed in another whiff of coffee. Right now the only decision he planned on making was whether to have two or three cups of coffee. It was about all he felt capable of.

"I hope there's enough coffee for two in that pot." Trace was seated at the oak kitchen table, a steaming cup in front of him.

"Help yourself. I don't quite function until I've had my second cup."

"I know what you mean." John sat down, cradling a cup between his palms, letting the warmth seep into his body. "Looks like the winds have died down."

"The weather report says they're gone for now," Trace said.

"Have you been outside? Is there much damage?"

Trace shrugged. "It's not too bad. A couple of broken branches and a section of the back fence down. Mike was— Mike was going to replace the fence this summer anyway." He picked up his cup and sipped at the steaming liquid.

"It's probably the same fence that was there when I was a kid and Dad was threatening to replace it then."

Trace grinned, the first openly friendly expression John had seen from him. "It's the same one. He almost replaced it about five, six years ago, but then he priced new fencing and swore he'd make the thing last till doomsday before he shelled out that kind of money for a few moldy boards."

John laughed. "Doesn't sound like he'd changed much."

"No, he didn't change a whole lot."

"So what do you do for a living?" John took a swallow of coffee, cocking a brow at the other man.

"I'm a cop." Trace glanced up. "Mike kept track of where you were through a friend of his at your company, but he never said much about what you did."

"I work for an import-export business. I handle a lot of the foreign side of things. When I'm in the States, I'm based in New York." The explanation tripped easily off his tongue. It was absolutely plausible, would even check out if someone did any digging, but Trace's eyes took on a shrewd glint that made John wonder how much of it he bought.

"Sounds interesting" was all he said.

"I enjoy it."

"Enjoy what?" The question came from behind him and John turned to see Lily standing in the doorway. She was wearing a pair of faded jeans that clung lovingly to her slim legs and a gray sweatshirt that should have concealed her feminine curves but somehow emphasized them instead. Her hair was pulled back in a low ponytail, her face untouched by makeup, and John didn't think he'd ever seen a more purely beautiful woman in his life.

"Enjoy what?" Lily repeated the question, making him realize that he'd been staring at her. He turned back to the table as she walked farther into the room.

"My work. I was just telling Trace that I enjoy my work. You teach, don't you?"

"Yes. I was thinking that maybe I'd check around and see if there are any positions open here, maybe something part-time." She poured herself a cup of coffee and took a sip, wrinkling her nose at the taste of it.

"I thought you'd be going back to England," Trace commented, his voice carefully neutral.

"No. I told the Fairfields I wouldn't be back." She leaned back against the counter and looked at him, her heart in her eyes. "I thought it was time I came home for good."

Trace didn't look up and John had the feeling it was deliberate, as if he were afraid of what he might see. Or maybe he was afraid of what his eyes might reveal. Interesting. Despite the fact that they'd spent the night before in the same room and presumably in the same bed, there were apparently still problems in paradise.

He shifted his eyes from Lily to Trace in time to catch the other man's look, and there was no mistaking the message there. Whatever was going on between the two of them, Trace was warning him off. The look in those blue eyes burned with possessiveness. John acknowledged the warning with a lift of his brow. He had enough problems of his own without coming between the two of them.

The morning was spent cleaning up the damage the winds had left behind. In the wake of the storm the sky was a brilliant blue, so clear it almost hurt to look at it. From higher in the hills it was possible to glimpse the pale blue of the

ocean across the Los Angeles basin. It was a day of crystal
clear beauty. Impossible to think of smog or summer days
when the heat threatened to smother the city.

Trace and John worked together easily, sawing the rough
ends off the snapped branches and shoring up the fence well
enough to get through one more year. Lily raked and swept
the brick patio. It felt good to have something positive to do.
In the simple, practically mindless tasks, there was a peace
that all three of them treasured.

It was a peace that wasn't destined to last long. In the
early afternoon they had a visitor. Trace happened to be in
the house when the doorbell rang. He glanced up, frowning
and debating on whether to answer it. They weren't expecting anyone and he wasn't sure he wanted to see anyone,
expected or otherwise. He shut the refrigerator door, carrying two bottles of beer in one hand and wiping his damp
forehead on the tail of his shirt with the other.

The bell rang again before he could get to it and he threw
the door open, prepared to get rid of whoever was on the
other side as quickly as possible.

"Captain Jacobs." He was immediately conscious of his
battered jeans, his unbuttoned shirt and the faint sheen of
sweat that coated his face. Not to mention the two beers
clutched in one hand. "Sir. I wasn't expecting you."

"No reason you should have been, Dushane. I hope you
don't mind that I've just dropped by like this."

"No, of course not. Come in, please."

Trace shut the door behind the older man, hoping he
didn't look as uneasy as he felt. Mike and Bill Jacobs had
worked together before Mike left the force and the two of
them had remained friends. It wasn't the first time he'd seen
the captain outside the station house, but he had a funny
feeling that this visit was not purely social.

"We were just cleaning up some of the storm damage. It's warm out." He gestured to his scruffy clothes and held up the two beers as illustration.

"Nothing too serious, I hope."

"Not really. We're pretty well done."

"We? You and Lily? I saw her at the funeral. I was glad she made it back from England in time for that."

Trace nodded, preferring not to remember the funeral. It was assuming a hazy image in his memory and he wanted to encourage that as much as possible.

"Mike's son got here last night."

Captain Jacob's bushy eyebrows shot up. "John? Good God, I haven't seen him in twenty years or more."

"I gather he hasn't been here in twenty years or more. He's in the back if you want to see him."

The captain nodded. "I'd like that."

Trace gestured toward the kitchen with the hand that held the bottles. "You know the way. Can I get you something to drink?"

"No, thanks. This is a semiofficial call and I'd better keep my nose clean."

"Is there some problem?"

The older man shook his head. "Not exactly. If you don't mind, I'm sure Lily and John will want to hear what I have to say, so I'll just wait and save myself having to say it twice."

"Of course." What Trace really wanted to say was that he minded very much. He reined in his impatience while Captain Jacobs greeted Lily and John and the two men swapped a few stories of the last time they'd met just before John left home. Trace took a long pull of his beer, his eyes narrowing as he watched them. It was clear that they shared a lot of memories and he found himself wondering, not for the first time, just why John had left home.

"Trace? Can I have a drink?" Lily's quiet request drew his attention away from John and the captain.

"Sure." He handed her the bottle, watching as she tilted her head back to take a swallow. Her face crinkled at the taste and he smiled, taking the bottle from her. "If you don't like the stuff, why did you want a drink?"

"I always think that maybe I've exaggerated how awful it tastes."

"You haven't." He took a swallow and then set the bottle down on the stone wall that ringed the property. Lily linked her hands through his arm. The casual touch burned through his shirt, leaving the imprint of her palm on his skin.

"They look like old friends." Trace was so aware of her touch that it took him a moment to realize what she was talking about. He forced his eyes to focus on the two men who'd wandered across the yard to study the patched fencing.

"Captain Jacobs has probably known John since he was a kid."

"You're not still worried about last night, are you?" The change of subject threw him off balance. She was looking up at him, her eyes a clear deep green that reflected her emotions.

"Lily—" He broke off, frustrated. John and the captain were moving toward them. This wasn't a conversation he wanted to cram into a few brief moments. He wasn't sure it was a conversation he wanted to have at all.

"Captain Jacobs wants to tell us what they have on Mike's murder." John's words proved an effective distraction. Lily's fingers tightened on Trace's arm and he put his hand over hers, squeezing gently.

By unspoken consent the four of them moved into the house. It didn't seem the kind of discussion to be held in bright sunshine. Once they were all seated in the living room, Captain Jacobs didn't waste any time.

"The three of you know that Mike and I went way back. We were partners and we stayed friends after he left the force. I want the person who killed him as much as any of you do."

"This doesn't sound like good news," John said dryly.

Captain Jacobs shook his head. "It's not. To be blunt, we don't really have anything to go on. No fingerprints, no apparent motive, nothing. And the one witness we have is turning out to be not much better than nothing at all."

Trace leaned forward, his expression intent. "I didn't know we had a witness at all."

Jacobs ran his hand over what little hair he had left. "A Mrs. Betty Levy. She came to us yesterday. She's kicking seventy in the teeth. She was out walking her dog the morning of the break-in and says she saw a man run from the building."

"Why didn't she say something right away?" Trace demanded. "Damn, we might have had a chance if she'd said something the day it happened."

"She doesn't know enough to give us an ID, Dushane. All she saw was a man running from the store. About the only good it's done us is that we can eliminate a gang-related incident. The man she says she saw was gray-haired and rather thin."

"What kind of a car?" Trace leaned forward, wanting, needing, something solid to grasp, but Jacobs shook his head.

"Blue. Medium-sized. Might have had two doors or then again it could have been four. He went east or maybe south. She didn't think anything of it until one of her neighbors told her what had happened and then she decided maybe she ought to tell us what she'd seen."

"I guess it's better than nothing," Lily offered.

"Not much!" Trace heard the snap in his voice and shook his head. "Sorry. I just hoped maybe we'd have something to work with."

"Where are those precocious twelve-year-olds with the eagle eyes when you need them?" John's dry comment brought reluctant smiles.

"Yeah, let's hear it for precocious twelve-year-olds." Trace leaned back on the sofa, reaching out to catch Lily's hand in an absent gesture. "So we don't have anything, then?"

"Not much. We're still working on it. We're going back through Mike's case files, looking for anyone who might have held a grudge, but he'd been off the force a long time. Anybody who was holding a grudge against him would most likely have done something about it years ago."

"So you have no idea who killed Dad and you don't really expect to have any idea." John's succinct summation didn't leave much room for hope. Jacobs backed away from anything quite so final.

"We aren't giving up. Not by a long shot. We're going to get this guy. Sooner or later something will turn up."

No one said anything for a long moment. They all knew just how thin Jacobs's promise was. No matter how much the police wanted to catch Mike's murderer, they couldn't do it without some clues, some evidence.

Jacobs left soon afterward, leaving a vague depression behind him. It was impossible to recapture the morning's calm. They finished cleaning up the wind damage but no one seemed to feel much satisfaction in the results of their efforts.

Dinner was a take-out pizza and it was eaten in virtual silence. They all went to bed early, and neither Trace nor Lily suggested they spend the night together. Perhaps she felt the same need for a little distance between them that he did.

Trace lay in bed, his hands behind his head, staring into the darkness. There were no winds tonight and the house was quiet. There was a waiting quality to the silence and he wondered if the others were as wide awake as he was. Too much had happened too quickly. He still hadn't dealt with Mike's death and now there was Lily.

Lily. He didn't have to close his eyes to remember the way she'd felt in his bed, in his arms. She'd felt so right, as if she were made to fit only him. But that was what he wanted to believe. Lily wasn't for him. Oh, maybe for a little while he could let himself pretend, but it could only be pretend.

Lily was sunlight and laughter. She was brightness. The angel on the Christmas tree. And he was none of those things. It didn't matter how many years had gone by or how many miles he'd traveled, there was a part of him that would always be poor white trash. He could never forget where he came from. Jed's face was clear and sharp in his memory— the bitterness, the weakness. He hadn't been the man's son but Jed was as close to a father as he'd known all his young years. What if the seeds of Jed's particular madness lay somewhere inside him, just waiting to come out?

He shuddered and pushed the thought away. It didn't matter how often he told himself that nothing on earth could ever make him like Jed, there was still a niggling doubt in the back of his mind. As the twig is bent, so grows the tree. The old truism came to mind. He couldn't have spent all those years living like trash and not carry the scars. Sometimes he could feel them burned deep into his soul as if they were something alive and eating into him.

Just thinking about Lily was enough to soothe the ache, and when she was with him, he could almost imagine the

marks weren't there. But she deserved someone who could
come to her whole and unscarred.

He could pretend for a little while, but that was all it could
ever be—just make-believe.

But it was one thing to know that was the way it had to be
and another to make his heart believe it. It was impossible
to just walk away from her. She was too much a part of him.
Too much a part of his life. So he told himself it was all right
to stay close to her, all right to be a part of her life for now.

"I DON'T KNOW about anybody else, but if I don't get out
of this house, I'm going to go nuts." Trace threw down the
deck of cards from which he'd been dealing his thirtieth
game of solitaire and looked at his companions. Lily
glanced up from the book she was supposedly reading,
though she hadn't turned a page in at least ten minutes.

"I could use some time out of the house."

John looked up from the television. His eyes swung from
Trace to Lily. "Count me out. I've got a lot of lost time to
make up for on *Dallas*. I'm still trying to figure out who shot
J. R."

Lily laughed. "You're not going to find that out from this
week's show."

"No?" He shrugged. "Who cares? I've been out of the
country a long time. This way I catch up on what people are
doing. You two go on without me."

Trace wasn't going to argue with him. It wasn't that he
disliked the man, but it felt strange to have a third person
always around. It didn't seem to make any difference that
he hadn't seen Lily in two years or that he'd lived apart from
her for much longer. In a way, it had always been the two of
them, even when he didn't see her every day. Not even Mike
had changed that feeling. Somehow, with John, things were
different.

He couldn't put his finger on what it was. He didn't know if it was the shift in his own relationship with Lily or if it was the fact that everything had changed around them, but John seemed to slip between them in a subtle undefinable way. Whatever it was, Trace was just as happy when he chose to stay home, leaving him and Lily to go out alone.

It was a cool night, but the skies were clear. Trace's '65 Corvette, his most prized possession, swooshed down the hill into Glendale. It was past rush hour and traffic on the Ventura Freeway was light. Neither he nor Lily spoke. It was enough to be out on the open road, alone together. The freeway curved north around Hollywood and swept into the valley. From there it was a short trip to Mulholland Drive. Trace heard Lily sigh with pleasure as he turned the 'Vette onto the famous road. It had always been one of her favorite places to go.

The 'Vette's engine was a low growl as it took the hills and sharp curves, as if born to run on a road like this. At the top of the drive Trace pulled into a shallow turnout and shut off the engine. The sudden silence was almost a presence of its own. The lights of the San Fernando Valley were spread out below them like billions of jewels on a swathe of black velvet. Seen from this distance, it was hard to believe that people lived and died under those sparkling lights.

"It's beautiful, isn't it?" Lily's voice was low, in keeping with the still night.

"It's about the only time the valley looks good."

They were quiet again, staring out at the stunning display beneath them.

"You know, you haven't— John's been there and all, but you haven't acted like you had any interest in me."

Trace didn't need to be a mind reader to hear the hurt beneath her words. He reached out to catch her hand in his.

"Lily, I— Sometimes I can be a real jackass, but the one thing in the world I don't ever want to do is to hurt you."

"I know that." He could see the curve of her cheek in the starlight as she looked down at their linked hands. "But it's not your fault if you don't feel the way I feel about—"

"Don't." Trace cut into her words. "It's too soon for anybody to be talking about the way they feel. Look, we've just been through a pretty rough time. Things have changed so quickly, there are times when I'm still not sure what's going on. Let's not rush into anything."

"We've already rushed into quite a bit," Lily said quietly without looking at him.

"I know, but let's take things a little slower from here on. We hadn't even seen each other in two years until the...until the funeral. Maybe we should get to know each other again."

As if he didn't know her in the innermost recesses of his soul already. She was part of every breath he took.

"You mean we should date?" He didn't need a bright light to see the way she wrinkled her nose in surprise.

"I...yeah, I guess that's what I mean." *Coward*. It wasn't what he meant at all. Why didn't he have the guts to tell her that they were all wrong? That they would always be friends, always be linked by their past—but it couldn't be anything more?

"So I guess we could consider this our first date."

"Yeah, I guess we could."

She tilted her head to look at him and he caught the glimmer of her eyes. "What's your sign?"

"What?"

"What's your sign? That's one of the questions you always have to ask on a first date."

"Really? I didn't know there was a handbook on it." Her mood had shifted so quickly from intense to humorous that

Trace felt as if he were stumbling, trying to catch up with her.

"There are just certain things you do. One of them is to find out the person's sign, and I need to know what kind of a car you drive and how much you earn a year. Of course, I can't ask that directly, so generally it's best to ask what you do for a living."

He relaxed back in his seat, catching the lightness of her mood. "Do you have a chart that gives you relative salaries for various jobs?"

"Naturally. Oh, and it's important to know where you come from and who your family is. A girl can't be too careful these days. If a guy tells you that he spends every summer with his mother, you can eliminate him immediately. Nobody wants mother-in-law problems."

"Well, you don't have to worry about that with me." Despite his best efforts, there was a bitter note lacing the light words. Lily must have heard it, too, because she was silent for a moment.

"How is your mother?"

"She's fine, I guess. I talked to her at Christmas. She seems to like Florida. I guess after the winters in Oklahoma she's still not used to being able to pick oranges right off the tree in January."

There. His tone had been light enough. Nothing to reveal the turmoil thoughts of his mother always brought with them.

"I don't remember much but I do remember that she was kind to me."

"She was a kind woman. Probably still is."

"You know, it's stupid in a way, but I've never asked you why we ran away." Lily's tone was thoughtful. She might have been commenting on the weather. Trace's fingers tightened around hers in shock before he pulled his hand away.

"It was a long time ago." A weak reply but the best he could come up with. There'd been a time, when she was in her teens, when he'd half expected her to ask questions and he'd tried to prepare himself with some stock answers. But that was years ago and he couldn't remember what he'd planned to say. Besides, she wasn't a teenager anymore, and the half truths and vague realities he'd intended to tell her then wouldn't do now.

"When I was a little girl, it didn't occur to me to question you. If you thought we should run away, I just accepted that that must be the right thing to do."

"Let's hear it for little girls." His humor held a gallows edge to it. He had a feeling he wasn't going to like where this conversation was going.

"Then, when I got a little older, I guess I was too busy with other things to worry too much about how I'd come to be where I was. But I thought about it while I was in England and I realized that I'd never asked you any questions. Why did we run away? What happened?"

"It was all a very long time ago, Lily. Does it really matter?" It was a last-ditch effort to avoid dredging up memories he'd spent years trying to bury.

"It matters to me. Whatever happened, it was part of my life and I want to know."

Trace stared out at the blanket of lights below them, wondering just what words to use. She had a right to know, but that didn't stop him from wishing she hadn't asked.

"How much do you remember?"

"Not much. I remember your mother was nice to me and she had a soft voice. And I remember spending a lot of time with you."

"That first day you came to the house, I thought you were the most beautiful thing I'd ever seen in my life." The lights faded, replaced by memories. Trace could almost smell the dusty yard and see the worn pickup. He remembered the way his heart had seemed to catch in his throat for an instant when he first saw her. She'd been so tiny and so perfect. He'd wanted to protect her and take care of her from the first moment he saw her, and the feeling hadn't changed over the years.

"Trace?" Lily's voice brought him back to the present. He glanced at her, catching her questioning gaze in the darkness.

"Sorry. A lot of memories. Do you remember Jed?"

"Some." In the 'Vette's small passenger compartment, it was possible to feel the faint shiver that ran through her. The strength of his old anger surprised him. After all these years he still wanted to feel Jed's bones breaking beneath his fists.

"Jed had . . . ideas he shouldn't have had."

"Ideas? About what?"

"About you," he told her flatly. There was a moment of dead silence and then he heard her quick catch of breath as she realized what he meant.

"But I was just a little girl." Her appalled protest echoed in the small car.

There was nothing he could say. He'd had sixteen years to come to terms with the past, yet all that time hadn't helped.

"Is that why we left?" she asked after a long while.

"It seemed like the best thing to do. I didn't know what else I could do to keep you safe."

"You were just a kid yourself."

"There wasn't anyone else," he said simply.

"What about your mother?"

Trace laughed, a short sound that held more bitterness than he liked to admit. Funny how he'd been far more tolerant of the choices his mother had made when he was a child. As he'd grown older, he'd realized just how great was the burden she'd allowed him to carry.

"She had about all she could handle just surviving, I guess. Standing up to Jed was more than she could do."

"And you hate her for it, don't you?" Lily's perceptive comment pierced right to the heart of the problem. But Trace couldn't hate Addie. There had been times when he wanted to, but he couldn't.

"No, I don't hate her," he said at last. "It might be simpler if I did. She did the best she could. You can't ask more of someone than that. But there are times when I remember how scared I was all the months we spent living on the street with never enough to eat, always wondering if we were going to live through another day, and I can't forgive her for that."

He stopped, hearing the fierce anger in his own voice. It had been a long time since he'd thought about his feelings toward his mother. He'd been home only once, after the car crash that killed Jed. He'd spent three days there, helping her pack up the house and then putting her on a plane for Florida. She had a sister there, an aunt he'd never met, and she seemed happy enough now.

"You weren't much more than a child yourself."

"I was all you had," he said simply. "There was no one else."

"And who was there for you?"

Trace shrugged. "I didn't need anyone. Besides, I had you."

Lily was silent for a long time. "You know, I never thought much about family," she said quietly. "I guess I always felt as if you were all the family I needed. And then there was Mike." She stopped, struggling to control her voice. "Only now Mike's gone and it's just the two of us again. My parents are dead and I don't remember them very much. I think I was feeling a little sorry for myself. But I guess maybe just the two of us is more than a lot of people ever have."

Trace reached out, his thumb catching the teardrop that slipped down her cheek, a faint glimmer in the starlight.

"It's enough." For him, it would always be enough.

Chapter Ten

The gun was blued steel. Light caught on the barrel, giving it a cold gleam. All Trace could see was the gun and the hand holding it. There was no sound but the heavy thud of his own heartbeat. He had to get to the gun, had to stop it, but it was so hard to move. The barrel shifted slowly until it was aimed at a point somewhere behind him. He turned, so cautiously, to see what the gun was pointing at. His heart stopped and then started to pound again, the beat deafening in his ears.

Lily.

He screamed her name but there was no sound. She stood there looking at him, her eyes bright and trusting. Didn't she see the gun? Didn't she realize the danger? And then, somehow, he could see both Lily and the gun behind him. He could see the finger tightening on the trigger and he lunged forward, desperate to protect her. But his body moved sluggishly, as if caught in quicksand.

The sound of the shot exploded in his ear, echoing over and over again like a drumroll. He saw the bullet slam into Lily's body, saw her eyes widen in shock. He'd promised to protect her, promised to take care of her. It was all in her eyes.

Lily!

His throat ached with the force of his cry but he couldn't hear anything. Bright red blossomed on the front of her blouse as she began to fall. He reached out to catch her but his fingers passed through her body as if through a mist. He stared in horror as she began to dissolve in front of his eyes, fading into nothing, until the only thing he could see was her eyes, wide and reproachful.

He looked back over his shoulder at the killer, rage clogging his throat. For a moment all he saw was a vague silhouette, and then the killer stepped forward so that the light hit his face. Trace was looking at a mirror. It was his own hand on the gun, his own finger that had pulled the trigger.

He woke with a start, sitting up in bed, his hand reaching out as if to catch hold of her before he realized it had been nothing more than a dream. He sat there, staring into the predawn darkness, his chest heaving as if he'd just run a marathon. A fine layer of sweat coated his body, then dried quickly in the cool air.

It was just a dream. He took a deep breath, trying to steady his breathing. Just a dream. He repeated the reassurance in his mind but it didn't help to fade the vivid images he'd carried into waking. Lily shot. Lily dying. He closed his eyes, trying to shake the pictures away, but that only made them more real, and he opened his eyes again. He shivered, more from nerves than chill, but he got up and reached for his robe anyway. It was clear he wasn't going to get any more sleep.

He belted the thick terry-cloth robe at his waist and padded barefoot to the window, where he tugged aside the curtain to look outside. It was still dark, that funny gray darkness that came just before dawn. It was possible to make out the outlines of things without really being able to see them.

He let the curtain fall and shoved his fingers through his thick hair. Lily had cut it for him yesterday and his face softened, remembering her look of concentration as she'd wielded the scissors. God, that had brought back memories. The first time she'd cut his hair for him had been during those nightmare months they'd spent on the street. He'd never forget that childish face puckered in an intent frown as she'd sawed the straggling ends from his hair with a pair of broken scissors they'd found in the trash.

His smile faded as the memory was replaced by the dream image. He flicked on a table lamp but the light didn't help to dispel the nightmare. Trace sat on the bed, leaning back against the headboard, stretching his long legs out on the rumpled covers. He didn't need an analyst to interpret the meaning of the dream. The fear that he was going to hurt Lily was something he'd been living with for a long time, but never more so than in the two weeks since Mike's death.

He reached out and touched the unused pillow, remembering the way her hair had spilled across the cool white linen, shining black silk on the plain cover. Lily had asked him if he regretted making love to her and he'd said no. It wasn't entirely a lie. He could never regret something that had felt so right. What he was afraid of was that Lily was going to regret it. He was all wrong for her. Maybe that was what his dream had symbolized—that, through him, she could be destroyed.

He leaned his head back against the wall and closed his eyes. It must be the hour that was making the dream seem so terribly significant. And maybe the fact that he was going back to work today for the first time since Mike's death. He'd have gone back sooner if it hadn't been for Lily. But she'd started working part-time at a school for handicapped children two days ago. She didn't need him home all the time, if she ever had.

He swung his legs off the bed. It was obvious he wasn't going to go back to sleep. There was no sense in lying there thinking. The world always looked a little better after a cup of coffee. Maybe the caffeine would help evaporate the last vestiges of his nightmare.

When Trace came down the stairs half an hour later, he was shaved, showered and dressed. He hesitated at the foot of the stairs. There was a light on in the kitchen and the warm scent of coffee drifted out to tantalize his nose. It was just barely light outside, still too early to be day and too late to be night.

He entered the kitchen quietly but Lily turned immediately, as if sensing his presence more than hearing it. For an instant he remembered his nightmare, the picture of her fading away. He frowned, trying to block it out. Lily's smile faded.

"I heard you get up and thought you might like some company. If you'd rather be alone, I could go away."

"No, don't go. I wasn't frowning at you. It was just something I thought of."

She smiled, relieved. "It didn't look like something pleasant."

"It wasn't anything important." He smiled. It didn't matter how often he told himself that it would be best for her if he stayed away, he couldn't help but savor the way her eyes lit when she saw him. "What are you doing up so early?"

"I woke up and couldn't go back to sleep and then I heard you stirring around. The coffee should be ready in a minute."

"Smells great." Trace got down a mug and set it on the counter.

"How did you sleep?"

The nightmare flickered through his mind but he ignored it. "Not too bad, if you don't count the fact that I woke up about an hour too early." The light on the coffee maker came on and he reached for the pot, pouring himself a cup of steaming black brew. Lifting the cup, he inhaled deeply. "Heaven."

Lily smiled and sipped at her cup of tea. "That stuff is terrible for you. You know that, don't you?"

"That's a false rumor started by tea companies. Coffee is the fifth basic food group. The human body actually needs it to survive." He took a swallow and sighed with exaggerated pleasure. "Guaranteed to put hair on your chest."

"I think you have plenty of hair on your chest already." The light comment brought a new element into the conversation. Trace's eyes met hers over the rim of his cup. Maybe it was the house. Maybe it was the lingering effects of his nightmare. Maybe it was the fact that he was going back to work today and everything was going to be different. Whatever it was, it suddenly didn't seem so important to keep a distance between them.

"You do, huh?" Lily's eyes dropped away from the gleam in his.

"I do."

"I'm glad you approve."

"I approve. I definitely approve." Her eyes swept up to meet his and Trace felt a sudden hard knot of desire in his stomach. How was it possible for one look to combine so much innocence and sensuality? Saint and sinner in one expression. His fingers tightened on the cup and he looked away.

"How do you like your new job?"

"It's nice. The children are wonderful to work with. Heartbreaking and uplifting all at once. The other teachers have been really helpful."

She continued to talk but Trace lost track of what she was saying. He was watching her mouth, remembering the way it felt beneath his. It wasn't until she licked her lips nervously that he realized she'd stopped speaking and he had been standing there staring at her mouth. He dragged his eyes away again.

"I'm glad you're settling in so well."

"Me, too. What about you? Are you looking forward to getting back to work?"

"Yes. I feel like I've been gone for months instead of a couple of weeks."

"You really like being a cop, don't you?"

"I can't imagine doing anything else for a living."

"It's pretty dangerous, isn't it?" Her tone was casual but he saw the way her eyes avoided his, studying the counter as if she'd never seen it before, and he knew there was nothing casual about the comment.

"Sometimes. But it's not as bad as it looks in the cop shows. And I'm not working downtown L.A. or anything. All in all, it's probably not that much worse than working construction."

"People don't shoot at you when you work construction," she told him, her voice muffled.

"They might if you did a lousy job." Her smile was perfunctory at best and he knew he wasn't going to be able to laugh away her concerns.

"Look, nobody has taken a shot at me yet. Contrary to television, most cops retire, they don't get shot. Maybe it's a more stressful job than most but the rewards are worth it. There's a lot of frustration but there's no better feeling in the world than seeing a criminal off the street or helping someone settle a family dispute without anyone getting hurt. The times when you feel like you really made a difference are what keep you going."

He stopped abruptly, flushing as he realized how impassioned he sounded. He shrugged, suddenly self-conscious. "Sorry. I didn't mean to get on my soapbox."

"You didn't," Lily protested. "I think it's wonderful that you love your job but—" She stopped, looking down.

"But what?"

"I can't help but wish that you really loved being an accountant or a bank teller or something a little safer. I worry."

"Do you?" He reached out to tuck a shiny strand of hair behind her ear, his fingers lingering against her skin. "Don't worry about me. I'm very good at taking care of myself. Remember?"

"I remember." She leaned her cheek against his palm, her eyes half-closed. "I've never forgotten the way you took care of me. But I know you're not invincible and I can't help but worry."

One of them—it was impossible to tell which—had shifted forward so that they were almost touching. Lily's head was tilted back, exposing the vulnerable line of her throat. Somehow Trace's fingers were tangled in her hair and it seemed impossible to move them.

"Did you know that statistically speaking, accountants have one of the earliest death rates of any profession? And there are more bank tellers in therapy than there are actors."

His lips feathered along her cheekbone before finding her earlobe and nipping gently. She moaned softly, her body melting into his. Trace reached out blindly and set his coffee cup on the counter before disposing of her tea in a similar manner. His hand slid around her back, pulling her closer still as his mouth found hers.

Her arms came up to circle his neck, her lips opening beneath the demand of his. Trace felt his whole body tighten with hunger too long denied. He wanted her with a sudden fierce need that took his breath away. Lily gasped as his hands caught her around the waist, lifting her onto the counter.

He stood between her open knees, their bodies pressed together as intimately as was possible with the barriers of clothing still between them. His arousal strained at his jeans and he heard Lily moan softly as he pressed against the heart of her. His open mouth slid down her arched throat.

Passion raged out of control. He couldn't get enough of her. Her taste, her scent, the feel of her against him. He was reaching for the buttons on her blouse when something penetrated the fog of need that was blinding him to everything but her.

He couldn't have said just how far it might have gone if the shower hadn't come on upstairs, reminding them that they weren't alone. The muffled sound acted like a dash of cold water in his face and he realized how close he'd come to taking her on the kitchen counter, half-dressed, their clothes tugged open and pushed aside.

He leaned his forehead against her shoulder, his breathing ragged as he fought to regain control. My God, this was Lily and he was treating her like a streetwalker. It was several long moments before he could lift his head, feeling the flush that mantled his cheeks. The look on her face stopped the apology he was about to offer. She didn't look shocked or horrified or offended. She looked as disappointed as he felt. She hadn't been an innocent victim of his lust, she'd been a willing participant.

Trace gave a half laugh, shaking his head at her questioning look. He couldn't explain it to her. It was his own idiocy and he'd keep it to himself. The shower went off upstairs and he put his hands on her waist, lifting her down from the counter. She kept her hands on his shoulders, clinging to him for a moment as if she weren't quite sure of the strength of her knees.

"We're going to have company pretty soon," he told her.

"Too bad." He caught the words with his mouth, kissing her briefly and thoroughly before setting her away from him. He backed away, not trusting himself until he'd put several feet between him and temptation. She smiled, recognizing the move for what it was. There was such a wealth of feminine knowledge in that smile that he almost swept her back into his arms and kissed it from her mouth.

A door shut upstairs and they could hear John's footsteps in the hall. Trace picked up his coffee, downing the rest of it in a gulp.

"I'd better get going or I'm going to end up late." He still had plenty of time to get to the station but he had the feeling he'd be safer putting some distance between him and Lily. He had to remember all the good, logical reasons why it was better to stay away from her. He lifted a hand to John as the other man entered the room. "I'm off. See you later."

"Sure. See you later." John moved to the stove to pour himself a cup of coffee. Trace turned in the doorway, aware that Lily had followed him.

"Is it true?"

"Is what true?" How was it possible that she was so utterly beautiful?

"That accountants have a younger death rate than cops."

"How would I know? I'm a cop, not an accountant." He ducked the playful swing she took at him, grinning down at her. For just a moment he felt young and carefree in a way he couldn't remember feeling in years. Lily's smile shifted, and her eyes took on a look of poorly concealed worry.

"Be careful. Okay?"

"Sure. I'm always careful." He glanced over her head but John still had his back to the door, giving a momentary privacy. Her mouth was too sweet, too tempting, and he couldn't resist giving her a quick hard kiss, tasting her response. He raised his head and looked at her intently, his thumb brushing over her swollen mouth.

"Have a good day."

The hackneyed words said so little when he wanted to say so much. Mostly things that were better left unsaid. He backed the 'Vette out of the garage and headed down the hill into Glendale, his thoughts more on what he'd left behind than on what he was going toward.

THE SCHOOL for handicapped children was on a quiet street in the hills above Pasadena. Jacarandas arched across the road, the first hints of lavender showing amid the pale green leaves. In another couple of weeks they'd make a spectacular display.

Trace parked the 'Vette beneath one of them and got out. The air was warm and there could be no doubting that spring was here. The school was a low building, the front yard neatly landscaped to blend in with the surrounding homes. Calendula and pansies bloomed in cheerful disarray in a bed that lined the walkway. The door was opened by a black woman in her mid-fifties who smiled a welcome when he asked for Lily.

"I'm Mary Leigh. You must be Trace. Lily has mentioned you. She's telling the children a story. If you'd like to come in and wait, she shouldn't be much longer. In fact, you're welcome to listen in on the last of the story."

"Thank you." He followed Mary's tall elegant figure down a hallway decorated in bright yellows and greens. She gestured to a doorway on his right, raising her finger to her mouth to caution him to silence before she moved off down the hall.

Trace approached the door hesitantly, hearing the soft rise and fall of Lily's voice. Inside the room was as bright as the hallway, this time yellow and red. Low murals graced the walls and the tile floor was decorated with an occasional painted flower in purple or orange. It should have clashed but somehow it gave an effect of cheery disarray. Despite the disabilities of the students, there was nothing clinical about the school. It was obvious that someone had gone to a great deal of trouble to make the place as warm and happy as possible.

At first the room seemed to be a sea of children, but they sorted out into fifteen or so. Several of them were in wheelchairs. There were two little boys whose legs were thrust straight out ahead of them, encased in steel braces. Trace looked away, his eyes finding Lily.

She was sitting on a low stool, her bright green skirt spread out on the floor around her. He wondered if she'd chosen the color to go with the room or if the room was just so bright that any vivid color seemed to blend in. There was a book open in her lap but it was obvious that she was telling the story from memory, her face animated, her eyes flashing with the proper emotions as she spun a tale of dragons and unicorns.

The children stared at her, as caught up in the story as she herself seemed to be. She hadn't seen him yet and Trace took the opportunity to watch her. He didn't think he'd ever seen her look more beautiful. She told the familiar tale with all the fervor of someone who was as eager to hear the ending as her young listeners. And when it came to the climactic moment when everyone was rescued and good won out over evil, she seemed just as relieved as they were.

There was a general shuffle of movement as Lily shut the book and stood up. She looked over to see Trace and froze. The children turned to see what had caught her attention and he found himself being scrutinized by sixteen pairs of eyes. He smiled weakly.

"Trace."

"Lily."

The children continued to stare at him and he nodded to them, smiling. "Hi."

Lily seemed to shake herself. "Children, this is a friend of mine. His name is Trace."

"Hello." A chorus of young voices piped the greeting.

He smiled again, feeling like a bug on display. It was clear that a friend of their teacher's was something new and interesting in their day.

"Trace. That's a funny name." The voice came from roughly knee level so he looked down. The little girl who spoke was tilted way back to look up at him. She was probably six or seven but her legs were tiny twisted things, making her appear much younger.

"Sara, you shouldn't make personal remarks." Lily's mild reproach brought a flush to the child's delicate face.

"That's okay." Trace knelt down so that he was at eye level. Dark gray eyes met his, full of curiosity. "You know, I used to know another little girl who thought it was a funny name." He glanced up, his eyes meeting Lily's, sharing a memory.

"Did you?"

"I did, but she got used to it after a while."

"Time for lunch, children." Mary Leigh's voice came from the doorway and food took immediate precedence over a visitor. There was a quick rush toward the door, those who were a little slower receiving help from their companions. Trace watched the exodus, surprised to find a sharp pain in his throat.

"They really get to you, don't they?" He turned at Lily's quiet comment to find her watching him.

"It makes you realize how fortunate you are, I guess. Like most people, I don't think about having two arms and two legs that work."

"They're good kids." She gathered up a few toys, putting them in bins along the walls. "I like working with them."

"Doesn't it ever get depressing? I mean, there's so little you can do for them."

"No. I usually come away from here with a renewed sense of how precious life is. They're so accepting of what life has handed them. Not that they don't get frustrated by their limitations, but more often than not they set their teeth and look for a way around them."

He looked at her, seeing a new side to her, wondering if she would ever cease to surprise him. Lily glanced up, catching his eye.

"Why are you looking at me like that?"

"I'm just thinking that you're a pretty incredible lady."

She flushed with pleasure, her eyes taking on a coquettish glint. "Are you just now figuring that out?"

"No, but I guess I forget sometimes."

"I'm THINKING about opening the store back up." John made the announcement over dinner. Trace's head jerked up, his dinner forgotten.

"Mike's?" The question was automatic. What other store would he be talking about?

"Mike's." John shoved his chair back from the table, reaching out to grab the coffeepot off the stove. He poured himself a full cup and reached for his cigarettes. Trace shoved his plate away, aware of Lily doing the same.

"I hadn't given the store much thought," Lily said, and Trace could have agreed with her wholeheartedly. Every time he thought of the store, he remembered Mike's body lying on the floor, all the life drained from him. It was not a memory he went out of his way to resurrect.

John shrugged, inhaling a deep lungful of smoke. "I've been thinking about it for the last week or so. It seems foolish to just leave the place sitting there. Dad worked hard to build up his business. Besides, it would give me something to do. With both of you at work I'm beginning to feel like a bum."

"Don't you have to get back to your job?"

Trace half expected the answer Lily's question received.

"I'm on a leave of absence, more or less. I had a lot of vacation time saved up." His eyes met Trace's for a moment but there was nothing Trace could read there. Not that he expected to see the truth written in blazing letters across the man's forehead, but he had his suspicions. There were a lot of little things that added up to someone in an unorthodox and probably highly classified job.

"When are you thinking of reopening?" Trace asked.

"I thought I'd go down to the place tomorrow and take a look around. Maybe open the next day." He paused, waiting for some comment, but no one said anything. "Dad's will left everything split among the three of us. I wouldn't reopen the place without your okay. That's why I brought it up with you."

"I've got no objection." Trace picked up the coffeepot John had set on the table and poured himself a steaming cup, aware of Lily's silence across the table.

"Lily?" John's voice was gentle and she looked up, her eyes a little too bright.

"I don't have any objections."

"Are you sure?"

She shook her head, the movement causing her hair to lift and settle around her face. "It's hard to think of anyone but Mike being behind that counter, but I know Mike wouldn't want the place just sitting there.'' She drew in a deep breath and forced a smile. "I think it's a good idea. I'm sure it's what Mike would want.''

Trace felt a sharp pain in his chest. It was almost a month now and the pain had settled into a dull sense of loss that had become so familiar he rarely noticed it. Lily's words brought it alive for a moment, reminding him of just how much they'd all lost.

John reached out to cover Lily's hand with his and Trace had to restrain the urge to punch him in the nose. "I know this isn't an easy thing. If it would bother you too much, I'll drop the idea.''

Lily smiled at him, her eyes bright with unshed tears. "No, I really think this is a good idea.'' She turned her hand under his, squeezing his palm. "I'm glad you're going to do it.''

Trace watched the exchange broodingly, tilting his chair back on two legs in a way that would have earned him a thorough scold when Mike was alive. But Mike was gone and everything was different now. Things had changed so quickly that he sometimes felt as if he were walking on quicksand, trying to keep his balance.

"How about you, Trace? Are you okay with this?'' John's hand slid away from Lily's as he turned to Trace. Trace looked at him, still plagued by that nagging feeling that they'd met somewhere before. John's eyes were an unfathomable gray, taking everything in but revealing little. Trace still hadn't decided whether or not he trusted the man, let alone liked him.

"I'm okay with it. It doesn't make any sense to leave the place sitting empty.''

So MIKE'S LIQUOR reopened even though Mike was gone. John leaned against the counter and wondered what they'd think of him back at the head office if they could see him now. Not that he doubted that they knew exactly what he was up to. They might have granted him the time he wanted but they had too much invested in him to back off entirely.

He looked around the small store, feeling a definite swell of pride. It had taken him two days of hard work before the place was ready for reopening. He still wasn't entirely sure he knew how to run the cash register but he had a fairly good handle on how his father had managed the stock. It was enough for now. The floors shone, the shelves were immaculate, and he was ready for his first customer.

People trickled in throughout the day. He was surprised and a little touched at how many of them mentioned Mike and expressed their condolences. The man he remembered hadn't been the type to inspire affection in casual acquaintances.

It started to rain in the late afternoon and the trickle of customers became a drip. For the time being he was keeping the same hours his father had kept, which meant that the store was open until eight. The darkness closed in by six, leaving the lights to gleam off the wet streets.

John glanced at the clock and stretched. There hadn't been a customer in half an hour. Another twenty minutes and he wouldn't have to feel guilty about turning the Closed sign over and calling it a night. He rolled his head to one side and then the other, stretching out the kinks. He was tired, but not unpleasantly so.

The bell pinged, signaling another customer, and he straightened, trying to look like someone who belonged behind the counter at a liquor store. The man who entered was typical of the people who'd been coming in all day. Past middle age but not yet in a category that could be labeled elderly. His gray hair was still thick and neatly combed back from a face that might have been handsome in its youth. He glanced up, catching John's eye, and smiled. John returned the smile with the vague feeling that he'd seen the man before. He watched as the customer selected a bottle of orange juice before coming up to the counter.

"One of the small bottles of Kamchatka, please."

"Screwdrivers, huh?" John set the bottle of vodka on the counter. It hadn't taken him long to learn that most of the people who came in enjoyed a moment or two of conversation. This man was no exception.

"I have a friend coming to dinner tonight and I know she has a fondness for them."

John rang up the sale and took the money the man handed him. As he gave him the change, their eyes met and he felt a twinge of uneasiness. There was something in the back of the older man's eyes that didn't seem right.

"You must be Mike's boy. Michael, isn't it?"

"John. My father was the only one who ever called me Michael."

The man smiled. "Mike always did like to go his own way."

"Did you know my father?" John asked, trying to pinpoint the source of his uneasiness.

"A long time ago. A very long time ago. I've been out of the area and we saw each other only once before he was killed." He shook his head. "A terrible tragedy, that. Do the police have any idea who was responsible?"

"They're working on some leads." Over the years he'd learned the hard way to trust his instincts. He didn't doubt his uneasiness but he couldn't find a source for it. There was just something about the man.

"Well, I'd best be on my way. I wouldn't want my friend to think I'd abandoned her. My condolences on your father's death."

"Thanks. Come in again." He spoke automatically, his eyes narrowed on the man as he walked to the door. There was nothing there to warrant the way he felt. The man turned at the door, the lights casting his eyes into shadow, giving him a vaguely threatening look. Or maybe it was the way his left brow kicked up at the outer edge, twisted by an old scar that ran toward his temple. Whatever it was, something about the man made him uneasy.

"I'll definitely be back." The bell pinged sharply and then the door was swinging shut behind him. John watched through the window as he walked up the street. Apparently he lived close enough to walk. *Or he'd parked his car out of sight.* The suspicious thought popped into his head but he shook it off.

He was getting paranoid in his old age. It was one of the hazards of his job and one of the reasons he was giving serious thought to a change of career. He crossed to the door and flipped the Closed sign outward before turning back to look at the store. Yes, there was a definite feeling of pride in having reopened the place and he'd enjoyed running it for the day, but he knew it wasn't something he could do forever.

In an odd way, he felt as if he were getting to know his father by running the store. It was surprising how much you could learn about a man by looking at the way he ran his business. Maybe it was a way to make peace with the past.

He'd asked for this time off to put his life in order. His father's death had punched home his own mortality and made him face the fact that he was getting too old for the kind of games he was still playing. It was time to make some changes. He knew that. The only question was, what kind of changes?

But he had time. All the time he wanted, they'd promised. And while he was thinking about what he might want to do with the rest of his life, he was enjoying the present, the first time off he'd taken in more years than he could remember. Trace and Lily were providing the closest thing he'd had to a family since he fought with his father and left home.

Trace didn't entirely trust him. It wasn't hard to read that wariness in his eyes. He should probably tell him that they'd met before, remind him of that snowy Oklahoma afternoon, but some perverse part of him wanted to see if Trace would figure it out on his own.

Lily was another story. She seemed to have accepted him without question. He was Mike's son and that was all she required. She was an interesting little thing. So young and yet so old. And her face... God, he'd traveled the world and he knew just how rare beauty like that was, yet she didn't seem to be aware of it. Under other circumstances he might have been tempted to try for more than friendship from her. Not that it would have done him any good. You simply had to see the way she looked at Trace to know that only a fool would bother trying to come between them.

He shook his head and reached out to shut off the lights. Thinking about Trace and Lily wasn't getting him home and it wasn't getting him any closer to a decision about his own future. He stepped outside, turning up his collar against the cold night air. He could worry about his future another time. For now, getting home was enough to think about.

Chapter Eleven

"Just what was stolen, Mr. Gillespie?" Trace tried to sound official and interested but his heart wasn't really in it. This was the sixth time in the past year that Gillespie's little Italian grocery had been robbed. No fingerprints that shouldn't have been there, no sign of forced entry, nothing but money taken.

Out of the corner of his eye he could see Gillespie's oldest son. Marty was nineteen and he had what Trace considered a severe attitude problem, the kind of attitude that might have been improved by someone giving him a quick kick in the seat of the pants. Trace wanted to be first in line. Marty was leaning against the outer wall of the store, his hands shoved into the pockets of his tight jeans, his back curved in an impossible slouch. His too-full mouth was twisted in a smug smile that made Trace want to bypass the kick in the pants and go straight for a punch in the lip. You didn't have to ask the boy if he was cool, everything about him shouted it.

"Did you or your wife hear anything last night? See anything that might give us a clue?"

"Not a thing. They were very quiet."

It probably helped that "they" had a key. Trace looked up, meeting Marty's eyes head-on. He didn't have any

doubts about who was responsible for the repeated bur-
glaries. The first officer to suggest it to Marty's father had
been harangued in Italian, and then the old man had called
the station to complain. Trace didn't make the same mistake. He didn't doubt that Gillespie knew what was going
on; the old man just wasn't ready to admit it yet. Until he
was, there wasn't a whole lot the police could do. Marty
looked at him for a moment and then shrugged his shoulders, widening his eyes in a mock-innocent stare before
peeling himself away from the wall and wandering into the
store, where Trace's partner, Sally, was questioning his
mother.

Trace looked back at the boy's father, seeing the hurt and
anxiety in the old man's eyes. The look doubled his urge to
knock a few of the kid's teeth out.

"He's a good boy. He's had a little trouble finding work
now that he's out of school." Trace made a few useless notes
and nodded. It wasn't easy to find a job, especially when
you didn't bother to look.

A movement in the street caught his attention and he
glanced up. That was the second time that car had gone by.
A pale blue Chevy Nova with a crunched right fender. It
must have cruised around the block. The angle of the sun
cast shadows over the driver's side. It was impossible to
make out more than just a vague outline of someone behind the wheel. He could see that the person was looking
this way but there was nothing surprising about that. The
squad car parked in front of the little grocery was enough to
catch the attention of any passersby. They were probably
hoping to see someone being handcuffed or a little police
brutality, something to liven up their day. Trace returned his
attention to the old man.

They were still standing in front of the store a few minutes later when the car came by again. Trace had put away

his notebook and was listening to Gillespie talk about the problems of fatherhood. It was about all he could do for the old man until he was ready to face the fact that his oldest son was stealing from him. Inside, he suspected Sally was being fed bites of Mrs. Gillespie's lasagna or her spaghetti sauce or whatever today's special was. Which meant that she was going to moan about the ruination of her diet for the rest of the afternoon.

He heard the car before he saw it. The engine had a miss that he hadn't consciously noticed but he remembered it when he heard the car turn the corner and start toward them. His back tightened as it crept closer. Stupid. The driver was just gawking, hoping to see something exciting. Nothing to justify the sudden anxiety he felt.

He turned his head, keeping half an ear on Gillespie's words. It was the same Chevy and he still couldn't see the driver clearly. The car was slowing again, barely creeping. The passenger window was open. There was nothing sinister about the car. Just a beat-up Nova that had definitely seen better days. He started to turn back to Gillespie when something caught his eye, a funny glint of light from inside the car, like sun catching on something metallic. Like a gun barrel.

Trace lunged forward, catching the old man at the waist and dropping them both to the pavement. The staccato explosion of an automatic weapon sprayed the air where he'd been only seconds before. Glass shattered in the store window, falling to the ground in a shower of tinkling sounds.

Trace didn't stop moving once he hit the ground. He rolled, taking the old man with him until they were both sheltered behind the patrol car. Assured that Gillespie was safe, Trace scrambled to his knees, drawing his gun. Keeping to a crouch, he moved toward the front of the patrol car. The Chevy was still there. He could hear the miss in the engine. The question was, where was the driver looking? Would he have time to get off a shot?

He took a deep breath, tasting the acid tang of fear in the back of his throat. He could hear the sound of his own heartbeat, a little too loud, a little too fast. He raised himself cautiously, making sure that he was still protected by the bulk of the car. A quick breath and then he hit the ground in front of the car in a diving roll that ended with him on one knee. He brought his weapon up and snapped off two quick shots. Both hit the windshield but they clearly didn't incapacitate whoever was handling the gun. His shots were answered with a spray of gunfire that would have torn him to pieces if he hadn't already moved. The bullets smacked into the pavement where he'd been but Trace was already behind another car.

There was a sharp report and the smack of a bullet biting into metal. Looking over his shoulder, he could catch just a glimpse of Sally's pale hair. She was still in the store, protected by the old brick. He saw her aim again and then the sound of a taillight shattering. It was apparently all the incentive the driver needed to cut his losses.

He floored the gas pedal and the car took off with a roar. Trace ran around the end of the car he'd been using as shelter. The license plate was clearly visible, the numbers imprinted on his brain. Not that it would do much good. He was willing to bet that the car was stolen.

"You all right?" He turned as Sally ran up to him. Adrenaline still pounded in him but he took a deep breath and nodded.

"No damage. Everyone okay in the store?"

HIS GUESS about the car turned out to be correct. The owner had reported it stolen three hours before the shooting. The Gillespies were all intact, though the same couldn't be said for their store. The squad car was towed off for repairs and Trace and Sally spent the afternoon giving reports and going over nonexistent details. In the end, the only guess anyone had was that it was a random cop killing. Or attempted cop killing.

That idea was worse than shootings where a motive could be found. Everyone was edgy, wondering if this was an isolated incident or the beginning of some kind of spree where the next cop might not be as lucky as Trace had been.

By the time he got home, Trace was worn-out. All he wanted was a tall Scotch, a hot shower and a bed, and he might even be willing to forgo the shower. He parked the 'Vette in the garage next to Lily's car and leaned his head back against the seat for a moment. He'd thought about what to tell Lily all the way home and he'd decided that there was no need to worry her. No one had been hurt. Why upset her over nothing?

He opened the door and climbed out of the low car, wincing as he straightened. Every muscle ached. He wasn't sure if it was tension or tumbling on the pavement that had done it, but he felt as if he'd gone forty rounds with a punching bag and lost.

He let himself in through the back door. The lingering scent of turmeric told him that John must have cooked dinner. The house always smelled like the local Indian restaurants after he cooked. Trace hadn't eaten since morning but he wasn't hungry. Too much had happened for him to be interested in food.

The low murmur of the television filtered through from the living room. He got out a glass and some ice, shutting the refrigerator quietly, though there was a good chance they'd heard the 'Vette and knew he was home. He was tempted to go straight upstairs but the Scotch was in the living room, so he carried his glass there.

John was sprawled in a chair, his long legs stuck out in front of him, his attention on the television, though he didn't look too interested in the sitcom that was dancing away on the screen. A burst of canned laughter didn't draw even the flicker of a smile from him. Lily was curled up on the sofa with a book in her lap. There was a lamp on over her shoulder and the light caught in her hair, finding blue highlights in the heavy black length.

She looked up, her mouth curved in a welcoming smile. It was enough to soothe some of his tension. How bad could the world be when Lily could smile at him like that?

"Hi. You worked late."

"Hi. I hope you didn't hold dinner for me." He moved to the small bar and poured himself a glass of Scotch.

"No. Lily and I polished off an excellent batch of chicken curry all by ourselves. I outdid myself, if I do say so myself." John pulled himself a little more upright.

Trace took a hefty swallow of his drink, feeling it burn its way down his throat before settling in a warm pool in his stomach. He turned, arching a brow at John.

"That's not saying much. The last time you cooked, it took longer to get the burned chicken off the bottom of the pan than it did to cook the stuff."

"Details." John waved his hand dismissively. "Actually, we did leave you some dinner. It's in the fridge."

"Thanks but I'm not really hungry." He settled himself in a chair, stretching his legs out and relaxing for the first time since the shooting.

"What happened to your face?" His feeling of relaxation evaporated with Lily's question. Damn. He'd forgotten about the scrape on his cheekbone. He reached up to touch it. He'd apparently gotten it when he tackled Gillespie, scraping his face on the concrete. It was nothing serious but it was a little sore. He smiled and shrugged.

"I had a small argument with a piece of concrete. Nothing serious."

Lily plucked nervously at the cover of her book. "There was a report on the news about a shooting incident in Glendale. They said there were officers involved in it. Was it anyone you know?"

Trace met her eyes reluctantly. He wanted to lie to her. He'd planned to lie to her. But he could see from the look on her face that she already knew he'd been involved. Damn the news. He hadn't thought of that, either, which just showed how tired he must be.

"Actually, I *was* involved in it." He shrugged. "It was really no big deal." With the simple phrase, he dismissed those moments when he'd thought his heart was going to stop.

"No big deal? They said someone shot at an officer. They showed the front of the store." Lily's voice was tight with the effort she was making to control it.

"It looked worse than it really was," he lied. His eyes met John's. He didn't think it was his imagination that put understanding there, but there wasn't anything the other man could do. "Reporters always like to exaggerate things, you know that. I was taking a burglary report and some fruitcake drove by and took a few shots at me. No one was hurt."

She twisted the book in her hands, her eyes wide and frightened. "You could have been killed."

"Guess it just wasn't my day to die." He regretted the flip words as soon as they were out of his mouth but it was too late to take them back. Flip was not what was needed right now. He downed a swallow of Scotch. He wasn't up to this.

No one said anything for a slow count of ten. The television continued to mutter in the background. Occasional bursts of mechanical laughter punctuated the silence. Trace couldn't look at Lily's pale face. He didn't know what to say to her. This had certainly punched holes in his assurances that his job wasn't more dangerous than any other.

"It's late. I think I'll go to bed." Lily stood up, the mangled book still clutched in her hands. "Good night."

Trace looked up at her, seeing the fear she couldn't hide. She was trying to be brave, trying not to show how frightened she was. But he'd known her a long time. He wanted to put his arms around her and tell her not to be scared. If John hadn't been there, he might have done just that. Lily left the room without another word and Trace listened to her footsteps as she climbed the stairs. Her bedroom door clicked shut.

He leaned his head against the back of the chair, holding the glass too tight. John reached out to snap off the television and the sudden silence was deafening.

"She loves you." The quiet words dropped into the silence. Trace didn't look at the other man. He focused his eyes on the blank television screen.

"She'll get over it." The words sounded harsh. "I'm no good for her."

"Maybe that's true, but then again, maybe it's not. She's a hell of a woman. You'd have to be either a fool or a very brave man to walk away from her."

Trace's mouth twisted in a bitter smile. "If I'm either one, it's got to be the fool."

"I wouldn't have thought that fifteen years ago."

John's words sank in slowly. Trace lifted his head, staring at the other man with narrowed eyes.

"Fifteen years ago?"

"I've been waiting for you to figure it out. A snowy road, two kids on their way to California." He leaned back in the chair and waited.

Trace stared at him for a long time, memories flipping through his mind. The truck driver who'd given them a ride to Denver, the man who'd given them Mike's address. It didn't seem possible and yet it all fit together. So much had happened to them after that. His memories of the truck driver were all tangled up in everything that had come after, and yet there'd been that niggling sense of familiarity ever since he'd met John. And there'd been the fact that the driver had been the one to give them Mike's address.

"Geez. That was you?"

"More or less."

"Why the hell didn't you say something when you first got here? It's been driving me crazy for weeks, thinking I'd met you somewhere."

"I don't know. I guess I just wanted to see if you'd remember first."

"My God." Trace shook his head. "I don't remember a lot of details about that time but I can't believe I didn't recognize you."

"It was a long time ago."

"True."

"You know, you may be underestimating yourself and Lily," John said. "When you think you know what's best for someone else, it's always a good idea to stop and think again. You're usually wrong." He stood up. "I'm going to go catch a late movie."

Trace watched him leave without saying anything. His head was spinning. It was incredible to think that John was the truck driver who'd helped them all those years ago. But it explained so much. He leaned his head back, listening to the sound of John's car pulling out of the drive. The house was quiet and he shut his eyes. Too much had happened today. There were too many things to think about, too many things to try to understand.

He gradually grew aware of something disturbing the quiet. Low, almost inaudible, it pulled at him even before he realized what it was. Lily was crying. She was crying because of him. His fingers tightened over the glass until his knuckles turned white. The sound tore him apart.

With a curse he stood up, setting the half-finished Scotch down. He took the stairs two at a time, the muffled sound of her sobbing growing more audible with each step. Standing outside her door, he hesitated, knowing he shouldn't go in, but he couldn't stand the sound of her tears.

There was only one lamp on, throwing a small pool of light next to the bed. Lily was stretched out on the bed, her face buried in her pillow, her slim shoulders heaving with the force of her anguish. She caught her breath with a gulp when the bed dipped beneath his weight.

"Go away." The muffled command was interrupted by a sob. Trace set his hands on her shoulders.

"I can't leave you here to cry. I can't bear the sound of it." He turned her over despite her weak resistance. She stared up at him, her eyes a dark and stormy green and swimming in tears.

"What are you crying for? I'm all right."

Her lower lip shook. "You could have been killed."

"But I wasn't." He brushed the tangled black hair back from her forehead, his expression tender. "I wasn't even close to killed."

"This time. But what about next time? I couldn't stand it if something happened to you." Her face crumpled and she put her fist against her mouth, trying to swallow the tears.

"Nothing's going to happen to me. I'm tough. Oh God, don't cry anymore. Please don't cry. I'm not worth it." He lifted her, holding her trembling body against his. She sobbed against his shoulder, the sound tearing at him until, at last, he could stand it no more. His hand tangled in her hair, pulling her head back, his mouth smothering her sobs. She gasped, her breath catching in her throat, and then her arms came up to circle his neck, her fingers burrowing into his thick hair.

Perhaps it was the lingering adrenaline left over from the afternoon. Perhaps it was the need that he always tried so hard to bury. Whatever it was, passion exploded in his gut, catching him off guard, giving him no time to regain control.

His tongue plunged into her mouth, tasting the honeyed sweetness of her. She responded, her tongue coming up to meet his, demanding even as she gave. They kissed until the need for air forced them apart. Trace stared down at her, his hand still tangled in her hair, his chest heaving with the effort of breathing. Somewhere, far back in his mind, a small voice spoke of the need to think, but the pounding of his pulse drowned it out.

His hands reached for her blouse.

This wasn't like the first time they'd made love. There was no hesitation, no uncertainty. He didn't need to soothe her fears and she didn't want soothing. Her fingers were as impatient with his clothing as his were with hers. But when the last garment hit the floor, some of the frantic need ebbed, and for the space of several slow heartbeats, they simply looked at each other.

Trace saw a woman, delicately formed, her fragile exterior masking an inner strength that still had the power to leave him awestruck. Her skin was pale ivory. Her hair spilled over her shoulders like a thick black cape. And her eyes... God, her eyes. They were emerald green, heaven on earth.

Lily saw a man, strongly muscled and broad shouldered. His hair a shade that hovered somewhere between gold and brown. His features were a little too rough, his jaw a little too strong. His eyes were summer-sky blue, clear and deep. The color of angels and heaven.

They reached out to each other at the same moment. Lily shivered as his hands cupped the weight of her breasts, his thumbs brushing across dusky nipples. Her palms rested on the thick mat of hair that covered his chest, learning the pattern of muscle beneath. His hands slid around her back as he eased her onto the bed, following her down, his chest covering her breasts. She moaned, arching upward into his body, and the moment's calm was gone.

Desire burned between them. Need was a living presence. Her legs parted, shifting restlessly, and his thighs slid between them. He stopped, just touching the threshold of her need. The ache built until he could stand it no more. Lily accepted him as he sheathed himself within her. She was made for him alone. He was complete only with her.

Their lovemaking was desperate, raw emotion exploding into physical action. They moved together in an age-old rhythm—give and take, thrust and parry. Nothing was given that wasn't returned a hundredfold. Nothing could be truly taken because each belonged wholly to the other.

Lily lay beside him afterward, her head on his shoulder, her body curled into his. He stroked her hair back from her forehead. Just like the first time they'd made love, this had been inspired as much by a sense of belonging to each other as by passion. Wrapped in Lily's arms, held tight within her body, he felt as if he belonged somewhere. Truly belonged.

"You know, maybe I should cry more often. You made love to me the last time I cried, too."

"You shouldn't ever cry," he told her, his voice husky. His thumb brushed over her cheek. Her tears seemed to wash away all the barriers he worked so hard to build.

"I love you, Trace." She said it quietly, without fanfare, as if the words weren't going to pierce him to his very soul.

Trace closed his eyes, his arms tightening around her. She loved him. The knowledge swelled inside him, filling him up, taking away the emptiness. And yet pain slid through him. It wasn't right for her. *He* wasn't right for her. Words trembled in his throat. He loved her. God knew he loved her. But he couldn't tell her that. Wouldn't tell her.

He said nothing and he wondered if it was his imagination that made him think that Lily shrank away from him a little. He felt like a worm. The last thing he wanted to do was to hurt her and he knew his silence was a hurtful thing. But wouldn't he hurt her more in the end if he told her how he felt? She'd get over her feelings for him. She'd find someone better. He couldn't tie her to his side.

"Trace?" Lily's questioning voice broke the silence that had built between them.

"I think it's too soon to be talking about how we feel." God, what a stupid thing to say. Too soon. As if they'd just met. As if she weren't already so much a part of him.

Lily closed her eyes for a moment, her face tight with hurt. When she looked at him again, the green of her eyes shimmered with tears he knew she wouldn't shed. Her pain was more than he could stand.

"Lily, I—"

"You're right. It's much too soon." Her mouth curved in a superficial smile. Behind the pain in her eyes, he thought he could see a kind of understanding, as if she knew what he was doing.

He brushed her hair back, unaware that the tenderness in the gesture revealed his love as surely as any words could have. He'd have given his soul if things could have been different.

"You are so beautiful." It wasn't what she wanted but it was the best he could give her.

She was quiet for a long time, and when she spoke, it was on another subject.

"I'm sorry I fell apart tonight. It's just that I couldn't bear it if something happened to you. You and Mike were the only family I had. And now Mike's gone. When I found out that you'd been involved in the shooting today, all I could think about was how I'd have felt if you'd been killed. I couldn't stand that."

"Nothing is going to happen to me." He set his cheek against the top of her head, his voice low. "Today was some kind of crazy isolated incident. Chances are, nothing like that will ever happen again. Hey, you know what John just told me?"

"What?" Her voice held only vague interest. It was clear she wasn't interested in talking about anything John had said, but Trace wanted something to distract her.

"You remember the truck driver who picked us up in Oklahoma and took us to Denver?"

"Vaguely."

"That was John."

"John? Mike's son, John?" She raised herself on one elbow and looked down at him, her interest caught. "You're kidding."

"Nope. It's the same guy. I should have made the connection ages ago but it's been a long time. I'd all but forgotten the guy's name. But ever since John showed up I've had this niggling feeling that I'd seen him before."

"Why didn't he say something right away?"

Trace shrugged. "I don't know. Maybe he just wanted to see if we'd figure it out on our own."

"Everything comes full circle." Lily's face was thoughtful, her eyes dark. "I still can't believe Mike's gone. Sometimes I expect to see him walk through the door and say that it was all a joke.''

"I know.'' Trace brushed her hair back, tucking it behind her ears, his hands lingering on the softness of her cheeks.

"Promise me you'll take care of yourself.'' Her eyes met his and it was impossible to ignore the intensity in them.

"I promise. Nothing is going to happen to me.'' He lifted her and placed a slow thorough kiss on her mouth, distracting her. It worked better than he'd hoped.

This time their lovemaking was slow and gentle. The urgent passion had been dissipated earlier, leaving them relaxed, more at ease with each other. There was time to savor, to explore.

Lily fell asleep in Trace's arms, her slim body lax against him, her head pillowed on his shoulder. He held her, drawing in the wonder of the moment like a drowning man would draw in oxygen. She loved him. He didn't doubt that. She loved *him*. It was incredible. It was miraculous. He fell asleep, holding the miracle close to his heart.

THE MORNING DAWNED warm and clear. Lily still slept beside him, her face burrowed into the pillow, the covers drawn up over her shoulders.

Trace felt at peace in a way that had been all too rare in his life. He looked around the room, savoring that feeling of peace. Lily's bedroom reminded him of her. Cool ivory walls, simple furnishings and a splash of color here and there that drew the eye. Enameled shelving covered most of one wall and was filled with books and knickknacks and mementos, all the small treasures a person collects in life.

Sitting on the top shelf, his pale pink fur mostly worn off, was Isaiah, his dark eyes seeming to look down at Trace with deep wisdom. Trace smiled at the stuffed dog, remember-

ing the first time he'd seen Lily, the toy held under her arm.
Isaiah had been through a lot with the two of them but his
sewn-on mouth still smiled. The smile was a little lopsided
now and Trace felt a pang, remembering Mike's clumsy
stitches as he'd attempted to repair the treasured toy.

His chest hurt. God, the things that stuffed animal had
seen. Oklahoma and the trip to Denver. The months when
their money was running out and then the months after it
was gone. Through it all Lily had clutched that dog to her,
drawing some strength from the matted bedraggled lump of
fur and stuffing. They'd been through a lot together—the
three of them. So many things that no one else could ever
share.

Lying beside Lily on a bright winter morning, Trace could
almost believe in miracles. They'd been through so much
together. They'd been so much to each other. There'd been
a time, before they found Mike, when they'd had nothing
but each other.

He remembered those times and all that had come afterward. All the years their lives had twined together. A tiny
hope flickered deep inside him. Maybe, just maybe— He
refused to finish the thought as if it would be bad luck. But
he nodded to Isaiah as if the two of them had just made a
pact. He felt younger than he had in years as he slipped out
of bed and gathered up his clothes.

Lily was still sleeping when he left the room. He stopped
in the doorway to look back at her and his mouth curved in
an irrepressible smile. She slept on her stomach, one knee
drawn up, her arms wrapped around her pillow. The sheet
had slipped down to bare a length of smooth back and her
hair spilled in a tangled black skein across her skin. There
was an innocent sensuality to her that made him want to
crawl back into her bed and wake her with a kiss. He re-

sisted the urge with difficulty and backed into the hall, shutting the door quietly behind him.

Trace was whistling softly under his breath as he let himself out of the house. The sun was shining with enough strength to make it almost possible to believe that it was June rather than February. He shrugged out of his denim jacket on the way to the car. He refused to put a name to just what he was feeling. If he labeled it, he'd have to look for its source, and right now he preferred not to look too deeply at his feelings.

The 'Vette sat in the driveway, gleaming black perfection. He felt a surge of satisfaction when he saw it. It had taken him two solid years to restore the car but it was showroom fresh now. He opened the door and tossed his jacket into the car. Before he could begin the morning ritual of folding himself into the low passenger compartment, he noticed the piece of paper wedged under the windshield-wiper blade. He pulled it out with only mild curiosity. It was probably someone who wanted to know if he was interested in selling. He'd had notes left on the windshield before. He unfolded the plain white sheet and all the vague optimism he'd been feeling vanished like mist under a hot sun.

IT SHOULD HAVE BEEN YOU. NOT HIM. BUT IT DOESN'T MATTER. YOU'LL PAY ANYWAY.

Chapter Twelve

The note was printed in block letters, the paper clean of fingerprints. There was no clue as to who had stuck it on his windshield or when they might have done it. Trace sat in the captain's office, his hands resting in his lap, his fingers deliberately relaxed. His face was carefully blank, giving no hint of the emotions seething inside. It was a look he'd perfected a long, long time ago when it had been important to keep his stepfather from seeing his fear. Jed was long gone but the look remained, a shield he still kept ready.

"It seems likely that the note is referring to Mike," Captain Jacobs said heavily. He looked at Trace from under bushy brows, trying to weigh the impact of his words, knowing what a powerful burden they carried.

"I don't see who else it could be." Trace glanced up, his eyes a cool clear blue, revealing nothing of his thinking. "I should have thought of it before. Mike took my car to work that day. Whoever killed him must have seen the car and thought it was me. They shot before they realized they'd made a mistake. Mike died in my place."

"Maybe." Captain Jacobs stroked his upper lip, his eyes thoughtful. "It looks like that may be the case at this point but there are some gaps in that scenario. Even from behind, you and Mike didn't look much alike. The killer would have to have had his eyes shut not to notice that it wasn't you. Besides, why would they be expecting you at the liquor store that day?"

"I don't know. Maybe they drove by and saw the 'Vette and thought they'd just take advantage of the opportunity. All I know right now is that it looks like Mike died in my place." There was a wealth of pain in the words, all the more powerful for the calm way he said them.

Jacobs shifted a few objects on the desk, his head bent over the task. Trace noticed the way the light exposed his pink scalp with merciless clarity. Jacobs was trying to think of something to say that would make his officer feel less guilty but there was nothing to be said. Nothing could change the facts. Someone had wanted him dead but Mike was the one who'd bled out his life all alone. Nothing could change that.

"Do you have any idea who might want you dead?"

Trace shrugged. "Not really. I gave a list of everyone I could think of to Martin and Castillo. They were investigating Mike's murder. There wasn't anyone who really jumped out at me."

"Too bad. It could be some nut case who's just decided he doesn't like you. You know, the note could mean nothing. It might just be a crazy who knew about Mike's death and saw this as an opportunity to make a cop squirm."

"What about the shooting yesterday at Gillespie's? Whoever that was, they seemed real sincere about wanting me dead. We thought it was just a random cop shooting but it could have been someone after me."

"Maybe. But spraying the pavement with an automatic weapon is a clumsy way to kill one man."

"Maybe they don't care who gets killed along with me. They must have known it wasn't me before they shot Mike but they killed him anyway."

"Maybe he saw their face. Maybe they were afraid he could identify them," Jacobs suggested.

"The report said that they opened fire when his back was to them."

Jacobs sighed. "At this point we're talking pure speculation. The note could be a crank with a grudge. It could mean absolutely nothing. We've got people going through your files looking for something we can work with. I want you to go home for the day, get some rest and let your mind wander. Maybe you'll come up with something."

"I'd rather stay here and go through the files again."

"Go home, Dushane. You've been at the files for almost five hours. Get out of here and clear your mind."

"Yes, sir." Trace stood up, his reluctance clear, but there was no arguing with Jacobs's tone.

He didn't drive straight home. His thoughts were twisting and turning in too many directions for him to just go peacefully home. There was so much to think about. He pointed the 'Vette's nose in the direction of the Angeles Crest and headed up the Glendale Freeway. It was still early afternoon and traffic was light. Lighter still on Foothill Boulevard, and the highway up over the crest itself was almost empty.

He drove faster than he should have, pouring all his concentration into the snaking turns that wound upward into the mountains. At this speed he couldn't afford to think about anything but his driving, which was exactly what he needed. The sports car clung to the curves, hugging the narrow road as if it were a lover. The temperature dropped as he climbed to snow level but he didn't stop to put on his jacket. He barely noticed the chill. Near the top of the crest, he turned off on a narrow dirt road and parked the car.

The snow lay in dirty white drifts on the ground, banking up in hollows and shaded areas, fading to almost nothing where the sun rested. The air was crisp but not bitingly cold. Even in the mountains, winter was losing the fragile grip that was all Los Angeles ever allowed it.

Trace got out of the car, tugging on his denim jacket. He shoved his hands into his pockets and stared at the grubby white landscape. The blankness he'd drawn around his emotions was fading. He tried to hold on to it for just a little while longer but it wasn't possible. It slid inexorably away, leaving him raw and aching.

Mike had died because of him.

The knowledge refused to be pushed away any longer. Mike's death should have been his death. He should have been the one to die. Had Mike known? In those last few agonizing moments, had he known that his death was a mistake?

Trace's hand knotted into fists in his pockets, his knuckles aching with the pressure. It wasn't right. It wasn't fair. It was Mike who had taken him in. Mike who'd taught him how to be a man. Because of Mike he'd become a cop instead of ending up on the other side of the bars. He remembered Mike's face the day he'd graduated from the academy. He'd been so proud, and that look had made all the training worthwhile. Superimposed over that memory was the last time he'd seen Mike, his face twisted in agony, his blood pooling around him.

"No!" The mountains echoed his cry. The sound bounced off the hills, full of anguish. Rage and denial boiled inside him. It wasn't right. Mike shouldn't be dead. Mike had given so much; he'd had so much more to give. *He* should be the one lying in that graveyard, covered with six feet of soil. It wasn't fair.

One thing to keep in mind, Trace, is that life isn't fair, and anybody who tells you it is is either a damned fool or a damned liar.

Mike's voice echoed in his mind but it did nothing to ease his torment. Nothing could change the fact that Mike had died because of him. Nothing could ease the guilt and pain of that knowledge. He stood there for a long time, his eyes focused on nothing, his vision turned inward. But he could find no comfort.

The sun sank behind the mountains and the air grew colder. Trace gradually realized that his ears were starting to feel numb, as were his feet. He turned back to the car and folded himself into the low seat. The engine caught immediately and idled with a deep roar that promised speed. Enough speed to sail right off any one of the sharp curves that led down off the crest. The thought slid in and was pushed away. He wasn't a quitter. No matter what else, he wasn't a quitter. He'd learn to live with the knowledge that he was partly responsible for Mike's death, just as he'd learned to live with other things in his life.

He drove home slowly. Pulling into the driveway, he looked at the small house and remembered how he'd felt when he walked out the door that morning. It seemed like aeons ago. He'd been so optimistic, even daring to hope that he and Lily—

Lily. God, what was he going to say to her? Would she hate him when he told her that Mike had died in his place? She'd told him she loved him but she'd loved Mike, too. Even more important was the fact that she might be in danger because of him. Whoever had killed Mike had probably been the one to shoot at him yesterday. They knew where he lived. What if they tried again while Lily was with him?

He closed his eyes. He could live with anything but the possibility of her being hurt because of him. Anything. Lily had to be safe. Which meant she had to stay away from him. As long as she was close to him, she was vulnerable.

He'd been a fool to think it could be otherwise. Even without a killer after him, he couldn't bring her anything but hurt. That was all he'd ever brought to the people he loved. His mother, Mike, Lily. He'd caused them all pain.

Trace pushed open the front door and stepped into the warm hallway. Lily was in the kitchen. He could hear her humming to herself and the sound of running water. John would still be at the store so they'd have the house to themselves. He left his jacket on as he pushed the door shut behind him. He didn't plan on staying long.

The sound of the door brought Lily into the hall. Trace looked at her, wondering how it was possible for one person to hold so much beauty.

"Hi. You're home early, aren't you?" He felt her smile go through him as if it carried a sharp edge. She looked so happy, and what he was about to do was going to wipe that look from her eyes.

"I . . . ah . . . had some things to do."

"Well, it's nice to have you home a little early." She crossed the hall with quick light steps and set her hand on his arm. "John won't be home for a couple of hours. Why don't you take off your coat and act like you're going to stay awhile?"

She tilted her head back, the look in her eyes pure invitation. Trace wanted to put his arms around her and hold her close. He wanted to feel her arms around him. He wanted a lot of things he couldn't have. He dragged his eyes from her face, moving away so that her hand dropped from his arm.

"As a matter of fact, I'm not going to be staying long."

"You're not? Are you going back to work?"

"No." *Tell her about Mike. Tell her you were the one who should have died.* But he couldn't bring himself to do it. She'd find out sooner or later but he couldn't be the one to tell her. He couldn't stand to see the look in her eyes when she realized it was his fault Mike was dead. She probably wouldn't blame him for it but it would change the way she looked at him.

And if she doesn't blame you? If she doesn't look at you any differently? That was no good, either. Then she'd worry about him being in danger and she'd want to be with him. She could be hurt and he couldn't live with that.

"Trace?" Lily's questioning tone made him realize that he'd let the silence stretch a long time. He refocused his gaze on her. "Is something wrong? Why aren't you going to be home tonight?"

"I'm moving back into my apartment. I thought I'd pack up a few things and go on over tonight."

"You're doing what?" Shock drove the lingering invitation from her eyes.

"I'm just going to get a few of my things and take them back to my apartment." He couldn't stand the hurt that was filling her eyes and he looked away. "I'll go pack." He took the stairs two at a time, feeling like someone who'd just stolen Christmas from a child.

He had his duffel bag on the bed and was throwing clothing into it more or less at random when Lily came to the door. He saw her out of the corner of his eye but he refused to look at her, instead tossing another handful of shirts into the bag. She watched for a long moment without saying anything, and when she did speak it was to ask a painfully simple question—one he couldn't answer, at least not with the truth.

"Why?"

Trace's fingers clenched over the bundle of socks he'd picked up. He felt her pain as deeply as if it were his own. He wanted to hold her and soothe her hurt but he couldn't do that. Not and keep her safe, too. Her safety had to come first. She'd get over the hurt. In the long run, she'd thank him for it.

"Why what?" He made his response deliberately obtuse.

"Why are you doing this?"

"I've been here quite a while, Lily. You've settled in okay. John is here. You don't need me anymore."

"I'll always need you." The simple statement caught at him, sinking into his soul, bringing both pain and comfort.

"Well, I'll be around. It's not like I'm moving to another state. I'm only fifteen minutes away." He stuffed the socks into a corner of the duffel bag and glanced around the room blindly, looking at anything but her.

"Why are you doing this now? Why now?"

"Why not now?"

"What about last night?" The quiet question held a wealth of pain. Trace had his back to her and he shut his eyes for a moment before turning to look at her, his expression as blank as he could manage.

"What about last night?"

Lily sucked in a quick breath, her eyes reflecting the hurt he'd inflicted. She knew it had been deliberate. It wasn't possible that it hadn't been deliberate. And the knowledge that he'd deliberately hurt her caused more pain than anything he said.

"Are you going to tell me it didn't mean anything to you?" Her voice shook despite her best efforts to steady it.

"Of course not. It meant a lot to me. *You* mean a lot to me. You always have." His tone was absent and he looked around the room as if making sure he hadn't left anything important.

"Trace, this doesn't make sense. Are you mad at me for some reason? Is there something I've done?"

"Of course not." He zipped the duffel bag with a quick movement. He had to get out of here before he broke down and told her everything, including just how much she meant to him. "I'm not mad at you. It's just time for me to move home again. I've been paying rent on the place and not getting any use out of it."

"Don't give me that! There's more to it than that. Last night I told you I loved you."

"I love you, too, Lily." The words came from deep in his heart but his tone sounded like someone soothing a fractious three-year-old, offering a lollipop to prevent a tantrum.

Lily flushed, anger and hurt warring in her face. He wanted the anger to win. If she was angry with him, it would hurt her less.

"You're just going to walk out? Just like that?"

'I'm not walking out. You make it sound like I'm abandoning you or something," he chided. "I'm just moving back into my own apartment. Like I said, I'm not far away. We'll still see each other."

"Sure. Let's do lunch sometime." Her tone crackled with anger and Trace felt a vague relief. He could handle her anger far better than he could handle that hurt look in her eyes.

"I'll have my people contact your people." His weak joke was delivered to the empty doorway as Lily spun on one heel and walked away. There was a distinct click as the door to her room closed. Trace picked up the bag and slung it over his shoulder. He hesitated in the hallway. Lily's door beckoned to him. She was hurt. When the anger eased, the hurt was going to rise to the surface and he wasn't going to be here to comfort her.

He gritted his teeth and strode down the stairs, shutting the door behind him without looking back. Sometimes you had to be cruel to be kind. The old cliché echoed hollowly in his mind as he threw the duffel bag into the passenger seat. The 'Vette roared to life and he threw it into gear almost before the engine had a chance to catch. The car jerked, the tires grabbing the pavement as he backed into the road and slammed it into first. The sedate pace he assumed did not reflect the turmoil he felt.

He was heading toward an empty apartment and leaving behind the only home he'd ever known and the one person in the world who meant something to him. But he was doing the right thing. It was hollow comfort at best.

JOHN PUSHED the door shut behind him and stretched. He'd never have guessed that running a liquor store could be so tiring. It wasn't the physical labor involved. He'd done a lot worse than sling around a few boxes of liquor. It was dealing with people all the time that exhausted him. It made him realize what a loner he'd become.

He dropped his jacket over the stair railing and walked into the kitchen. Lily was standing at the stove, stirring a steaming pot. She hadn't heard him come in and he watched her for a moment, reading her mood in the slump of her shoulders.

"Hi. What are you cooking?"

She jumped at the sound of his voice. Her back straightened and he could see her gathering herself together before she turned to look at him.

"Hi. I was just throwing together a tuna casserole. Nothing fancy."

"Sounds great." He opened the refrigerator and took out a beer, twisting the top off before turning to her again. What had happened to put that look in her eyes? "Something wrong?"

"Nothing." Her mouth edged up in a false smile before she turned away and stirred the noodles again. He'd seen a chef pay less attention to a hollandaise sauce.

He took a long swallow of beer and studied her again. In the weeks he'd known her, he'd learned that Lily was one of the most even-tempered women he'd ever met. She took life calmly, seeming almost to view it from a distance, letting a lot of it flow around her rather than wading right through the middle of it. Except when it came to Trace. When it came to him, her emotions were right on the surface.

"Where's Trace?" The spoon clattered to the stove top, telling him that his guess was right on the money. There was a long silence.

"He moved back to his apartment." Not even all her self-control could keep the lost note from her voice. "He left this afternoon."

John didn't say anything. When he'd left them alone last night, he'd hoped that maybe they'd work things out between them. He wasn't sure just what their problem was, though he had a few guesses, but he'd figured some time alone just might help them. So much for his figuring.

"What happened?"

"Happened? What do you mean? Nothing happened. He just felt that it was time he moved back into his own place." She snatched up a can of tuna and attacked it with the can opener. "By the way, he told me about you being the one who picked us up all those years ago. Why didn't you mention it before? It's a pretty incredible coincidence, don't you think?"

"Moderately. I knew if you came to Dad he'd help you. We may have had our problems but he never turned away a kid who needed help."

"Just what kind of problems did the two of you have? You've never said anything and Mike didn't talk about it much." The question was a measure of her desperation to keep the subject away from Trace. She seemed to realize that she was prying and she looked up, her face flushed. "I'm sorry. That's really none of my business."

John shrugged, unoffended. "I don't mind. You met Dad after he'd mellowed quite a bit. When I was a kid, he was quite a martinet. Not exactly harsh, but rules were rules and God help you if you broke them. My mother was just the opposite. She belonged to the school that felt that a child should be left to grow in whatever direction seemed natural."

He took a swallow of beer, his expression thoughtful. "Naturally they had more than a few arguments about it. And naturally I liked Mom's ideas considerably better than Dad's. What kid wouldn't? I resented what I saw as his attempts to control me and he fought all the harder. We both went a little too far.

"When my mother was killed, I didn't deal with it real well. If there's a good age to lose your mother, sixteen isn't it. I know Dad must have grieved but I didn't believe it at the time. I felt that since they'd fought so much, he must not have loved her. Actually, they argued about everything under the sun. I don't think they were very well suited. When I got older, I realized that they stayed together because of me more than anything else.

"Anyway, we grew even further apart. He wanted me to go to college and I thought it was a waste of time. To spite him, I joined the marines and shipped out to Vietnam. We never spoke again. The rest, as they say, is history."

He finished off the beer and tossed the bottle in the trash before looking at Lily. She was watching him with those eyes that always seemed far too old.

"When I was little, I used to dream about being part of a real family. My parents traveled so much, I hardly knew them. When they were killed, it didn't have much impact on me. Then I went to live with Trace and his mother and stepfather. It wasn't a happy home. It wasn't the way I'd pictured a real family at all. But it didn't really matter because I had Trace and I didn't need any more family than him. He took care of me and protected me and that was enough.

"You had the family I always thought I wanted, but I think, in some ways, maybe I had more than you did."

John stared at her, struck by the truth in her words. He'd never felt part of a family, never really felt part of anyone. There'd been a woman once but she'd died before he could find out just what they might have had. All his life he'd walked more or less alone. Maybe that was what he'd seen in Trace and Lily all those years ago. There'd been a bond between them even then.

"Maybe you did at that." He leaned back against the counter and watched her stir the tuna, noodles and peas together before adding a can of mushroom soup. He waited until she'd slid the casserole in the oven before speaking again.

"You want to tell me what's going on with you and Trace?"

She rinsed her hands and wiped them on a towel, her expression guarded. "I'm not sure I know what you mean."

"I'll explain. It's obvious to any idiot that the two of you are in love. Hell, even when you were kids, it was obvious that there was a special kind of bond between you. So why aren't you engaged or married or living together or something?"

Lily bit her lower lip, her eyes filling with tears that were blinked back before they could fall. "Don't ask me. Ask that pigheaded creep who packed his things and walked out of here today."

"You want to talk about it?"

"No... Yes... I don't know." A smile flickered wanly. "Nothing like being decisive, huh?" She twisted the towel in her hands, looking down at the aimless movement.

"I've always known I loved Trace. When I was little, he was my knight in shining armor, always there to protect me and keep me safe. As I got older, my feelings changed and I began to love him in a different way. I think Trace's feelings changed the same way. Only he won't admit it. He keeps acting like loving him is the worst thing I could do, like he's bad for me or something."

"Maybe he thinks he is."

"Well, he isn't." The look she gave him dared him to argue. John lifted his hands.

"You don't have to convince me."

"I know. But I'm not having much luck convincing Trace. And I'm beginning to wonder if I'm seeing things that aren't really there because I *want* them to be there."

"If you want my opinion, I think he loves you at least as much as you love him, but I think he's got a hang-up about not deserving you. He thinks you could do better than him."

"I don't want better than him. I want *him*." Her lower lip quivered and John reached out automatically, pulling her into his arms. She buried her face in his shoulder, sobs shaking her slim body. John's mouth twisted in a rueful smile. He must be getting old when he could hold a beautiful woman in his arms with nothing in mind but comforting her sorrow over another man.

"I know that and you know that but it may take a while for Trace to believe it. Have some patience. No man in his right mind would resist you for long."

TRACE MIGHT HAVE AGREED with him. Turning his back on Lily was surely the hardest thing he'd ever done and there were times when he wondered if it wasn't also the stupidest.

As the days passed without seeing her, he had to keep reminding himself that the best way to keep her safe was to stay away from her.

He didn't doubt the wisdom of his choice when the second note was left on his windshield. A repetition of the first, this time it mentioned Mike by name, so there could no longer be any doubt that the bullet that had killed him had been meant for Trace. Soon after the second note, someone put a bullet through the windshield of the 'Vette while it was parked in the garage beneath his apartment building. A neat round hole just about where his head would have been if he'd been in the car.

Then the right front tire came off the car while he was driving down the freeway. If the traffic had been heavier or he'd been driving faster, it could have resulted in a serious accident. As it was, he was able to keep the car from spinning out completely and get it to the side of the freeway with nothing more than some torn fiberglass and a badly damaged wheel to show for it. When the tire was fished out of the gully it had bounced into, it was easy to see that the lugs had been filed just enough so that they would sheer off under pressure.

He took to looking over his shoulder wherever he went and sleeping with his gun under the pillow. Whoever it was, they didn't seem to be in any hurry to kill him. He had the feeling that they were enjoying tormenting him for a while before they moved in for the final kill.

The search for someone with a reason to want him dead had drawn a blank. There was no one in his files who fitted the mold. No one who had a strong enough motive. So far, the best anyone had been able to come up with was that it was someone who'd picked him more or less at random and was working off some kind of a grudge against cops in general.

Worse than the knowledge that someone was trying to kill him was the aching hole in his gut that cutting Lily from his life had left. The hurt in her eyes haunted him. The need to call her, to talk to her, to put his arms around her tore at him, making sleep a thing of the past. Even when she'd been thousands of miles away in England, he hadn't felt this same aching loss.

But then, he hadn't held her, loved her, slept with her beside him when she left for Europe. He'd had only that one kiss to remember and he'd almost managed to convince himself that that had been little more than a dream. He couldn't convince himself that making love to her had been a dream. It had been too real, too vital. Too right.

Trace rolled onto his back and stared up at the dark ceiling. The sheets were twisted from his restless movements but he didn't notice the discomfort. It was minor compared to the aching emptiness that filled him every time he thought of Lily. He could see her face above him, suspended in the darkness, as clear and sharp as if she were really there.

The harsh ring of the phone popped the image like a soap bubble. He stirred sluggishly, exhaustion making his movements slow and awkward. There'd been too many nights with too little sleep. He fumbled for the phone, his movements becoming more coordinated as he registered the late hour. Phones didn't ring at midnight unless there was something wrong.

"Hello?"

"Trace? It's Lily. I'm sorry it's so late."

He sat up, the sheet falling away from his bare chest. "What's wrong? Are you hurt?"

"No, it's not me." Her voice shook and she stopped to regain control. Trace waited, his fingers knotted over the receiver. "It's John. He's been in an accident."

"How badly is he hurt?" Trace was reaching for his jeans as he spoke, thrusting his legs into them and grabbing for a shirt.

"I don't know. I'm at the hospital but I just got here and the doctor is still with him."

"Stay calm. Chances are he's going to be fine. I'll be there as soon as I can."

He hung up the phone and shoved his feet into a pair of boots before snatching up a heavy jacket and the keys to his motorcycle, since the 'Vette was still out of commission. The freeways were empty and he pushed the motorcycle past the speed limit. He barely noticed the chill night air rushing by his face.

Lily needed him and he had to be there for her.

Chapter Thirteen

The waiting room was softly lit as if perhaps the dim light would help to soothe the anxieties of those who had to wait there. It didn't help. When Trace strode into the room, Lily was sitting on the edge of a soft chair, her feet set neatly together, her hands in her lap. The very composure of her position made her tension all the more obvious.

"Lily." He called her name softly and she looked up.

"Trace!" She flew across the room and into his waiting arms.

Trace held her close. Her slim body was trembling and his arms tightened around her, offering what comfort he could. Forgotten was the need to keep his distance from her. Forgotten was the fact that he wasn't good for her. She needed him and he had to be there for her. It wasn't a choice so much as a deep visceral compulsion.

"It's going to be all right, honey. It's going to be all right." He held her, murmuring quietly, until the trembling had eased. She drew back, looking up into his face with such love and so much trust that he felt as if his heart would stop.

"I knew you'd come."

"Of course I came." He brushed the hair back from her forehead, struggling with the urge to tell her he loved her. "I'll always be here when you need me."

"I'll always need you."

Trace shut his eyes in pain as she laid her head against his shoulder. How could he fight such simple honesty, even when he knew he had no choice?

"Tell me what happened." He chose to avoid the issue. Now was not the time to confront it. He led her over to a chair and sat down next to her, holding her hand.

"I don't really know much. The hospital called me. I guess the phone number was in his wallet. All they told me was that he'd been in a car wreck. I got here as soon as I could but they don't really know that much more. There was a highway patrolman here waiting to ask John some questions but the nurse told him it was going to be a while before the doctors were through examining John and I guess he left. He said John's car was pretty well totaled."

"That doesn't mean that John was badly hurt. I've seen people walk away from cars that looked like they'd been through a trash compactor. Was John unconscious when they brought him in?"

"I think so. I don't know. They really haven't told me much."

"I'm sure he's going to be all right."

"As a matter of fact, we're pretty sure he is, too."

Trace had been concentrating so much on Lily that he hadn't noticed the doctor stepping into the doorway. He stood up and turned to face her, keeping Lily's hand in his.

The doctor was younger than he'd have expected and quite pretty, not the grizzled emergency room veteran he'd been picturing.

"I'm Dr. Levine. I presume you're friends or family of John Lonigan?"

Lily couldn't seem to find her voice so it was Trace who answered her. "More or less family. As close as he has, anyway. How is he?"

"He seems to be all right. He's got a nasty bump on the head, a few cracked ribs and a leg that's just short of broken. All in all, not too bad for someone who ran his car into a mountainside."

"When can he come home?" Lily asked, her voice shaky.

"Tomorrow, I think. We're going to keep him in overnight for observation and he should be able to go home tomorrow."

"Can we see him?"

Dr. Levine shook her head. "I think it would be better if you didn't. He's pretty groggy and we're trying to coax him into going to sleep. He needs rest more than anything else right now. Why don't the two of you go home and get some sleep and we'll call you in the morning?"

Trace nodded, sensing Lily's reluctance but seeing the logic in the doctor's suggestion. "Come on. We'll come back the minute they let us know he's awake."

"I just feel like he ought to know we're here. He doesn't have anybody else."

"We'll tell him," Dr. Levine offered. "You've both had quite a fright. Get some rest and come back tomorrow."

Trace left his motorcycle at the hospital and drove Lily's compact home. There was no question of leaving her alone. He could sooner have cut off his own arm than walk out on her now.

"I could use something hot to drink." Lily hung her coat in the hall closet, looking over her shoulder at Trace as she spoke.

"Sounds good to me. I could make some of my world-famous hot chocolate."

"World-famous?" She arched her brow, her pale face taking on a touch of humor.

"Semi-world-famous?"

"Hot chocolate sounds great, even if it's only locally well-known."

They drank their cocoa without talking, each wrapped in thought. And when the cups were rinsed and put away, it seemed the most natural thing in the world for them to climb the stairs together. Trace hesitated outside her door. His common sense told him that he was playing with fire, but looking at Lily's pale face, he couldn't bring himself to just turn and walk away.

"I could stay with you tonight, if you'd like." He didn't look at her as he spoke, half hoping she'd say no. Staying with her tonight would only make it hard to walk away again. And he *had* to walk away in the morning. At least until whoever was after him had been caught.

He felt Lily's eyes on him, full of questions he couldn't answer.

"I'd like that. I don't really feel like being alone tonight."

So he followed her into her room, slipping off only his shoes before lying on her bed. Lily took her nightgown into the bathroom, and when she came out, he thought he'd never seen her look more beautiful. The plain blue cotton gown covered her from neck to toes, hinting at feminine curves without revealing anything. She crawled into bed without questioning the fact that he was still dressed, and Trace reached out to shut off the light.

In the darkness, it was possible to pretend that he belonged here. It was possible to forget that someone wanted him dead, forget that Mike's death lay on his conscience, forget everything but Lily's slim body cuddled so close to his, her head on his shoulder. He fell asleep with his arms around her, his face against her hair.

IT WAS MIDMORNING when Trace came downstairs. He'd slept more deeply than he had in days and he felt rested. It was a feeling he'd almost forgotten. Lily had already gotten up when he woke and it was a measure of his exhaustion that she'd managed to rise and dress without disturbing him.

The scent of fresh coffee floated from the kitchen but he hesitated at the foot of the stairs. The barriers he'd tried to build between them were showing signs of cracking and he wasn't sure about the wisdom of letting those cracks widen.

Lily looked up from the morning paper as he walked into the room. Her eyes reflected the wariness he felt. So much lay between them. So many questions that couldn't be asked or answered.

"Good morning." Trace moved to the stove and poured himself a cup of coffee.

"Good morning." Lily folded the paper and set it aside. "I called the hospital. They said John is doing just fine and they'll call and let us know when he's ready to be released."

"Great. That's great." Trace took a swallow of coffee, almost choking as the scalding liquid hit his throat. There was something in the set of Lily's jaw that made him uneasy.

"I want to talk to you, Trace."

The uneasiness increased and he took another gulp of coffee. "About what?" His voice sounded raspy, which didn't surprise him. The way his throat felt, he was surprised he had a voice at all.

"I think we need to talk about what's been going on."

She fixed him with a look that demanded honesty and Trace glanced away. "Going on?"

"You blow hot and cold. It's a wonder I haven't caught pneumonia from the way your moods change. I thought about it at the hospital last night. I thought about how I'd feel if it had been you they were working on, and it made me realize that life is too short to play around with it."

"I agree, but I don't think this is a good time for this conversation."

"Why not?"

"Why not?" He stumbled over the simple question. "Well, we're going to have to go get John in a little while."

"The hospital will call us. Trace, I love you. And I think you love me. I *know* you love me. Why do you keep fighting it?"

Trace stared down into his coffee, wishing he could just drown himself in the dark liquid. Maybe he was still suffering from the strain of the past few weeks. His brain didn't seem to be working as well as it normally did.

"You want to know what I think?"

"Do I have a choice?" he asked with a weak attempt at humor.

"No, you don't. I think you're afraid of what you feel for me. I think you're afraid that you're going to get hurt or you're afraid that I'm going to get hurt. I'm not sure which it is."

"Lily, this really isn't a good time—"

"It seems like a good time to me."

Why hadn't he ever noticed how persistent she could be?

"Do you love me?"

"Lily, I—"

"Do you love me?"

Trace set his cup down and ran his fingers through his hair, avoiding her eyes. How could he answer her?

"I don't think—"

"Don't think, just answer me." She pushed her chair back and stood up. She was right in front of him. If he took a deep breath, he could inhale her scent. If he moved just a few inches, they'd be touching. "Trace, please. Do you love me?"

He felt crowded, hemmed in, pressured. Everywhere he looked, she was there, her eyes demanding honesty, asking for the truth.

"Lily—"

"Do you?"

"Yes. Dammit, yes." The admission was pulled from him. He felt a certain release that he'd finally told her how he felt. Lily stared at him, her eyes wide, as if she hadn't really believed he'd say it. He watched elation fill her face, turning her eyes a bright sparkling green. "But it doesn't mean anything," he added weakly.

"It means a lot to me. Oh, Trace, don't you see? All you had to do was say it. Why didn't you tell me? Why have you been acting like you couldn't care less?"

"Lily, just because I've admitted that I love you, that doesn't mean there's some kind of fairy-tale ending to this. All the same problems are still there."

"What problems?" She smiled up at him and set her hands against his chest. "Trace, whatever you think the problems are, we can work them out. This is right. We're right. Don't you feel it?"

He didn't trust what he was feeling. Life had taught him that when you wanted something bad enough, you could convince yourself of almost anything. The feel of her hands seemed to burn through the fabric of his shirt, warming his skin, making it easy to forget reality. He shifted, moving away from her, away from that tantalizing scent, away from her touch.

"Lily, I can't be the kind of man you need."

"What?"

"I can't be what you need. I'm not the right man for you." He got the words out with difficulty, aware of an aching wish that he *could* be what she needed, what she deserved. He might have expected several different reactions. Denial, hurt, even acceptance. He hadn't expected anger.

"Who the *hell* do you think you are?" She spit the words out and Trace turned to look at her, startled by the violent tone of her voice.

"What?"

"Just who the hell do you think you are to start telling me what I need and what I don't need? I'm a big girl now, Trace. I don't need anyone to tell me what I need or what I want."

"You don't understand. I didn't mean it like that." How had he come to be on the defensive?

"Just how did you mean it? And what makes you think you aren't what I need?"

"Look at you, you're beautiful, you're intelligent, you could have anyone."

"And I want you. If I'm so intelligent, why do you assume I've made the wrong choice?"

"Lily, I'm a nobody. A white trash farm boy from a town in Oklahoma that nobody ever even heard of. My father wrapped his car around a telephone pole, my mother married a drunken wife beater and stayed with him because she didn't have the guts to get out. I didn't finish high school, I didn't go to college. I haven't traveled anywhere—"

"Stop it!" Lily broke into his words, facing him with her hands clenched into fists, her face flushed and angry. "That's a lot of nonsense. Who cares what your father did? And your mother did the best she knew how. Not everyone is as strong as you are. And you are strong. Look at what you've done. You took care of your mother the best way you knew how, and when I came along you took care of me. You ran away rather than see me get hurt. You were just a kid yourself but you took responsibility for me and I never felt frightened as long as you were close.

"I may not remember everything about the time before we found Mike but I remember enough to know that it must have been pretty scary for you. But you never let me down."

"I—" She gestured sharply, cutting off his attempt to get a word in.

"I'm not through yet. After we came to Mike, you worked hard to gain his respect and to keep it. Mike loved you and he thought you were worthwhile. Are you going to say he was wrong, too?"

"It's got nothing to do with loving." He thrust his fingers through his hair, ruffling it into dark blond waves. How could he make her understand when he wasn't even sure he understood himself? "It's got to do with who I am. What I am. Deep inside I'm always going to be a white trash farm boy. Can't you see that?"

"No. I can't see that. Deep inside you're a warm wonderful man with a lot of love to give someone if you'd only let it go. You're afraid to let it go. You're afraid you'll get hurt."

"No!" He took a deep breath, trying to regain control. "I'm afraid I'll hurt you."

"How? How could you hurt me? The only way you'll hurt me is if you keep denying what's between us."

"What if I end up like Jed? What if I start beating you?" Until the words were out, he hadn't even acknowledged that fear to himself.

"Trace, it takes two people to allow what happened to your mother and Jed. Your mother stayed with him. She gave him a kind of permission to do what he did to her. Even if you wanted to beat me up periodically, do you see me allowing it?"

"I—" He broke off and stared at her, realizing the truth in her words. "No, I don't." She was knocking down his arguments one by one but there was still one argument she couldn't get by, one she didn't even know about. And he didn't want her to know about it.

"Trace, don't you see? Whatever is wrong, we can work through it."

"No. No, we can't. Can't you just take my word for it? It's never going to work. There are reasons why it can't work."

"What reasons? Tell me."

He thrust his fingers through his hair again, feeling as if he were on a merry-go-round that was spinning faster and faster. There'd been too many pressures for too long. His self-control was getting thinner and thinner, stretched taut.

"What reasons?" she repeated. Her delicate jaw was set with a stubbornness that spoke of infinite patience. "I'm not giving up until I know what reasons. Whatever they are, we can work them out."

"No, we can't." The words were spaced a little too far apart and spoken a little too loud. "We can't work out the fact that Mike's death was my fault."

Lily stared at him, her mouth open to refute his argument, but nothing came out. He watched her, waiting with a kind of morbid fascination to see what her reaction would be.

"Your fault? How do you figure?"

"There was a note left on my windshield the day after the shooting at the grocery store."

"The day after we made love."

He nodded. "The day after we made love. It said that it should have been me, not him, but that I'd pay anyway."

"What did it mean, you'd pay anyway?"

"Someone is apparently trying to kill me. Mike got in the way. I was the one supposed to die that day, not Mike. He died in my place."

He waited to see anger or distaste or even hatred come into her eyes. She looked at him for a long moment. "Do you think I'm going to hate you for this? You can't possibly believe I'm that stupid. Even if it was you they were after that day, it's not your fault that you weren't there."

"Technically, maybe, but the end result is still the same. It was supposed to be me."

"Trace, you can't believe even for a moment that this would change the way I feel about you."

He stared at her, his heart full of a confusing tangle of emotions. Elation—she still loved him. Guilt—no matter what she said, he couldn't help but feel responsible for Mike's death. And fear—how could he keep her at a distance? How could he keep her safe?

And beyond that, there was a part of him, deep inside, that knew he wasn't right for her. He couldn't be right for her. It wasn't possible.

"This person who killed Mike and left the note—do you know who it is?"

"No."

"Are you still in danger?"

"Yes, and that's another reason we can't be together."

"But if you're in danger, I want to be with you." She set her hand on his sleeve and looked up at him, her eyes the deep green of a forest.

He steeled himself against the plea he saw there and shook her hand off his arm. "I'm not going to have your death as well as Mike's on my conscience. Besides, this is all wrong. All of it. I shouldn't have made love to you. I had no business getting involved with you like that. It's wrong. All wrong."

Lily opened her mouth to argue but the phone rang, cutting her off before she could say anything. Trace turned away, reaching for the coffeepot.

"That's probably the hospital," he said. "You'd better get it."

He felt the frustrated look she threw him, though his back was to her. She answered the phone while he poured another cup of coffee and gulped it down.

"They're ready to release John as soon as we get there."

"Good. We'd better get going. I'm sure he doesn't want to stay there any longer than he has to."

"Trace—"

"Lily, I don't want to talk about this anymore. I've had a rough couple of weeks. I'm tired. There's some nut out there who wants me dead and I just don't have the energy to deal with this anymore. What's between us isn't going to work. I know it, and if you weren't so stubborn you'd know it."

"No, I wouldn't, but I'll leave it alone for now. But not for good. Sooner or later you're going to see that I'm right. In the meantime you just make sure you stay alive, Trace Dushane."

He lifted the coffee cup in a tired salute, willing to take the half victory she offered rather than push for more. "I'll do my best."

"See that you do."

DESPITE THEIR best attempts, the atmosphere between Trace and Lily was thick enough to cut with a knife. John could practically smell the tension in the car during the drive home. Lily talked cheerfully enough but Trace was silent unless asked a direct question. And all the time Lily was talking, her eyes would flick to Trace and then away.

John limped into the house, trying to favor his leg, his ribs and his aching head all at the same time. When he closed his eyes, he could still see the mountainside coming at him, but, he told himself, he'd survived worse than this. Once he was settled in a chair in the living room, Lily cast Trace another one of those sidelong looks and then announced that she was going upstairs to make sure John's room was ready for him.

Maybe it was his aching head but John suddenly found himself out of patience with the two of them.

"You know, you're a damned fool if you keep pushing her away."

Trace threw him an enigmatic look. "Stay out of it."

"Fine. I'll stay out of it, but I still think you're a damned fool."

"That's your privilege." The phone rang before John could say more, though he wasn't sure he was all that inclined to add to what he'd already said. It was a brief conversation and Trace's end of it seemed to consist mostly of an occasional grunt of agreement or disagreement. When he hung up, his features seemed tenser, harder. He went straight to the bar and poured himself a stiff Scotch, downing it in one gulp.

"It's a little early for that, isn't it?"

"That was Captain Jacobs. Someone set fire to my apartment last night. The smoke alarms went off and the damage isn't too severe but the place isn't going to be livable for a while."

John watched him, his eyes narrowed. Despite the pounding in his head, his instincts were still working and they were telling him that there was more here than met the eye.

"You don't seem all that surprised."

"I suppose I'm not. Someone is trying to kill me. As a matter of fact, someone was trying to kill me the day your father was killed. It should have been me who died that day."

"You want to explain that?"

Trace told him the whole story in short terse sentences, biting the words off as if they tasted foul in his mouth. When he was done, there was a long silence. Above them they could hear the sound of Lily's footsteps. Trace finally turned to look at John, his lean body taut with rage and pain.

"I suppose you're waiting for me to revile you, to heap loads of guilt on you. Well, you're not getting it from me. What happened, happened. It sure as hell wasn't your fault if some crazy killed Dad when they were gunning for you. Dad would have been the first to tell you that. You know it as well as I do."

Trace's mouth twisted and he stared down at the empty glass. "I know it logically but I can't seem to shake the feeling that it's my fault somehow."

"It's not, but you'll just have to learn that in time. Does this have anything to do with what's going on between you and Lily?"

Trace shrugged. "More or less. It's part of it."

"Let me give you a piece of advice. It's always a mistake to lose time with someone you love. Thinking you can make up for lost time tomorrow isn't a good idea because you don't always get a tomorrow. God knows, I can speak from experience on that. Don't let it slip away, Trace. You may not get a second chance."

"I'm well aware of my own mortality. That's why it's more important than ever to keep Lily away. I can't risk something happening to her because of me. Until this nut is caught, she's better off at a distance.''

John leaned his head against the back of the chair and didn't argue any further.

Chapter Fourteen

Trace walked up to the door, reluctance and anticipation struggling for supremacy inside him. He hadn't been back here since picking up John at the hospital almost a week ago. He'd called once to see how John was getting along, and luckily John himself had picked up the phone.

He'd kept busy. Between attempting to repair the damage the fire had done in his apartment and going through files he'd already gone through half a hundred times trying to come up with someone who might want him dead, he'd had plenty to keep him occupied. But always, in the back of his mind, his argument with Lily played over and over.

She had sounded so sure. As if there could be no doubt that loving him was the right thing to do. He wanted to believe that she was right. He wanted to believe it so badly that he knew he couldn't trust his own judgment anymore. When you wanted something that much, you could convince yourself of almost anything.

He slid his left hand into the pocket of his jacket and opened the front door with his right. He wouldn't be back here now if John hadn't called to tell him that the lawyer had papers they all needed to sign—something to do with Mike's estate. It was too soon. He needed more time away from Lily, time to regain his equilibrium, time for her to think about what he'd said. Maybe she'd see the sense in his arguments. He ignored the pain that thought brought with it.

The house seemed to welcome him. This place was home in a way no other place had ever been. The feeling had changed with Mike's death but the welcome was still there. He shut the door quietly but apparently not quietly enough.

"Trace?" Lily's voice preceded her by only a moment. As always, Trace felt a funny little catch in his throat when he saw her. She was wearing jeans and a loose gray sweatshirt, her hair held back from her face with combs. Nothing fancy. If she was wearing makeup, it was too subtle for him to notice. On some women, the casual attire might have looked sloppy. On Lily, it looked like . . . Lily. Exquisite.

"Hi."

"Hi." She watched him, her eyes a little uncertain. "How are you?"

"Fine. Just fine." He started to shrug off his jacket, then remembered his hand and left it on. "Is the lawyer here yet?"

"No. I guess he's running a bit late."

"Must be." He looked at her and then looked away. What was he supposed to say to her? It wasn't possible to ignore the things they'd said to each other the last time they'd talked, but that was what he had to do. "How's John?"

"Fine. Just fine. He's in the living room."

There was a long silence while Trace tried not to look at her—and found it impossible. How could he look at anything else? It took all his willpower to drag his eyes away from her.

"I guess I'll go say hello to John."

"Trace, I—"

"Not now, Lily. Not now." He was unable to resist the urge to touch her, even if just for a moment, and his fingers trailed across the softness of her cheek. She closed her eyes as if savoring the light touch. Before she could open them again, he was gone.

John was seated in an overstuffed chair—the one Mike had always favored—a newspaper spread across his lap. He glanced up as Trace came into the room and Trace had the uneasy feeling that John saw a lot of things that he'd just as soon have left unseen. He was immediately aware of the dark circles under his eyes and the hollows in his cheeks.

"How's the leg?" He nodded to where John had his injured leg stretched out on a hassock.

"Not bad. A little stiff but that's about it. How's the apartment?"

"What's wrong with your apartment?"

Trace winced at Lily's question. John shrugged. "Sorry."

"Sorry about what? What's wrong with your apartment?" Lily came to stand between the two men, one dark brow arched in question.

"Nothing much. A small fire. No big deal. The damage is already pretty well cleaned up."

"A small fire? Does this have something to do with someone trying to kill you?"

Trace shook his head. "Not unless they're doing an incredibly clumsy job of it. I wasn't even home the night it happened." He didn't mention the fact that there'd been quite a few incidents that had stopped short of being actually life threatening. That they were connected to Mike's murder, he didn't doubt, but there was no reason to tell Lily that.

"Then why didn't you want me to know?"

"Because I knew you'd worry," he answered honestly.

"You were right." To his relief, she was willing to let the subject drop. The relief dissipated with her next words. "You want me to take your coat?"

He thought of the bandages on his left hand, considered how odd it was going to look if he kept his coat on in the comfortably warm living room, and surrendered to the inevitable.

"Sure." He shrugged the coat off.

"Trace! What happened to your hand?" The coat was tossed in the direction of the sofa as she took his injured hand in hers, looking at the bandage that circled his palm.

"It's no big deal. I cut myself."

"You don't put a bandage like this on a little cut. This looks like a professional job. What happened?"

She looked up at him, her green eyes wide with concern, cradling his injured hand in her palms. Trace wanted to sink into her eyes and leave all his troubles behind him. Instead he pulled his hand away from her, flexing it to show how minor the injury was, trying not to wince at the protesting twinge of pain as the stitches pulled at his flesh.

"It took a couple of stitches, that's all. I grabbed the wrong end of a knife."

"It must have hurt a lot."

Her words brought the pain to mind, the instant when he'd reached into his mailbox and felt the blade bite into his palm. Instead of a handful of junk mail, he'd drawn back a bloodied palm. It could have been worse. That's what he told himself, what he told the detectives when they came out to examine the booby trap, what he told Captain Jacobs when Jacobs wanted to put him in a safe house. It could have been worse. And if he went into a safe house, how were they going to draw this nut out?

His eyes met John's over the top of Lily's head and he read more comprehension there than he liked.

"Any clues as to who is trying to kill you?" John asked.

Trace frowned. He didn't want to talk about it in front of Lily. He didn't want to worry her any more than she already was. But the question had been asked and she was looking at him with as much interest as John.

"No real progress. We're still going through the files. We haven't turned up much yet."

"Well, they've got to do something. You shouldn't be walking around on the street like this. I mean, you should have a guard or something. Just what are they doing to protect you?" She looked so upset on his behalf that Trace couldn't help but take some pleasure in her concern.

"Captain Jacobs suggested that I go to stay in a safe house, but if I do that, then this guy might just go underground until I show up again. There's the same problem with armed guards. Not to mention the fact that we don't have the manpower to do that twenty-four hours a day."

"Well, you can't just walk around waiting to get shot." She wrapped her arms around her midriff and Trace knew she was trying to conceal her trembling. He wanted to hold her and tell her that everything was going to be all right but he couldn't do that.

"I'm being careful and I'm wearing a bulletproof vest. It's not like I'm walking back and forth on the street like a duck in a shooting gallery. I'll be fine. Sooner or later this guy will show himself and we'll nab him and then we'll have Mike's killer."

"Just make sure you get him before he gets you." Lily's stern words didn't match the pleading in her eyes. Trace's heart melted and he had to draw on every ounce of willpower he possessed to prevent himself from taking her in his arms and holding her close.

"Isn't this lawyer pretty late? Has he called or anything?" Trace quickly diverted the conversation.

John shook his head. "Nope. Not a word. He should have been here twenty minutes ago. Maybe he got caught in traffic."

"Could be. He'll probably be here any minute now."

But twenty minutes crept by and there was still no sign of the lawyer. The three of them sat in the living room making increasingly labored conversation. At least it seemed labored to Trace. He was painfully aware of Lily every moment. It was heaven and hell being so close to her and yet still so far apart. Lily seemed distracted, inclined to lose the thread of the conversation, her sentences trailing off into nothing.

Only John seemed at ease, carrying the conversation practically by himself when necessary. And when a silence occurred, he seemed just as comfortable with that. Another twenty minutes crept by and it was becoming pretty clear that the lawyer wasn't going to show up.

"Maybe his car broke down," Lily suggested.

"Could be. I'm going to call his office and see if they know anything." Trace crossed to the phone, checking the number in the address book written in Mike's scrawled hand. "Did he say what he wanted?"

John shrugged. "Just that he had some papers for us to sign, some final stuff about the estate, I guess."

"Probably." But the lawyer's office had no idea what he was talking about. They weren't aware of Mr. Lavery's having an appointment to see them; besides, they said, he rarely called at a client's home.

Trace set down the phone, quizzical. He told Lily and John what the secretary had told him and the three of them looked at one another, none of them willing to voice their suspicions.

"Maybe he just forgot to tell his secretary," Lily said.

"Maybe." Trace glanced at his watch. "One way or another, I'm not going to hang around here much longer."

He made it sound as if he had other, far more important things to do, though the truth of the matter was that his only plans were to go back to the station house and sift through files for the thousandth time.

Lily stood up abruptly. "You know, I told the other teachers I'd only be gone an hour or so and it's already been almost twice that. I think I'll go ahead and get back to work. If the lawyer shows up, tell him he can bring any papers he has down to the school and I'll sign them there." She spoke rapidly, her tone a little too clipped, a little too hurried.

"I thought you took the afternoon off?" It was John who asked the question. Trace was busy studying the toes of his boots.

"No." She looked at Trace, her heart in her eyes. He glanced up and then away, steeling himself. "No, I really should be getting back." Trace looked up as she left the room, her back ramrod straight, her steps brisk. But he knew it wasn't his imagination that her eyes were a little too bright. The front door shut behind her and the room was silent.

"You're a hell of a lot stupider than I think you are if you let her go like that." John's tone held a bite.

"It's for the best," Trace told him.

"Like hell it is. I don't know the details of what your problems are but I know she's hurting, and if you let her walk away like that, you may never be able to repair the damage."

"Mind your own damned business," Trace snarled, but he was already on his way out the door.

Lily was just opening her car door when he stepped outside. He didn't need to see the hunched set of her shoulders to know that she was either crying or very close to it. No matter what, he couldn't let her go away in tears.

"Lily." She looked up as he called her name. She seemed to hesitate for a moment, as if debating about ignoring him,

and he came down off the steps, calling her name again.
"Lily."

She turned, wiping her face on her sleeve, and Trace felt
like a beast. All his talk about never wanting to hurt her and
yet it seemed that was all he did. She took a few steps toward him as he strode across the lawn.

And then the world seemed to explode around them.

Afterward Trace could remember every second of what
followed as if he'd seen it played in slow motion. There was
a hollow roar and the car seemed to swell and bulge like
some bizarre kind of insect shedding its skin. The roar became an ear-shattering boom and he saw Lily thrown forward, heard her scream at the same instant the ground
seemed to disappear from beneath his feet.

He hit the lawn with enough force to knock the wind out
of him, but he was struggling to his feet even before he could
register what had happened. His one thought was to get to
Lily. His only need was to have her in his arms, to protect
her, to shelter her.

"Lily!" He wasn't aware that he screamed her name as he
threw himself across the short distance that separated him
from her still figure. The car was burning, throwing off a
fierce amount of heat. Lily was sprawled facedown on the
grass, her hair spread around her like a black mourning
cloak. Trace caught her under the arms, aware of the heat
beating against his face. He dragged her several yards away,
praying that he wasn't adding to any injuries she might already have.

"Come on, baby. You're going to be all right. You have
to be all right." If anything happened to her, his life
wouldn't be worth living. There'd be nothing left in the
world for him. Nothing. Lily was everything. Everything
bright and beautiful and precious. "You've got to be all
right. You just have to be."

He knelt on the grass, turning Lily over and cradling her across his lap. She was so still and pale, her lashes forming thick black crescents on cheeks devoid of color. His hands were shaking too badly to find a pulse but when he bent to lay his head against her chest, he could hear a heartbeat, a little too fast but there.

"Is she all right?" Trace looked up as John hobbled to a halt beside them.

"She's alive."

"Thank God. How badly is she hurt?"

"I don't know." Trace ran his shaking fingers over her arms and legs. He could find no obvious injuries but that didn't mean there wasn't something internal.

"I'll call an ambulance." He barely acknowledged John's words. All his concentration was on Lily. She had to be all right. She just had to be.

He was still kneeling beside her when John returned with a blanket. He was vaguely aware of the crowd that was gathering on the lawn, some of them watching the car burn, some of them watching him and Lily. One of the neighbors came over and asked if there was anything he could do. Trace hardly heard him. It was John who asked him to make sure that the paramedics could get through when they arrived.

Trace couldn't—wouldn't—pull his gaze from Lily. He had the strange thought that she might slip away from him if he wasn't looking at her every moment. As if the fact that he was concentrating on her could keep her tied to him.

Sirens wailed in the distance, coming nearer. John and a few others herded the crowd back, clearing plenty of room around Trace and Lily and the still smoldering wreck of Lily's car.

Lily's lashes fluttered and she took a deeper breath, which seemed to catch in the middle. Trace leaned closer, stroking the hair back from her forehead.

"Lily? Sweetheart? Can you hear me?"

Her eyelids flickered and then opened slowly. She stared up at Trace, her eyes dazed, her face still pale as mist.

"Trace?"

"I'm here, sweetheart. How do you feel? Do you hurt anywhere?"

"I . . . I don't know." Her hand wavered as she lifted it to her forehead and frowned. "What happened?"

"Your car exploded. Do you feel any pain?"

"No, I don't think so. A little bruised, maybe. What do you mean my car exploded?" She struggled to sit up but he pressed her back down.

"Hold still until the paramedics have had a chance to take a look at you. We don't know if there are any internal injuries."

"I'm fine." She pushed herself up on one elbow, brushing aside his attempt to make her lie back down. "Why would my car explode?"

"At a guess I'd say a bomb." The reply came from John, who now knelt across from Trace. Trace threw him a quick angry look but John met it with one that held just as much determination.

"No good is going to come of lying to her about it."

"And no good is going to come of worrying her right now when we don't really know what happened."

"Stop quarreling, you two," Lily admonished them, her eyes on the smoldering ruin of her car. "If you hadn't called my name, Trace, I'd have been in there when it exploded."

"The bomb was probably activated by you opening the door," John explained. "It was likely tied into the courtesy lights, and set to go off a few seconds later when you'd have gotten in. A little more risky than setting it to go off with the ignition but fairly functional.''

John's expression was distant as he studied the smoking ruin and Trace had no doubt that this wasn't the first time he'd viewed the aftermath of a car bomb. Whatever kind of "import-export" business he was in, Trace would have laid bets that it didn't have anything to do with fancy French chocolates.

Lily shuddered and reached out to take hold of his hand, and the look he gave John was as searing as the heat from the car. John met the look calmly. "Whatever is going on here, it obviously involves more than just you. Someone had to set that bomb. And it's Lily's car they set it on."

Before he could say more, the paramedics had arrived and were politely but firmly pushing them both aside. Lily clung to Trace's hand, throwing him a pleading look, but he detached himself. "I'll be close. I promise."

He backed away, giving the paramedics room to work. The fire department was spraying the car with foam and a couple of squad cars had arrived and the officers were dispersing the curious crowd of onlookers. Trace nodded to them but he was in no mood to make polite conversation.

He stood off to one side, watching everything with a feeling of detachment. The only thing that seemed real was that Lily had almost died. What if he hadn't come after her? What if she'd been just a few feet closer to the car when it blew? He shoved his hands into his pockets, oblivious of the twinge of protest from his injured palm. So close. He'd come so close to losing her forever.

"Dushane?" Captain Jacobs had to repeat his name before Trace responded. He turned slowly to look at the older man.

"Captain. What are you doing here?"

"I heard the call and recognized the address. How is she?" He nodded to where Lily lay on the grass, the paramedics still kneeling over her.

"I don't know yet. I couldn't find any obvious injuries."

"I'm sure she's fine. She's a lot stronger than she looks."

"Yes, I think she is."

"What happened?"

The two men turned their attention to the remains of the car. "A car bomb, it looks like," Trace replied. "John seemed to have a pretty good idea of how it might have been set. If I hadn't called her name, she'd have been in the car when it blew." He hunched his shoulders. "Just a few seconds one way or the other and she'd be dead."

Jacobs slanted him a shrewd look. "You've been under a lot of stress these past few weeks. How's your hand?"

"My hand?" Trace pulled his left hand out of his pocket and stared at the bandages as if trying to remember what they were doing there. "It's okay. It's just a couple of stitches."

"I wanted to talk to you."

"About what?" Trace was watching the little group around Lily and his tone was absent.

"We've got some new information that may relate to this case."

Trace's head jerked around and he fixed the older man with a fierce gaze. "Mike's killer? You know who it is?"

Jacobs shook his head. "Unfortunately, nothing that concrete, but there are some things we should discuss. Actually, I think John and Lily should be in on the discussion, also."

"I'm not going to the hospital." Lily's voice rose clearly over the murmur of those around them. "I feel fine and I'm not going to the hospital."

Trace moved toward the small group on the lawn, Jacobs's words not forgotten but filed for future examination. Lily was sitting up, her hair in disarray, her delicate chin set in a determined expression he knew well. The paramedics were muttering admonitions and suggestions, resorting almost to pleas, but she was clearly not in the mood to listen. She looked at Trace as he stepped up to the group, her eyes lighting.

"Trace, explain to these nice men that I'm not going to the hospital."

He knelt down in front of her, filled with relief to see her looking so normal. "If they think you need to go to the hospital, maybe you should go."

"There's nothing wrong with me. They even admitted they couldn't find anything wrong with me. And I'm not going to the hospital just so they can observe me. You can keep an eye on me here, can't you?"

"I really think you should let us take you to the hospital, miss," one of the paramedics advised.

"Trace, please. I want to stay here. I want to be at home." Her eyes fixed pleadingly on his and there was just the hint of a quiver about her chin. He really should insist that she go to the hospital.

"Would it be really dangerous for her to stay here if I keep a careful eye on her?"

The older paramedic shrugged. "We can't find anything wrong with her but she'd be better off in a hospital just in case. If you want to keep her here, that's your decision."

"I've had some medical training." John's voice came from behind Trace. "I know what to watch for."

"It's your decision." The two paramedics packed their equipment back in their truck and left, their expressions making it clear that they didn't agree with the decision. Trace watched them leave, wondering if they weren't right.

"Help me up. I'm going to catch pneumonia sitting on this cold grass."

Trace stood up and bent to take Lily's hand, helping her to her feet. She staggered slightly, putting her hand to her forehead. He bent, catching her behind the knees and scooping her up into his arms.

"Trace. I'm perfectly capable of walking. I just felt a little dizzy when I stood up."

"I'm not taking any chances," he told her, his voice stern. "If you won't go to the hospital, then you're just going to have to do as you're told here."

"Yes, sir." Her meek tone was at odds with the rather pleased look in her eyes, but she subsided against his chest and allowed him to carry her into the house and lay her on the sofa.

Half an hour later, the last of the firefighters were gone and the house had settled into a more or less peaceful state. If it hadn't been for the battered condition of the lawn, which had seen far too many feet tramping over its surface, and the burned-out hulk of Lily's car in the drive, it would have been possible to believe that the explosion had been a nightmare.

Trace leaned against the mantel, a cup of steaming coffee in his hand. John sat in Mike's old chair, his sore leg resting on a hassock, his coffee cradled against his chest. Lily lay swaddled in a blanket on the sofa, a cup of weak tea on a table near her head. If Trace had had his way she would have been upstairs in bed, but she'd refused to be moved. She wanted to know what Captain Jacobs had to say just as much as he did. Jacobs was settled into a chair across from John.

Though it wasn't particularly cold, Trace had set a fire in the fireplace, more out of a psychological need for warmth than a physical one. The heat from the fire didn't seem to do much to warm the chill he felt.

"At this point, the new information we have just seems to confuse the issue more than clear it."

Jacobs stopped and took a sip of coffee, gathering his thoughts together before he continued. "We got the report back on your car, John. You said the brakes failed you."

"That's right. I was lucky they went out where they did. Running into a mountain was a lot better than running off a cliff."

"They went out because someone put a hole in the hydraulic line. Every time you stepped on the brakes you were losing brake fluid. It was pure chance that they went out when they did."

"So someone wanted me dead." It was more a statement than a question but Jacobs answered it as such.

"Maybe. It's a chancy way to try and kill someone. They had no way of knowing just where you'd go after they put the hole in the line. Brake failure isn't automatically fatal. You're living proof of that." He lifted his cup in salute.

Trace frowned. "So where does this put us? The attempts on my life, the notes. Brake lines tampered with on John's car, Lily's car rigged to explode. Just who the hell are they trying to kill? And why? And where does Mike's murder fit in to all of this?"

Jacobs shrugged. "I don't know. Like I said, it doesn't really clear anything up. The notes indicate that it's you they're after, Trace. But when you factor in what's happened to John and Lily, it doesn't seem to add up."

"It's scary to think that there's somebody out there who can't even make up his mind as to who he wants to murder." Lily's words held a macabre humor but no one was laughing.

"You know, I can't help but think that we're missing some piece of this puzzle," John said. "Something we're not seeing. Maybe something that goes all the way back to my father's murder. There were things about it that just didn't add up."

"Like what?" Trace asked.

"There's no way anyone could have shot Dad thinking he was you. You're a good six, eight inches taller than he was, the hair color is wrong, the build is wrong. Even from the back, you don't look anything like him.

"Maybe we've been looking at this the wrong way. Maybe there's more to this whole thing than just somebody wanting you dead. What if it's someone who wants all three of us dead?"

"But why?" Lily asked, her brows drawn together in a frown. "Why would anyone want the three of us dead? What's the connection? You didn't even come home until after Mike was killed."

"The first note said it should have been you, not him, right?" John asked Trace.

Trace nodded, his eyes intent. "There didn't seem to be anyone else it could have meant but Mike. Besides, some of the notes since then mention Mike by name."

"This whole thing smacks of someone out for revenge." John frowned, rubbing his injured leg, his expression absent, as if he were working something out in his mind. "What if this is someone who wants revenge on my father, not Trace?"

Jacobs stared at him for a moment before nodding slowly. "I see where you're going with this and it could make sense. Twisted but possible."

"I *don't* see it." Trace's voice was sharper than he'd intended. He wanted—needed—to believe that Mike's death was not his fault, but the very desperation of that need made him cautious.

"Think about it," John said. "What if someone meant to kill us off one by one and make my father suffer while they did it? Instead, they killed him first."

"Why? As you pointed out, there's no way they could have mistaken Mike for me."

"Maybe they couldn't resist killing him when they saw him." Lily shuddered at John's blunt suggestion and he threw her an apologetic look. "We're obviously dealing with a very sick mind here."

"I know." She drew the blanket closer around her, her eyes dark. "Poor Mike. I wonder if he knew."

"He probably did." There was a long silence, each of them wondering what those last moments must have been like. Trace stared down into the fireplace, his features set. Was it possible that John's theory was right? If there was some truth in it, any truth... He stopped. Too much hope could be as painful as too little.

"That's another thing that's strange." Trace looked up as John spoke again. "Why did Dad spend his last seconds getting out his wallet? What was in it that seemed so important?"

Jacobs shook his head. "I don't know. I've asked myself the same thing. Mike would have tried to leave us a clue if he could have but I'm damned if I can figure out what kind of a clue his wallet is."

"What *was* in his wallet?" John asked.

"Not much. Some money. Credit cards, pictures of the three of you, a picture of your mother, John. A few old receipts. Nothing unusual."

"Nothing that would help us," John muttered in disgust.

"Still, there's got to be something here that we're not seeing." Trace's tone carried an element of frustration that they all shared. There was a long silence and then Jacobs sighed.

"Well, I'm going to head home. My wife hates it when I'm late." He set his cup down and stood up. "I've got a squad car outside. They'll be relieved at midnight by another car so you should at least be able to get a decent night's sleep tonight. Tomorrow we'll put our heads together and check out this new angle. Maybe we can come up with something. There's got to be something here that we're just not seeing. Maybe a night's sleep will help."

No one had much to say after he left. The three of them sat watching the fire, each wrapped in his own thoughts. Dinner was suggested and dismissed. The events of the day had been enough to discourage anyone's appetite.

"I think it's time for you to go to bed. That's the second yawn in the last five minutes."

Lily looked up as Trace approached the sofa. If she had any thoughts of arguing, his determined expression must have changed her mind. Another yawn forestalled anything she might have said.

"Maybe you're right. It was a pretty rough day... Trace!" Her voice rose in surprise as he bent and scooped her up, blanket and all. "What are you doing?"

"I'm taking you up to bed."

"I'm perfectly capable of walking."

"Maybe. But you're not going to. Hold on to me."

Her arms circled his neck obediently as he settled her against his chest. She looked at John, her face flushed a delicate shade of pink.

"Would you tell him that I don't need to be carried upstairs?"

John shrugged. "Not me. Hell, I'm tired enough that if someone offered to carry me to bed, I'd take them up on it. Sleep well." He lifted his hand in farewell as Trace carried Lily into the hallway.

The stairs creaked in all the familiar places, reminding Trace of the thousands of times he'd climbed them. There'd been a few times when he'd cursed the way they revealed his presence, but tonight the faint moans spelled home.

Lily rested in his arms, her slight weight a reassuring burden. Just having her here, warm and alive, was something to give thanks for. Nothing had ever frightened him as much as seeing her fall today, the car exploding behind her. For an instant, a split second, he'd known what it felt like to lose her. It was an unbearable thought.

He stopped, aware of her throwing him a quick questioning glance before she reached out to open the door. Trace carried her inside, kicking the door shut behind them. Lily said nothing as he walked across the room and set her on his bed. Still wrapped in the blanket, she looked up at him.

"Why did you bring me here instead of taking me to my room? I'm fine, Trace. Really I am. A little bruised maybe, but there's nothing wrong with me. You don't have to watch me every second. I'd be okay in my own room."

"I wouldn't." His expression was calm but there were lingering traces of fear visible in his eyes. "I want you in here where I can keep a watch on you."

Lily looked at him a moment longer, her eyes unreadable. "I have no objections to that."

So Trace held her throughout the night and it would have been impossible to say who gained the most comfort from their being together.

Trace lay awake long after Lily slept peacefully in his arms, his eyes on the darkened ceiling. She was a warm precious weight against his side. Every time he closed his eyes, he saw the car blossoming fire behind her, her slight body thrown forward.

Maybe he'd been wrong. Maybe a love as strong as the one he felt for her could make up for everything else.

Chapter Fifteen

Trace leaned back in his chair and reached for his coffee, his eyes on the file in front of him. Around him the station bustled quietly. Outside, dawn was just breaking, but the only way to know that was to look at a clock. Crime didn't take the night off and neither did cops.

Trace was barely aware of the activity. All his attention was on the file that lay spread across the table. Harry Smith: Caucasian, male, convicted of first-degree murder, sentenced to life in prison. Convicted of murdering Maryann Lonigan.

Trace sipped the bitter coffee and studied the photograph. A fairly ordinary-looking guy. Not the kind of face you'd notice in a crowd except maybe for the fact that his left eyebrow kicked up at the outer corner, tugged upward by a small white scar that ran toward his temple. Other than that one small thing he could have been Joe Ordinary.

He and the victim had allegedly been having an affair; she'd decided to end the affair and he'd shot her twice in the face. Not a pretty way to go. The evidence had been clear: the murder weapon with Smith's fingerprints, a motive and a witness who saw him leaving the scene of the crime. An open-and-shut case. The jury had apparently thought so, too. They'd come back with a guilty verdict after a short deliberation and Harry Smith had gone to prison.

Trace reached out to flip to another page of the report. Nothing special there. Smith had been a quiet prisoner, causing no real problems. He'd been paroled for good behavior five years ago and he'd been a model parolee. He was living somewhere in the San Diego area at last report. That would seem to be the end of it. Case closed.

So why was this the file he was looking at? Out of all the files he'd gone through in the past three hours, why was this the one that kept drawing his attention? He rocked his chair back on two legs and took another swallow of coffee, staring at nothing in particular. His eyes felt gritty and there was a vague pasty feeling in his brain.

He'd had, at a generous estimate, maybe two hours' sleep. When he'd finally given up trying to get any more rest, it had still been the dead of night outside. Lily had been sleeping heavily, her breathing even. He'd allowed himself a few moments just to watch her in the light of the small desk lamp he'd turned on, savoring her presence in his bed, reassuring himself that she was really there, safe and sound. And then he'd dressed and come down here, too restless to stay in the house.

Mike's files hadn't turned out to be much more helpful than his own had been. No one who had obvious motives to cook up any bizarre revenge. Still, this one file kept drawing his attention. It was certainly the most personally relevant file he'd found. But it was over and done with. A closed case. Still, there was something there that drew him, and right now that was more than anything else he had to go on.

Trace yawned as he shut the folder. Not even adrenaline could make up for the strain of these past weeks. He was feeling the lack of decent rest. He stretched and then glanced at his watch. It was going to be another couple of hours before he could expect Captain Jacobs to be in his office. Maybe he'd go out and get some breakfast, plenty of black coffee, and then take a brisk walk. He stood up, picking up the file and tucking it under his arm. He could take a look at it over breakfast and see if he could put his finger on what it was that caught his attention.

The street was empty, the air cool and damp. A rare fog drifted around lampposts and cars, giving a surreal look to the sidewalks. Trace turned the collar of his jacket up around his ears, reaching into his pocket for his keys as he approached the 'Vette.

His fingers had just closed over the metal key ring when he heard a slight noise behind him, not quite a footstep but definitely a sound. He started to turn when something caught him behind the ear. There was a moment of blinding pain, an instant to wonder if this was what it felt like to die, and then a heavy blanket of darkness descended, blanking out everything.

THE FIRST THING Trace was aware of was pain. His head ached. Not a vague pain across his forehead but a demanding throb of pain located somewhere in the back of his skull. His arms felt stiff and something was poking him in the back. His tongue felt thick and dry. It took a great effort to force his eyes open and he almost changed his mind when the action only intensified the pain.

But the same stubborn determination that had led him at fifteen to take a little girl and run away from home refused to let him give up now. He opened his eyes the merest slit, letting them adjust to the light before he tried to force them wider.

He was lying on his side on the floor, a cracked vinyl floor that looked as if it had been installed sometime before the flood and hadn't been cleaned since. He stared at the worn gray-and-black print, his mind slowly shifting into gear.

His arms hurt because they were tied behind his back. The cloth in his mouth accounted for the dryness of his tongue. He couldn't guess what was poking him in the back but the ache in his head was centered just behind his right ear and he had no doubt that there was a sizable lump there to show for the pain.

He didn't move but tried to use his eyes and ears to give him as much information as possible before he let anyone know that he was conscious. His field of vision was limited to the floor and the edge of a table with two rickety chairs pushed next to it. He listened carefully but he seemed to be alone. Still he waited, his muscles screaming for some movement to relieve the tension.

He moved at last, first turning his head as far as he could. No one spoke or moved, and after a time he came to the conclusion that he was alone. Once that was determined, movement became imperative. He had to find out as much as he could before whoever had trussed him like a Christmas turkey returned.

The struggle to sit up intensified the pounding in his head, leaving him faintly nauseated when he was at last more or less upright. His feet were bound together at the ankles, which placed severe limitations on his mobility, but he leaned back against the wall and studied the room from his new position.

Shabby did not do it justice. Tumbledown, perhaps. Ratty might be suitable. Pit was the description that occurred to him first. The antediluvian flooring was actually just about the most attractive component of the small room. The furniture consisted of a sofa whose springs looked poised to do fatal damage should anyone be so foolish as to sit on it. The table and two chairs stayed upright by sheer willpower. The curtains hung in shreds from the windows, one of which was boarded up. There was a kitchenette in the far corner, almost out of his line of vision. He rather wished it had been completely out of sight as well as out of smelling range. His nose wrinkled as the scent of old food drifted to him.

Not the Ritz but he was alive and, apart from considerable discomfort, in reasonably good shape. It was a safe bet that whoever had brought him here didn't intend for him to stay that way, however. Tugging experimentally at the ropes that held his wrists, he felt an encouraging give. He twisted his hands again, feeling a twinge of protest from the stitches in his left hand, which he ignored.

Trace couldn't have said how long he sat there, twisting his hands back and forth, trying to loosen the knots that bound him. His wrists were rubbed raw and he could feel the slow seep of blood running down to soak the bandages on his palm before he heard a key in the lock of the door.

He froze, his eyes on the door, his thoughts crystal clear. He didn't doubt that whoever was entering the room was the same person who'd shot Mike and left him to die all alone, the one who'd written the notes on his windshield, who'd cut the brake lines on John's car, who'd planted the bomb in Lily's car.

The door opened with a whine of old hinges. The man who entered was much older, his hair grayer, his skin showing the pastiness of someone who'd spent too much time indoors, but Trace recognized him. He wasn't in the least surprised to see that the left brow kicked up at the outer corner above dark eyes that were completely, totally insane.

Harry Smith. The man who'd killed Mike's wife nearly twenty-five years ago.

Smith looked up and saw that Trace was conscious. "Well, so you're back with us. How are you feeling?"

He shut the door behind him and set the bag he was carrying on the table. "I didn't think you'd wake up quite so soon or I'd have hurried back. I was just getting a few things I thought we might need."

His tone seemed to imply that they were old friends. Vaguely apologetic with an underlying friendliness that turned Trace's stomach.

"I bet that gag is uncomfortable. I'm sorry I had to do that but I couldn't have you making noise and disturbing the neighbors. Not that there are any neighbors, but you never know when someone might wander by."

He came over and knelt down next to Trace, and it was all Trace could do to keep from drawing away as Smith reached for the gag. The fabric fell away from his face and he forced his tongue to push the wad of cloth from his mouth.

"There. That's better. I bet your mouth is dry. Let me get something for you." Smith moved away, continuing to talk as he poured juice into a dirty glass. "I should warn you not to try and call out. As I said, there's really no one for you to disturb, but I dislike loud noises."

Reluctantly Trace took a swallow of juice when the glass was held to his lips. It tasted slightly rancid but it was wet and his mouth felt parched. The liquid trickled down his throat, moistening dry tissue. He drank again, his eyes never leaving Smith's face. That the man was going to kill him, he had no doubt. Why he was taking the time to give him something to drink now he couldn't begin to guess, but then, perhaps madness followed its own logic.

He didn't doubt that Smith was mad. It wasn't only the things he knew the man had done. Even without that, the insanity was easy to read in his eyes. They glittered with a light that wasn't natural.

"How are you feeling now?" Smith still knelt beside him, his mouth curved in a smile. "I hope your head doesn't hurt too much." He reached out to touch Trace's hair and Trace jerked back. Smith's smile widened. "Don't worry. I just wanted to see if you had a bad lump."

"It's fine." His voice rasped in his throat, the words slurred by his stiff tongue.

"Suit yourself. Would you like some more juice?" He would have all but killed for some more moisture in his throat, but more than that, he wanted Harry Smith at a greater distance. He shook his head.

"No, thanks."

"If you'd like some more later, just ask." To his relief, Smith moved away. "Of course, don't make it too much later because I have other plans."

He was unloading the sack as he spoke, his tone conversational. He might have been discussing the weather or the possibility of the Dodgers winning the World Series in the fall.

"I'm afraid my plans may not suit you. I'm sure you've realized that I'm going to have to kill you." He stopped and turned to look at Trace, his expression regretful. "It's too bad really, but it can't be helped."

"Couldn't we talk about this?"

"Certainly. I don't mind at all, but the end result will be the same."

Trace waited until Smith turned away again before going back to work on the ropes, twisting and turning his wrists, praying it wasn't his imagination that made it seem that the bonds were loosening.

"Why do you have to kill me? I don't know you."

"True, but it's not because you know me. It's because of someone else."

"Someone else?"

"Michael Jonathan Lonigan. Sergeant Michael Lonigan." The way he said the name sent chills up Trace's spine. His tone was almost caressing and yet he could all but smell the hatred.

"Why would you want to kill me because of Mike? He's dead." He was barely aware of what he was saying. All his concentration was on the ropes at his wrists but it seemed like a good idea to keep Smith talking.

"I know he's dead." There was real regret in the words. "I killed him. I didn't mean to kill him. At least not so soon. I had other plans. It was supposed to be you, you know," he said with a touch of petulance. Trace wondered if he should apologize.

"I had it all planned. It was going to be you and then the girl and then his son. I left his son for last because I thought that might hurt the most. Besides, I knew it might be difficult to find him. He seems to move around so much. I thought he might come home to comfort his father over your deaths and then I'd kill him. Neat, huh?"

Smith didn't seem to expect a response, which was just as well. He picked up a box of .38 shells and began taking them out of the box and setting them on the rickety table in front of him, lining them up in neat little rows.

"I had it all figured out and then I drove by the liquor store and saw your car parked out front. It was so perfect. I thought you were opening up the store and it seemed so neat to kill you there. Mike might even have been the one to find your body.

"I went in and saw it was Mike and I just couldn't stop myself. I knew I shouldn't do it. It wasn't part of the plan, but I couldn't help it. I pulled the trigger and then I couldn't stop pulling it. He knew it was me. I was the last thing he saw. The very last face. Even after all these years, he rec-

ognized me. It was almost worth ruining my plan to see the
look in his eyes.''

His hands had stopped moving and he was staring at the
wall, clearly seeing other things. A trickle of saliva ran down
his chin, unnoticed. Trace looked away, swallowing hard on
the acid taste of bile that filled his throat. The picture Smith
painted was vivid. He had no trouble imagining Mike's last
few seconds. His realization of who his killer was, the desperate need to leave some clue, some message so that his
knowledge wouldn't die with him.

The answer had been right in front of them all the time.
Mike had been trying to get to his wife's picture, trying to
tell them that Maryann's murderer was also his own.

''But then, after he was dead, I realized that I'd spoiled
my plan.'' Smith reminded Trace of a child who'd just broken his favorite toy. The comparison was nauseating. ''I'd
wanted to watch him suffer, the way I suffered all those
years in prison. I watched my whole life drift away. I
couldn't do that to him. But I could destroy his life. Everyone who meant anything to him.''

He started methodically arranging the bullets again. ''I
spent a long time planning all this. I didn't really have anything else to do, you know. I'd have done it as soon as they
let me out but that would have been too obvious. I don't
want to go back to that place. I won't go back. So I waited
and watched. I learned all about you and Lily, how Mike
had taken you in.

''It was really a perfect plan and then I had to spoil it all
by killing Mike first.''

Trace froze as the madman turned to look at him. The
bonds at his wrists were giving. His hands were slipping out
of them, their path softened by the blood that was oozing
downward from his raw skin. The pain was negligible, un-
important.

"I thought for a while that I'd ruined everything. I was very depressed. With Mike already dead, there didn't seem to be much point in killing the three of you. And then it hit me!" He smiled, his eyes alight with insanity. "Do you believe in the afterlife?"

Trace nodded warily and Smith's smile widened. "I do, too." He turned back to the bullets. "So you see, it's going to work out after all."

Trace went back to twisting the ropes, keeping his eyes on Smith's profile. "I'm not sure I understand."

"It's obvious. If you believe in an afterlife, then you've got to believe that Mike knows what's happening in the world he departed. So even though he's not here, he'll know what's happening to the people he loved the most." He stopped, frowning down at the tidy rows of bullets. "It's not quite as pleasant as my first plan because I don't get to see him suffer, but it's still quite good. Now I can imagine his pain. And after all, one has to make the best of things. When life hands you lemons, you make lemonade and all that."

Trace felt a moment of dizzy unreality. The homey little saying had no place here. Not in the midst of murder and madness.

"What do you plan to do with me?"

"Well, I've changed my plan a bit. Even after Mike died, I was going to stick with the original idea and kill you one by one, but then I thought about it and that seemed rather unkind. Then the three of you would suffer watching your loved ones die. After all, I'm not trying to punish *you* and it seemed unfair that you should be made to suffer. So I set the car bomb yesterday. That was supposed to kill Lily. I thought it only fair that she should go first and therefore suffer the least. Then I was going to kill the two of you last night.

"Only the car bomb didn't work so I decided that it might be easiest just to get all three of you in one place and kill you all at once. While you were taking your little nap, I called your two friends and told them that I had you. I suggested that if they wanted to see you alive again, they should meet us here."

"Only you have no intention of them seeing me alive, do you?" Trace got the words out between gritted teeth.

"Certainly I do." Smith threw him an indignant look as he picked up a blued-steel .38 and began stroking a cloth over the barrel. "I always keep my promises. They'll get to see you alive, right before you all die."

Trace was barely listening. His right hand slid free of the ropes, scraping skin all the way. After that, it was only an instant before his left hand was loose. The rope dropped to the floor behind him with a whisper-soft sound. Pain flooded his wrists and he ground his teeth together, fighting the need to move his arms and massage the blood back into them. Until he figured out just what he was going to do, it was imperative that Smith not know he was no longer tied.

He had to do something soon. Lily would come for him. He knew it as surely as he knew that he loved her more than life itself. No matter what the danger to herself might be, she'd come to him. And John would follow her. Even if they called the police first, they were walking into a trap.

Smith's plan was full of holes, but in some ways the very weakness of it gave it strength. No one would expect such a simple flawed plan.

Smith continued to babble, sometimes humming to himself, sometimes repeating some particular portion of his plot. All the time he stroked the cloth lovingly over the .38, caressing it as one would a lover.

Trace watched for an opportunity, racking his brain for a plan. Something—anything—that would stop Smith before this madness went any further. His feet were still tied. Whatever he came up with would have to take that into account. There had to be something.

But he was suddenly out of time.

"Trace?" Lily's voice came from the other side of the door, fear lending it a sharp edge. Smith's head jerked up and he stared at the door, seeing the culmination of all his plans, all his dreams. Trace saw the moment as if it were frozen in time. Lily was on the other side of the door, a few feet away from death. No matter what, he couldn't let that happen.

"Trace? Are you in there?"

Without Lily there was nothing. In an instant he saw how foolish he'd been. No matter what, he should have taken every moment he could have had with her. He should have done everything he could to make her happy. It was his pride that had come between them, that had kept them apart. And now, in a dingy room, he saw his second chance slipping away. He could lose everything, including Lily's life.

Smith stood up, the gun drooping loosely in his hand. Trace tensed, knowing he had to move now, knowing he didn't stand a snowball's chance in hell of succeeding. Smith took a step and Trace lunged upward, pushing himself up with all the strength in his arms. He hit Smith at waist level, heard the man's startled cry and the heavy thud of the .38 as it hit the floor, and then they crashed against the table.

The table served only to break their fall. The thin legs gave way and the two of them fell to the floor with a crash of splintered wood. Still tied at the ankles, Trace fought to keep his hold on Smith. Fear for his life and Lily's lent him strength, but Smith's was the power of insanity and he wasn't hampered by ropes.

They rolled back and forth, their breath coming in guttural grunts. Trace struggled to get a better grip on the other man, using his weight to try to pin him to the floor. Smith clawed at him, his fingers groping for Trace's eyes. Trace jerked his head back, loosing a precious fraction of his hold.

He could hear Lily calling his name, her tone more and more frantic, but he couldn't spare the breath to call out to her, to tell her to get back. Smith pulled one hand loose and groped over their heads. Trace could hear his fingers scrabbling against the floor and he knew what he was looking for. The gun. He'd dropped it and now he was trying to find it amid the wreckage of the table.

Trace got a grip on the front of his opponent's shirt and jerked him forward, slamming his forehead into the other man's. His own ears rang with the impact, but Smith, unprepared for his action, went limp. It was only for a fraction of an instant but it was all Trace needed. He rolled away, his right hand brushing across the gun and then grabbing it.

Smith screamed in rage, his eyes glittering wildly. Like a bizarre punctuation mark, the door crashed inward, the lock shattered by a well-placed foot. John lunged through the doorway, an automatic in his hands.

Smith moved and Trace's eyes came back to him. The madness in the other man's face was terrifying. Spittle dribbled down his chin and the sounds he was making were not even human anymore.

"Give it up. It's over." The words rasped out of Trace's throat. He was half lying on the floor, braced on one elbow, his bound feet in front of him, but the .38 was absolutely steady.

Smith looked from Trace to John and back again. Neither gun wavered. In the distance the wail of sirens drew ever closer. Smith was crouched on the floor, all humanity drained from his face, hell looking out of his eyes.

"Never! Never!" Without rising to his feet, he flung himself toward the sofa, his movement blindingly fast. Trace saw his hand slide under a cushion and then the glint of light on a barrel. There was only a fraction of a second in which to react. An instant in which to make a choice. And there wasn't a choice.

The sharp bark of the .38 blended with the heavier boom of John's .45 into one deafening sound. Bright red blossomed on the front of Smith's shirt. A gun dangled from his fingertips for an instant before falling to the floor. He stared at Trace, his eyes full of shock and a strange look that could almost have been relief. There was a long frozen moment where eternity seemed to walk the room and then Smith toppled forward, his madness stilled forever.

Trace dragged his eyes from the body and looked up at John. "Nice timing," he said hoarsely.

Before John could answer, there was a movement behind him and Lily flew through the doorway. She stopped abruptly, her eyes on Smith's body for an instant before jumping to Trace.

"Trace." In one word, everything was said.

"I told you to stay out of the way until I called you." John's chastisement was absently given and ignored.

"Are you all right?" Lily asked.

Trace nodded, sitting up and tugging at the ropes that held his feet. "I'm all right."

The ropes fell away and he climbed to his feet wearily, feeling decades older than his years.

"I thought you were going to die." Lily's words came out on a sob and she took a step toward him. Trace raised his head to look at her. She was everything in the world to him. All that mattered, all he ever wanted or needed. In the past few days they'd almost been parted in the most final of ways. All his doubts and fears seemed petty in the face of that.

He opened his arms to her and she flew across the room to him. She buried her head against his chest, sobs shaking her slender frame.

"I thought I'd lost you."

He bent his head over hers, his expression full of such tenderness that John looked away, feeling as if he'd intruded on a very private moment. Outside, the sirens screamed to a stop. There was going to be hell to pay as soon as the cops got up here. He glanced at Smith's body and then looked at Trace and Lily before turning and walking out into the hall, his gait a little stiff.

Neither of them noticed his departure. For them, there was nothing in the world but each other. Trace nuzzled her hair, his arms holding her so close that not even a whisper could have slid between them.

"Don't cry, sweetheart. I love you. I love you."

She shifted her head, her eyes the color of a stormy sea, all gray green and damp. "You said it. You really said it." Happiness began to come up in her eyes like the sun after a shower. "Oh, Trace, I love you so much and I was afraid you were never going to see how right we are for each other."

He brushed his thumb over the dampness on her cheeks, his smile a little twisted. "Nothing in the world is ever going to convince me that I deserve you but I could work on it."

"You don't need to work on it, but I don't care if you want to try. Just so long as we're together."

He glanced over her shoulder at Smith's body. It had come so close. So very close. Trace put his arm around Lily's shoulders and led her from the room, walking away from a past that had held too much darkness and toward a future that held nothing but light.

"Didn't I always promise you that we'd be together? Always, Lily. Always."

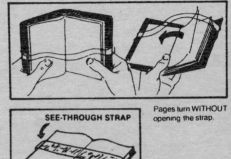

ABOUT THE AUTHOR

An episode on TV's *Beauty and the Beast* inspired Dallas Schulze to write *Together Always*. The moving way in which poor, unfortunate street children were handled caused Dallas to look at the protective nature of sibling relationships. And Trace Dushane and Lily Roberts were born.

Books by Dallas Schulze

HARLEQUIN AMERICAN ROMANCE
154–MACKENZIE'S LADY
185–STORMWALKER
235–TELL ME A STORY
263–LOST AND FOUND